DARK HORSE

DARK HORSE

MIKE LANGAN

FIVE STAR
A part of Gale, Cengage Learning

GALE
CENGAGE Learning™

Detroit • New York • San Francisco • New Haven, Conn • Waterville, Maine • London

GALE
CENGAGE Learning

Set in 11 pt. Plantin.
Printed on permanent paper.

LIBRARY OF CONGRESS CATALOGING-IN-PUBLICATION DATA

Langan, Mike.
  Dark Horse / Mike Langan. — 1st ed.
    p. cm.
    ISBN-13: 978-1-59414-664-0 (alk. paper)
    ISBN-10: 1-59414-664-0 (alk. paper)
    1. Lawyers—Crimes against—Fiction. 2. Personal injury lawyers—Fiction. 3. Judges—Election—Fiction. 4. Fugitives from justice—Fiction. 5. Eccentrics and eccentricities—Fiction. 6. New York (State)—Fiction. I. Title.
  PS3612.A558D37 2008
  813'.6—dc22   2007036333

First Edition. First Printing: February 2008.

Published in 2008 in conjunction with Tekno Books and Ed Gorman.

Printed in the United States of America
1 2 3 4 5 6 7 12 11 10 09 08

For my parents

CHAPTER 1

Doreen Pardy called Rigopoulos & Magnarella, the one with the fancy TV ads, more than a year after she'd tripped in a hole in a sidewalk in the City of Syracuse. She'd waited so long, she said, on account of the pins in her ankle only hurt when it rained and, frankly, she hadn't been looking where she was going at the time of the accident. But then her son Dale was released from the Jamesville Pen and asked for a loan so he could buy some "business equipment"—a plow for his pickup, a lawnmower ramp, and maybe a set of monster tires with spinning chrome rims.

So six months and two depositions later, there was Nicky Rigopoulos, sitting in court across the aisle from some kid lawyer for a lousy insurance company. The lawyer was Porter Boyd, from the law firm of Trollope & Secore, LLP. Porter stood up, buttoned his Hickey Freeman poplin suit, and opened a binder of typed notes.

"May it please the court, I represent James Satterfield, who owns the property next to the sidewalk on which plaintiff claims to have tripped and fallen. Opposing counsel and I are here this morning because Mr. Satterfield has moved for summary judgment. I think the legal issues before the Court have been thoroughly framed by the parties' motion papers. But I'd just like to make two final points that are not in the papers."

Porter waited for Judge Francis Nichols to look up from the papers in his hand, then Porter turned and opened his hand.

"My first point is that the seat next to me is empty."

Judge Nichols slid his bifocals down his nose. "I can see Frolic & Detour is still hiring only the most observant law school graduates."

Porter's face—normally pale from countless hours in his firm's library—reddened.

"Thank you, Your Honor. What I mean is, who are we missing? Plaintiff tripped in a hole in a sidewalk owned by the City of Syracuse, but she hasn't sued the city. Why not? Maybe it's because her counsel didn't study the deed to my client's property, or maybe it's because she's barred from suing the city by not serving it with a notice of claim within ninety days of the accident. In any event, having failed to sue the responsible party, she's now coming after my client, an innocent bystander, an upstanding member—"

"I get your point, Counselor. Leave the speeches to Mr. Rigopoulos and move on."

"Thank you, Your Honor."

"Mr. Boyd, do you know why your trial professor in law school taught you to always thank the judge, even when he's criticized you?"

"Your Honor?"

"And don't say 'to be polite.' "

Porter closed his mouth.

"It's to give the jury the impression you haven't screwed up, isn't it?"

"Yes, Your Honor."

"Mr. Boyd, do you see those empty chairs over there?" Judge Nichols nodded at the jury box. "Who are we missing?"

A cackle rose from the back of the gallery.

"Proceed, Counselor."

"Yes, Your Honor. The second point I'd like to make is, I hope, less obvious than the first." Porter forced a pained smile.

"Under the relevant city ordinance, a property owner like my client has a duty to the *city* to maintain an abutting sidewalk. A property owner has no duty to a *pedestrian* to maintain that sidewalk. The only way for a property owner to be liable to a pedestrian for a defect in a sidewalk is if the owner *created* that defect. Here, plaintiff swears defendant created the defect in question by driving over the sidewalk. The problem with this 'evidence' is that a *lay* witness such as plaintiff isn't qualified to testify about the cause of a defect in a sidewalk. Only an *expert* witness can do that, but plaintiff hasn't bothered to hire an expert. Nor has plaintiff . . ."

As Porter droned on about the rather severe deficiencies of plaintiff's case, Nicky Rigopoulos tilted his head back and admired the courtroom. Not one of those modern things you saw on *Court TV* with blond wood, low ceilings, and track lighting. But a genuine piece of Americana, recently refurbished to its turn-of-the-century splendor. Mahogany seats, marble dais, brass light fixtures. And the part Nicky liked best, green walls and drapes, which he hoped made judges and juries think of the same thing. The reason they were all there. Not statutes of limitations, or city ordinances, or even justice, whatever in the world that was. But the green stuff. Defendant had it, and plaintiff needed it, simple as that. And best of all, she deserved it, if not in a legal sense at least in a moral sense, which wasn't required for him to represent a client, but was always a nice bonus.

"As a result," Porter was saying, "plaintiff has introduced absolutely no evidence that my client created the defect in question. For this reason, her case must be dismissed."

Nicky waited for Porter to sit down before he rose and stretched his arms, suppressing a yawn. "Morning, Judge."

"Mr. Rigopoulos. I hope Mr. Boyd wasn't boring you."

"No, Judge, he was good. Very academic."

"It's always nice to have the law on your side. I didn't expect to see you here this morning."

"I wasn't expecting to be here, Your Honor," Nicky said. He could still see his law partner's panicked look when he'd strolled into work at nine-thirty. "Lottie—Ms. Magnarella—signed our response papers, but she's upstairs arguing a motion in the Onondaga Furniture case. Judge Merritt took it off the regular calendar and reserved the Appellate Courtroom because of the, you know, magnitude of the case."

"So she dusted you off. I didn't know you were still practicing. Thought all you were doing these days was shooting commercials and kissing babies."

"All cheeks are the same to me," Nicky said, getting a snigger from the bailiff. "Speaking of which, I hope I can count on your vote in November."

"Save it for Rotary Club. I don't want to think what would happen to the doctors and businesses in this city if the people draped a black robe over your shoulders. I'm only sorry my retirement is going to open a spot on the bench for you to fill. It leaves a sour taste in my mouth, to have you as my legacy after all these years."

Judge Nichols shifted his stern look from Nicky to the court reporter, who had already stopped typing, knowing when to leave something out of the record. Now Nicky knew why Judge Nichols hadn't given in to the trend of replacing pricey court reporters with cheaper recording machines. An uncomfortable silence had come over the room.

Nicky smiled. "Thank you, Your Honor."

There was more laughter, then a crack of the gavel. Judge Nichols glared at something over Nicky's shoulder, in the back of the gallery.

"The gentleman with the muscle shirt and mullet is kindly advised that he may be seen, unfortunately, in my courtroom but not heard. Proceed with your argument, Mr. Rigopoulos."

"Judge, I could use Porter's flair for the dramatic to show you that, at the very least, a question of fact exists about whether Dr. Satterfield created that hole in the sidewalk in front of his residence on Sedgwick Drive, which caused Doreen Pardy's painful and debilitating injuries, preventing her from returning to her grueling work as a house cleaner. I could open Dr. Satterfield's deposition transcript to the page where he admits driving a Saab over the sidewalk at least twice a day for ten years. Or the page where he admits putting rock salt on the sidewalk during the winters—except when he was at his condo in Hilton Head. Or maybe I could waive a stack of dealership repair bills showing his leaky engine. But I'm not going to do any of those things."

"That so?"

"No, instead I'd like to talk about a subject near and dear to Your Honor's heart."

The judge's law clerk looked up from her nails. The bailiff opened his eyes. Porter put down his silver pen. Even the guy in the back row closed his monster-truck magazine. Nicky had waited for this moment all morning—ever since Lottie had thrust the file onto his chest two hours before. It had been months, maybe years, since he'd said anything in court other than *I submit on the papers, Your Honor,* or maybe *I'll get you a draft order, Your Honor.* None of his cases went to trial anymore. That was the way he liked it—no risk. Just put your John Hancock right there and we'll withdraw the complaint. But he missed something, being on his feet in court, having a pit in his stomach. It made him feel young again. He was only sorry his motion was last on the docket, so that the other lawyers on the cattle call couldn't hear it. He loved an audience.

Then again, so did Judge Nichols, who said, "And what

subject is that, Counsel? Tort reform?"

"You did what?" Lottie said.

"Settled it," Nicky said. "Fixed it, made it go poof."

Judge Nichols had just withdrawn to his chambers, sending everyone to lunch except for the guy in the gallery, who seemed to know the show wasn't over yet. Nicky had been packing up when Lottie had appeared and breathlessly asked for a word-by-word recitation of the argument.

"You voluntarily withdrew the complaint," she said. "How could you?"

"I just explained how we'd come down graciously from a million to seventeen-five, while the defendant was stuck with lock jaw at seventy-five hundred. How all we're fighting over is a lousy ten grand—which is probably close to the lawyers' fees for the motion, the way Trollope charges. The judge split the baby is all. Made Porter step into the hall and call his client's carrier."

Lottie glanced at the gallery and lowered her voice. "But what right did you have? Did you even think of calling Doreen first?"

"I'll call her. She came down to seventeen-five. She'll come down five more."

"Listen to yourself. It's too late for what she *will* do. The case is over. Only you would convert a motion argument into a settlement conference."

"Yeah, Judge Nichols laughed. Porter tried to stop me. Actually objected. Judge asked him on what grounds. Know what Porter said? 'I'd be happy to brief the court on that point.' So much for editor of the *Law Review*."

"Amazing. You have no regret whatsoever. That's it. I'm talking to the judge. The settlement isn't binding because you didn't have authority. It's as simple as that. We'll move to reinstate the complaint."

Nicky put a hand on Lottie's arm. "The case is now off the court's docket, which is three hundred cases long. You're going to ask to put it back on there? You're going to ask *Frank 'Knuckles' Nichols* to put it back on there, to undo some of his personal handiwork? The man loves knocking heads together and settling cases. And you want to deprive him of one of his little joys in life? All because of what, five grand? Your case against Onondaga Furniture is worth a thousand times that. Shouldn't you be upstairs focusing on that? Why did Merritt adjourn it until after lunch anyway?"

"Let go of me. The asshole scheduled a motion ahead of us, a takings case. And don't change the subject."

"No kidding, a takings case? In the city?"

"More painful than a slow divorce. Lawyers for the city lying about how a developer can't do without a dozen properties. Owners whining about a few dollars. I was this close to standing up and saying, 'Your Honor, we're talking about a slum on the south side. If I agree to pay the owners the difference between their selling price and the developer's buying price, can I argue my fucking case?' Marty talked me down from the ledge," she said, referring to one of the firm's associates, Martin Newberg.

"The city needs to clean up that block's crack houses," Nicky said. "If you really want to help, I know a nonprofit you can call. Tax deductible."

"And somehow you'll take the credit. Don't give me your bullshit. I give to real charities—the Rescue Mission, Vera House, the Chadwick Residence."

Nicky was offended. He gave to those types of charities, too, and not just a pittance but ten percent of his income.

"I don't know why you're so worked up about a trip and fall," he said. "Twelve-five is all the case was worth. We all knew it. Permanent injury, maybe. But liability?"

"That was a question for the judge. Which you aren't, yet."

The door between the gallery and counsels' tables swung open, and the man with the mullet stepped through it. He stabbed a grimy finger into Nicky's chest. He had the stringy frame of a heroin addict, and a tattoo on his shoulder. Nicky thought he caught a whiff of a Grateful Dead concert.

"I'll tell you what you are is a sell out," the man said.

"And you are?" Nicky said.

"Son of Doreen. Remember her, your client? She couldn't make it. She's at work, making calls from her trailer for one of them telemarketing companies. All the work she can get since they fused her ankle shut. And lucky to get that with this national Do Not Call List crap. Do you know she can't even baby sit 'cause the women say she can't move fast enough?"

"Really? How's the money in telemarketing?"

As the man fumed, recognition flickered in Lottie's eyes. She stepped between the two men.

"Nick, this is Dale Pardy. Mr. Pardy, I'm Carlotta Magnarella. We spoke on the phone."

"I know who you are. And you can put your damn hand away 'cause I ain't shaking it."

"I'm sorry for the awkwardness. We didn't know you'd be here."

"Awkwardness? Lady, I come to watch the famous Rigopoulos & Magnarella in action. What did the commercials used to say? 'We fight for every penny.' Shit, I didn't know what I was hearing 'til she showed up and 'splained it. You broke the law is what you did. You're just Bonnie and Clyde with a moustache."

Nicky liked that one. He stroked his moustache and wondered if that could have been a commercial. Guns ablaze as they ran from a bank. No, it would've been too . . . criminal. Better would've been Robin Hood and Maid Marian, stealing from the rich and giving to the poor. Except that didn't really matter now since commercials like that were barred by New York State's new rules on lawyer advertising. As of February 2007, lawyers could no longer depict fictionalized events without a distracting disclosure (even if the events were really funny). Nor could lawyers use paid testimonials or endorsements of clients without another disclosure (even if the client was really hot and you had sex with her in a Jacuzzi in Vegas). Everything Nicky did, someone was there to criticize him.

"Much as I enjoy being dressed down by my client's children," he said, "I have a date with a corned beef sandwich." He snapped a rubber band around an accordion folder, then paused. "Mr. Pardy, you're not happy with your mother's settlement, I'm sorry. If your mother's not happy, on the other hand, have her call me. I'll make it right."

Dale knocked the business card out of Nicky's hand.

"We don't want your handouts. We wanted *them* to pay. Besides, we could a got more if there was a jury."

"A jury?" Nicky stopped. "Dale—can I call you Dale? Let me tell you something, Dale. This case was never going to a jury. Your mother was going to lose that motion and get nothing. Dr. Satterfield didn't create that hole in the sidewalk. The only one your mother could hold legally responsible for her injury is the City of Syracuse, but she dropped the ball by not coming to us in time. The only reason she sued, apparently, was to get you some money. Well, we gave it our best shot but defense counsel did his homework and Dr. Satterfield dodged the bullet. It was only through a miracle that his insurance carrier agreed to give us anything. If you sat there and saw everything that happened and still don't understand that, I can't explain it to you. Now if you'll excuse me—"

Just like that, Dale was around a chair, in Nicky's face again.

"You think you can just spew some gobbledygook at me and

walk away? Like I was cuffed to my chair. This ain't over."

"I know, I've lost another vote in November."

Dale stuck out his jaw and gave Nicky another whiff—this time of day-old liquor. "Mister, I can't vote on account of I'm on parole. Know what for? Breaking a guy's jaw with a pool cue. Know why? 'Cause he stole fifty cents from me. You wanna know what I do to a guy who steals five grand from me?"

CHAPTER 2

"Then what?" said Lottie's older brother, Sal Magnarella. "Guy swing at you?"

"Nah," Nicky said. "He just wanted someone to shout at."

"How'd you know that?"

"I could see it in his eyes."

"I didn't know there were Greek gunfighters."

"Just good judges of character, like Aristotle."

"The guy that married Jackie Kennedy?"

"Student of Plato, teacher of Alexander the Great. Father of psychology and ethics."

Sal took a toothpick from his mouth. "All that stuff's Greek to me. All I know, I wouldn't have been so—what's the word?—magnificent."

"Magnanimous."

"Punk gets riled up in my place, I smack him up side the head. Then I take his collar and show him the door. Or, if he deserves it, the alley where we can, you know, talk it over."

"You're a perfect host."

"I didn't last this long in my business being a perfect anything."

"You're a perfect ass."

Sal laughed. "I'm a fat ass."

"There's no point making fun of you if you're going to be self-deprecating."

"You saying I shit myself?"

This was their thing, Nicky playing the brainy stiff, and Sal the dumb thug. But it was just an act. Sal was rougher around the edges than Lottie, but he had her brains.

They were in Sal's bar in Armory Square, an old section of the city that had been redeveloped the decade before. Sal had sold a couple clubs near the University to avoid more lawsuits from barroom brawls and to ride the wave of urban renewal. He'd done a good job—the place, called Lucky's Bar & Grill, a fixture now in the city, its walls exposed brick, its tables dark wood, its ceilings green tin. At the end of the bar, where Nicky and Sal sat, a clip of an SU football scrimmage played on TV.

"How do you think they'll do next weekend?" Nicky said.

"Spread is fourteen points."

"Don't you ever just bet them to win?"

"In the season opener? Against Miami?"

"But you're still going to paint your face and wear that wig."

"We get a good crowd before the game. Helps get people in the mood. The spending mood."

"You're all about school spirit."

Sal made a face.

"You haven't even tasted it yet," said a busty bleached-blonde, setting down their sandwiches. "Usually people wait until after the first bite to grimace."

"That's what the booze is for," said Sal. "Wash the taste out of your mouth."

"I thought it was to give guys an excuse to squeeze my ass."

"No one needs an excuse to do that."

Monique batted her lashes and thrust a hip towards Sal, who leaned over the bar and slapped her butt.

Nicky raised his eyebrows at Sal, who said, "Nick, meet my new girl, Monique. Used to be my personal trainer."

"And before that I was a stripper," Monique said. "In case you were wondering. I could see it in *your* eyes. Nice to finally meet you. Seen your commercials on TV."

"And you're still shaking my hand?" Nicky said, noticing the silver bracelets jangling on the girl's wrist.

"Advertising spreads the word about valuable public services while expanding emerging markets. Besides, the one you used to have where you chased that ambulance waving your business card, that always cracked me up. I don't know, maybe it was the white Reeboks and the black moustache. What I like best, the way you seem so friendly, unlike other lawyer ads, guys screaming and slamming gavels."

Nicky would've complimented the girl on her intelligence, and taste, but he became distracted when she mentioned his moustache. It was the second time that day someone brought it up. That hadn't happened since law school, when he'd grown it. By the time he'd opened his own firm, he'd stopped thinking about it. All the men in his family had one—his father, his grandfather, even his brother, the pro bowler. They grew good ones—thick and black. The only time he'd ever considered shaving it was a few months before, when the girl at the ad agency had said it reminded her of Saddam Hussein . . . only better looking.

Nicky said, "Lottie wanted to pull them after that editorial in the *Post-Standard*. The one where they called me a stain on the fabric of society. I said to Lottie, 'Why not double them? This is who I am. This is how I help people.' "

"I totally agree, except for that last part, which is pure baloney."

"It is?"

"Excessive personal injury verdicts drive up insurance premiums. Businesses then pass the cost on to consumers, who don't notice because they're too busy trying to make a living, or maybe playing the litigation lottery themselves. The whole game is rigged, with the only winners being the lawyers."

Nicky had been wondering how an ex-stripper had gotten so smart when, again, he'd become distracted—this time by her curvy figure. He tore his eyes away from Monique's skin-tight cashmere sweater, and saw hazel eyes blink back at him—aware but not accusing. He was grateful she didn't say anything.

He said, "Some people think what's driven up premiums in the past five years is insurance company losses in the stock market."

"Fat chance, since insurance companies invest about eighty percent of their assets in bonds, not stocks. Besides, historically, in states with caps on damages, premiums have risen about a quarter as much as in states with no caps."

Nicky should've seen that response coming, but he had a canned reply ready, the words rolling off his tongue so easily that they had almost lost their meaning to him. "Maybe so, but the problem with the system isn't lawyers but derelict doctors, corner-cutting contractors, and money-grubbing manufacturers. More people die each year as a result of medical error than from car crashes. What's going to stop careless doctors if lawyers don't? Comparative shopping by sick patients?"

"But don't only about twenty percent of cases against doctors have merit?"

"Depends what you mean by merit."

"Resulting in settlement or verdict," she said.

That sounded about right to Nicky.

"Then why sue the other eighty percent?" she said. "Threatening doctors with lawsuits only makes them cover their ass. Demand informed-consent waivers. Order tests you don't need. And sometimes, no tests when you need them. Like if you're a woman, they avoid giving you a mammogram because it can lead to false positives."

"What about that woman in Wisconsin? The one who had a double mastectomy and then learned the cancer had been in another woman's breasts. Did you know that, under most tort reform proposals, she could've sued only for the cost of her medical treatment, her lost wages, and no more than a quarter mil in pain and suffering?"

"Sounds fair to me," she said. "Besides, I didn't say there shouldn't be personal injury verdicts, just not excessive ones."

"Who's to decide what's excessive?"

"The legislature."

Nicky shook his head, preferring to tackle the problem from the front end, with court-appointed evaluators who screened cases when they were filed. But Nicky knew there were problems with that solution, too. He said, "The only thing legislators care about is businesses leaving their district."

"That's democracy," she said.

"It's not what people want."

"How do you know?"

"Because I talk to them."

"You talk to them?" she said.

"At shopping malls and senior centers," he said. "Baseball games and bowling alleys. Fairs and farmers markets. They want a chance if they're injured. They don't want their damages capped before they get to court."

"You've talked to people all around the state?"

"Not yet, but most of central New York."

"Nicky's going to be governor someday," said Sal. "Or bigger. Like that John Edwards guy. Suing doctors one day, then running for president the next."

Monique shrugged and turned back to Nicky.

"Then you should know more than anyone that if voters want, they can elect legislators who'll give juries discretion, and judges who'll use that discretion."

"Don't tell me you're not voting for me, either. What a day."

"No, I am."

"Yeah? How come?"

"I'm betting you get a case of shyster's remorse when you take the bench."

"I'll take that bet," said Sal.

"You already owe me five bills," she said. "Don't make me call my boys in Utica."

"Don't mind Monique, Nick. She was an economics major in college, when she wasn't doing handsprings behind the bench. Show him your pom-poms, honey. You're spooking the man. He's got to keep his confidence up. He's got a trunk full of them fliers to hand out. What're they called? Palm cards. And voters can smell weakness."

Monique spread her arms and showed off five grand of saline. "Be excessive! Be, be excessive! B-e e-x-c-e-s-s-i-v-e!"

Scattered applause came from the other end of the bar, where someone called for another round. Sal and Nicky watched Monique bounce away, then Sal hung his head.

"Maybe I should give her a spot on the bar instead of behind it. Place is dead at lunch."

Nicky spun around on his stool. Of the three dozen tables, only one was taken, by a little old lady drinking tea, no doubt waiting for her hair appointment across the street. A dozen other patrons sat at the bar, enjoying the Monique Show. Nicky bit into a corned beef and Swiss on rye, wiping Russian dressing off his chin. "Food isn't that bad."

"I'm on my second cook this year. Been through four waitresses, three bartenders, and I don't know how many bouncers and barbacks. They don't show. And, if they show, they don't work. And, if they work, they steal from you."

Nicky wondered what a *barback* was. He pictured a kid washing dishes, like he used to do. "How do you know? The register short at the end of the day?"

"Actually, it's when there's a surplus. See, they put the money in the drawer without ringing up the sale, then they forget to take it out at the end of their shift. For the other times, when they actually get away with it, I put cameras there in the ceiling, aimed right at the registers. Cost a mint."

Nicky wondered what Sal did to the culprits, then decided he didn't want to know.

"I haven't been in the black since before I remodeled," Sal said. "Contractors are sending me collection letters."

"Anything I can do?"

"Lottie's taking care of it. Had me sign some sort of confession for half the debt."

"Confession of judgment. I didn't mean legal help."

"You're asking me if I want a loan? No fucking way. And it's not because I'm too proud. I just don't want to mess things up between us. Me and Lottie are already on thin ice because of her so-called help."

"I wouldn't ask if I cared when you pay me back. I owe you for all the fund-raisers you've let me do here."

"Lottie convinced me to do them, and she was right. It's been the most action this place has seen in months."

"Still, you had to pay your staff." Nicky took out a leather billfold and left a blank check on the bar.

Sal kept eating, staring absently at the bottles behind the bar.

"What are those green ones up there?" Nicky said. "Glenfiddich and Glenlivet?"

"They're so dusty you can't read the labels. It's too bad. I used to make a nice profit on the top shelf. Pour Mohawk Vodka from the well, which you buy for about six bucks a bottle, into the Grey Goose, which you sell for five-fifty a shot, about a hundred bucks a bottle."

"Can't people tell the difference?"

"Maybe straight up but not with a mixer."

"Nice to have a bartender finally admit that. I wish mechanics would be that honest."

"Or lawyers."

After a moment, Nicky said, "I know what it's like to be on thin ice with Lottie."

"She's not pissed at me. Just doesn't have it right now."

Nicky stopped eating and watched Sal stuff the rest of a sandwich in his mouth. The man had his sister's impenetrable veneer. How could Lottie be strapped for cash? She and Nicky had been splitting everything for more than ten years. More money than most people saw in a lifetime. She was divorced with no kids. Drove an old VW Cabriolet—the *ultimate chick car,* Sal called it. And her house—a modest colonial on the east side—was paid off. Other than the slew of charities she supported, what was she spending her money on? He used to know everything about her.

Sal saw Nicky's perplexed look in the mirror behind the bar. Before Nicky could open his mouth, Sal held up a hand.

"Don't put me on the stand, all right? I already said too much. You're going to have to talk to her. I don't want to get in the middle of you two. Remember how it was when you dumped her?"

How could Nicky forget?

CHAPTER 3

"One of the oldest companies in central New York," Bartholomew Crawford was saying, "and one of the best furniture companies in the country, as good as Stickley and Harden, despite its smaller size . . ."

Nicky took a seat in the back of the Appellate Courtroom, next to a woman with a spiral notebook on her lap and a laminated ID on her chest. In the front row sat a couple of guys in ugly golf shirts. One of them lifted a hand to work out a kink in his sunburned neck, showing Nicky nails stained black. Not your usual peanut gallery, but this wasn't your usual case. On the other side of the bar, at one of the two counsel tables, sat Lottie Magnarella in a tight blue suit. Next to her were three grey suits—the lawyers for Cosmic Vacuum, Three Alarm Fire Systems, and Niagara Sprinkler. They were all staring at the ceiling or doodling on their legal pads, pretending to not be impressed by Barth Crawford's argument for why Onondaga Furniture should be dismissed from the case.

Barth was from the same high-priced firm as Porter Boyd—Trollope & Secore. It was the biggest firm in upstate New York—the product of a merger between two regional players in the late nineties that had earned the new monstrosity the nickname *The Evil Empire* among other members of the bar, and its managing partner the epithet *Barth Vader,* which was particularly appropriate due to his fondness for black suits. As managing partner, Barth spent most of his time demeaning other partners in committee meetings, courting new clients at country clubs, and firing associates who weren't making the grade. In his office hung a framed medical record verifying that a lawyer who had once gone up against Barth in a deposition had suffered a heart attack during the ordeal, causing him to withdraw from the case. Now, Barth was called to court every blue moon, when one of the firm's top clients was in mortal danger.

"Plaintiff was one of Onondaga's apprentice chair makers," Barth was saying. "She was at the end of the evening shift when smoke started pouring from one of Cosmic Vacuum's defective machines. Fire spread rapidly throughout the factory, undetected by Three Alarm Fire's defective warning system, and unstopped by Niagara Sprinkler's defective water system. Onondaga's evening-shift fire marshal called the fire department and quickly evacuated everyone from the building except for plaintiff, who chose to stay behind to rescue her Jack Russell terrier, which she had smuggled into work against company policy. Onondaga had no reason to believe that its vacuum machine, fire alarm, and sprinkler system weren't working properly."

"I'm aware of the facts of the case," said Judge Lamond Merritt. "But I couldn't help notice you glossed over a few things. Like the fact that Onondaga purchased the vacuum, subscribed to the alarm system, and helped maintain the sprinkler system. The least its workers can expect is that their company take its fair share of responsibility, don't you think?"

"It has, Your Honor, by paying plaintiff a fair amount through workers' compensation. What she wants is for us now to pay a second time. Under the law, the only reason we would have to do that is if you decided that Cosmic, Three Alarm, and Niagara owe plaintiff something, and that we have to reimburse them because plaintiff's injury was 'grave.'"

"I know the law, Counselor. What I'd like from you is a

straight answer to the following question—plaintiff has sustained several serious injuries, right?"

"Plaintiff alleges several injuries, yes."

"They're more than allegations," the judge said. "These hospital records say she sustained third-degree burns over more than fifty percent of her body, burning off her fingertips. Inhaled carbon monoxide and toxic compounds. Suffered a miscarriage and developed ovarian cancer. Endured a dozen skin-graft operations and got hooked on pain killers. As a result, when she got out of rehab, she was—how does plaintiff's counsel put it?— 'jobless, childless, husbandless, and infertile.' "

"But her medical claims are supported by junk science, at least as they relate to being *caused* by the fire."

"By 'junk science,' you mean an affidavit from her treating physician and a report from an expert—both concluding to a reasonable degree of medical certainty that chemical poisoning from furniture varnish caused her miscarriage, cancer and infertility?"

"And we have our own expert report concluding otherwise."

"Yes, I've read it. Your expert report says nothing about plaintiff's burns. Those burns are a fact, right?"

"Your Honor, although those injuries may be significant, serious even, they're not 'grave' under Section Eleven of the Workers' Comp. Law."

"You actually want me to hang my hat on the difference between 'serious' and 'grave'?"

"Only as defined by *Webster's Dictionary, The American Heritage Dictionary* and—"

"I read your brief, too, Counselor. And I'm still not convinced that the difference between the two terms is anything more than semantics."

"It's more than semantics, Your Honor. It's common sense. If you had to pay a 'serious' tax penalty or a 'grave' tax penalty, which one would you choose?"

"I'd declare bankruptcy and reorganize outside of New York State, like most of our businesses."

Snickering snuck into the courtroom, causing Judge Merritt to launch into a diatribe about counsel who narrowly define terms to support their arguments. Nicky was surprised. That was twice in one day that a judge had made a political comment from the bench. Maybe it was because of the upcoming elections. Not that Nicky didn't agree with the man about the exodus of business from the region. Since the new millennium, central New York had lost—what? Four thousand jobs that Nicky could count off the top of his head, having memorized the numbers for campaign speeches. About twelve hundred at Carrier, five hundred at Oneida Limited, four-fifty at Nestle, four hundred at US Airways, three hundred at Learbury, three hundred at New Process Gear, three hundred at Marsellus Casket, two hundred at Owens-Brockway, almost two hundred at Emerson Transmission, a hundred-fifty at Church & Dwight, a hundred at Wabash Alloys and almost a hundred at Bristol-Myers. And in the nineties, it was worse. Three thousand at GE alone, thirteen hundred at GM, nine hundred at Miller Brewery, almost nine hundred at Smith Corona, seven-fifty at Carrier, five hundred at Buckbee-Mears, and he didn't know how many at Lockheed Martin.

Granted, some jobs had come back to the area. Like Northeast Biofuels' decision to convert the former Miller brewery in Volney into an ethanol production plant. That meant 450 construction jobs, 100 permanent jobs, and a demand for 20 million bushels of corn from local farmers. Stuff like that was great, the way of the future. Like the windmill farms in Madison County. And the plan to expand Carousel Mall using only renewable energy sources. It was important to focus on positive change, Nicky knew. But the loss of jobs still stung, like a slap in the face.

The cuts had affected everyone. Larger companies that served as suppliers. Smaller companies that served as distributors. And all the businesses around the plants—stores, bars, restaurants. Like his parents' restaurant, Spanakopita. Then the neighborhoods would start to die, becoming infested with crime, alcoholism, divorce. Economist-types like Monique the stripper-turned-bartender would say that blue-collar layoffs were a good sign, evidence that the region was moving toward a post-industrial society. One where educated people designed new products and sold services to people around the world. *What services?* Nicky wanted to ask. Energy distribution like Niagara-Mohawk and Agway? They had more than a thousand cuts. Or maybe telecom services like Telergy and Philips Broadband? They had close to a thousand cuts. Maybe it was just over Nicky's head.

But Judge Merritt had come back to earth, focusing his wrath on the case at hand, and laying into Barth for his fancy word play. "I'm less concerned with whatever dictionary is convenient for you to cite, or your carefully chosen examples of common English usage, than with what the statute says. I have it right here. Section Eleven of the New York State's Workers' Compensation Law defines 'grave injury' as including a dozen injuries. 'Permanent and total loss of use of a hand,' 'loss of an index finger,' et cetera."

"Yes, Your Honor, the statute is very specific."

"So specific that it uses the term 'loss of multiple fingers.' "

"I know where you're going, Your Honor, and the Court of Appeals addressed that very issue a few years ago."

"You mean the *Castro* case, the one in which the worker lost the tips of his fingers while operating a die-cutting machine, and the Court held that the loss of five fingertips is not the 'loss of multiple fingers.' Sure, you love that decision, but I can see that Ms. Magnarella is itching to claim that the facts of that case are not the same as ours. In our case, the burns on plaintiff's hands extend well past her fingertips, resulting in permanent nerve damage and restricted mobility. It's as if plaintiff lost those fingers, or even the use of her hand. But relax, Mr. Crawford, I'm not about to ignore the spirit of a Court of Appeals' decision, even if it is wrong. What are plaintiff's damages?"

"Your Honor, plaintiff alleges her damages total ten million, but Onondaga doesn't concede—"

"Counselor, let's stop beating around the bush. We have a woman here with serious debilitating injuries. Isn't it true that the manufacturer of the varnish and the village fire department have already been dismissed from the case? Isn't it true that, if Onondaga wins this motion, Ms. D'Angelo will get little if anything because the other companies are barely solvent?"

"Maybe so, Your Honor, but legally that doesn't matter."

Judge Merritt laughed.

"As I explained," Barth said, "Onondaga has already paid plaintiff. The New York State legislature, in passing Section Eleven, intended to protect businesses and limit employers' liability—"

Judge Merritt waved a meaty hand. "Even more than I hate dictionaries, I hate legislative histories. Some politician telling me what his words mean. If that's all you have—"

"But, Judge, you can't—"

There they were, the four most deadly words in a court of law. Barth stopped himself mid-sentence.

"Yes, Counselor, I can. Tell me one last thing. Isn't it true that Onondaga is thinking of moving production to China?"

"I—I'm not sure that's even relevant to this case."

"I'm sure it's relevant to the company's two hundred employees, some of whom are sitting behind you."

The guy with the black fingernails elbowed his buddy.

"Yes," Barth said, "as one of several options, the company is thinking of moving production to Southeast Asia to accomplish its goal of expanding into the global market, and to avoid the cost of rebuilding its damaged and aging facility in Willow Glen."

"Where it must pay its workers higher wages, offer them a competitive benefits package, and run the risk of paying huge personal injury verdicts from its own funds since it's self-insured."

"The company would never hold that over the plaintiff's head, Your Honor, but yes, a large verdict for plaintiff would be a factor weighing in favor of moving production to Asia."

"As a company spokesman recently told a *Post-Standard* reporter. If it's one thing I hate more than dictionaries and legislative histories, it's defendants who threaten to raise prices, fire workers, or close their doors if they don't get their way. Sit down, Counselor."

Barth smoothed out his silk tie and did as he was told.

"Ms. Magnarella?"

Lottie was already on her feet. "I'm encouraged by the fact that Your Honor recognizes the injustice of letting an employer off the hook for making one of its employees 'jobless, childless, husbandless, and infertile,' simply because of a poorly drafted statute."

"Don't be. I was playing devil's advocate. My job isn't to insure justice, it's to apply the law."

"The plain terms of the statute?" she asked.

"That's the way it works."

"And, here, the statute provides that a 'grave injury' includes 'permanent and severe facial disfigurement,' right?"

The judge raised an eyebrow, apparently not having thought of that one. As he mulled over the term's relevance, Lottie nodded at Martin Newberg, who popped up and did his best Vanna White imitation—setting up an easel in front of the jury box, placing on it a blank white poster, then turning the poster over.

"This is a blowup of plaintiff's face," Lottie said.

"Objection," Barth said. "I wasn't given a prior opportunity to examine this exhibit. Ms. Magnarella kept it hidden over there behind her assistant."

Barth pronounced this last word with such venom that Nicky was reminded of the fact that Barth had personally recruited Martin when he'd come to Syracuse. Martin had declined T&S's offer because of discontent among its associates, who had just seen a ten-percent increase in their billable-hour requirement, with no increase in pay, to boost the new firm's profitability and justify the merger. Now that T&S was rolling in dough, it probably wouldn't even interview an ambulance chaser like Martin.

"You can have an opportunity to examine it now," said Judge Merritt.

Barth walked to the easel and took out his glasses. "Even based on a cursory review, it's clear the reproduction doesn't fairly and accurately depict plaintiff's face."

"What's wrong with it?"

"The coloring, for one. It's too light. Plaintiff has brown hair, not red. Also, the resolution has been distorted. See, the lines of her lips have been blurred. The result is that the blemishes here and here have been highlighted and enlarged."

"Blemishes?" Lottie said. "Those are scars. But never mind the exhibit, Your Honor. Look at the photo in the motion, taken by Onondaga's own counsel, produced electronically to us, and printed by Industrial Color Labs, which used the latest technology without any enhancements, as shown in the attached affidavit of their lab tech. Defendant didn't object to the accuracy of this photo in his reply papers and shouldn't be permitted to do so now. As you can see, the photo clearly shows the scars around Maria's lips. Scars, I might add, that have resulted in permanent numbness. The inability to feel a kiss. People have to tell her when she has food on her face."

As Barth objected as to relevancy, Lottie held up the photo for the judge, leaving the exhibit on the easel behind counsel's table.

"Sit down, Mr. Crawford," said Judge Merritt. "I've seen the photo, Ms. Magnarella. And while it may be accurate, Mr. Crawford would probably respond that the Appellate Division has ruled that worse scarring was not a 'permanent and severe facial disfigurement.' In that case, as you'll recall, the employee sustained facial fractures that required extensive surgery. Doctors inserted seventeen metal plates in the employee's face. Left him with a scar that started here and ended here."

Judge Merritt traced a finger from under his chin to beneath his ear. The gesture reminded Nicky of the sign for death, which he thought was appropriate since the decision the judge was talking about was from the Appellate Division—Lottie's next hurdle on her way to the Court of Appeals.

"Yes, Your Honor, but that case is distinguishable for several reasons. It involved a man, not a woman. And although the law may be blind to gender in other cases, it's not blind to gender in disfigurement cases. Another thing, the scar in that case was hidden, tucked under the man's chin. In fact, the court may have ruled for the employer because the scar wasn't even on the man's face. That isn't clear from the decision, which is very brief, but the statute does require 'permanent and severe *facial* disfigurement.' Most important, the scars here are multiple and more prominent—located on Maria's cheeks and lips. These scars are unable to be masked by makeup, due to Maria's many skin grafts—which have made it difficult for her epidermis to breathe. That, Your Honor, certainly is relevant."

Judge Merritt raised the photo and inspected it with a frown.

"Thank you, Ms. Magnarella. Let's take a ten-minute recess

before I hear argument from counsel for Cosmic, Three Alarm, and Niagara."

"All rise," said the bailiff.

When the judge had shut the door to his chambers, Lottie circled counsel's table, planted her fists, and leaned over. Her low-cut V-neck suit gave co-counsel a good idea why she was known as *Lottie the Body*. As if sensing their distraction, she pounded the table, causing the men to jump in their seats. Her voice fell back to a whisper, and Nicky could only imagine what halftime speech she was giving them. *Ve must stop der Roossians before dey reach der Mutter-land!*

He had to stop *her* before she made them cry. He sauntered over and clapped the shoulder of Martin Newberg, who sat behind counsels' table, wedged against the bar.

"Hey, boss," Martin said. Martin had spent a dozen years in the Army, and it had taken Nicky a good four years to get him to drop the *sir*.

"Bet you never got to man the exhibits at a motion argument in the JAG Corps."

"No, they only let me try murder cases."

"Keep up the good work and someday she may let you carry her litigation bag."

"Don't get my hopes up."

Nicky edged behind counsel's table and leaned in close to Lottie's ear. He said, "Like what you did with that exhibit."

She turned and scowled.

"Keeping it up there during the rest of the argument," Nicky said, "so plaintiff's scarred face will keep staring back at the judge. Did I teach you that?"

"A cheap trick," Barth said. He was grinning at them from the other table.

Nicky had thought he'd been talking in a hushed tone. He straightened. "It may be a trick," he said, "but it's got you against the ropes. Be a good time to put something on the table."

"You always think it's a good time for defense counsel to put something on the table," Barth said. "But in this case maybe it's not such a bad idea." Barth looked at Lottie, then gestured toward the bench. "This guy's a loose cannon."

"You should know," she said. "He's aimed at you today." She turned her back on Barth and lowered her voice. "Damn it, Nick. What do you want?"

"To talk to you," Nicky said.

"Not now."

"What's the deal? You're all done."

She let out her breath. "In his reply, Barth tried to reject our analogy to New York's Insurance Law."

"He's right—it has different language, and a different legislative purpose."

"Thanks for your well-researched legal opinion, Nick. I know our counter-argument. I have to plan how we're going to deliver it."

You have to plan how your co-counsel are going to make an argument? Nicky wanted to ask. Wasn't that their job? And hadn't they done that days ago—in legal briefs, in coffee-cup littered conference rooms, and in front of bathroom mirrors while shaving? Still, who was going to tell Lottie Magnarella to butt out? Nicky saw the doe-in-the-headlight expressions on the faces of Lottie's co-counsel. He wondered if her dire financial condition was causing her increased stress level lately. Maybe it was impairing her judgment, threatening the amount of money she could recover. Hell, it was his duty to the firm to be nosey.

"It's important, Lot."

"No."

"It'll only take a minute."

"What part of 'no' don't you understand?"

At some point after her divorce, this had become Lottie's

repartee of choice. It was now the bumper sticker on her car, her mantra in firm meetings, her zinger on cross-exam. For a while, the word had merely been a joke between them. *No, not yet,* she would say, in the throes of passion. *No, no, no!* Nicky recalled those times fondly, feeling a tenderness that surprised him, a sad memory of the girl inside the guerilla.

"Lot," he said, touching her arm.

She whirled around, back stiff, elbows wide—like he was a bouncer trying to escort her from a bar. He hadn't seen that much anger since the day he'd suggested they cool things down for a while.

"How many times do I have to tell you?" she said. People stopped talking and turned their heads. "Touch me again and I'll show you a *grave injury!*"

CHAPTER 4

"She sounds pissed," said Dara.

"It's the second time today someone threatened me," Nicky said, "and don't use that word." Nicky pinched the phone between his chin and shoulder, and tapped a handful of settlement checks against his desk.

"Peeved, perturbed, piqued, whatever."

"I don't know why she's so uptight."

"You settled her case, embarrassed her in front of her client."

"Client's son."

"Even worse. She's going to hear about it from someone else."

"Whose side are you on?"

"Why, is there going to be a custody hearing?"

"Don't sound so hopeful. Besides, you already have a mother."

"A stepmother, and ha! She's only six years older than me."

"She loves you."

"She loves her ATM card, her pharmacist, and the maitre d' at the Horned Dorset."

"You shouldn't be so hard on people."

"You sound like my principal. That reminds me, did I tell you what happened this morning? I feel awful."

As Nicky watched incoming calls light up his phone, he listened to his daughter tell him about her day at work. One of her students had Tourette's syndrome, which made him blurt out the word *whoop* every five seconds. He kept interrupting her lesson—passing notes, whispering, giggling. So she told him to keep his mouth closed for the last three minutes of class or he was going to be in big trouble. When she remembered his Tourette's, the poor kid was rocking back and forth with his hand over his mouth, like his head was about to explode. As soon as the bell rang, he screamed *Whoop!* so loud he fell off his chair.

"I'm basically going to hell," Dara said.

"You got him to stop, didn't you?"

"It doesn't work that way. He has a disease. He can't help it."

"Teach him to say 'objection' instead of 'whoop' and he'll make a heck of a living some day."

"Why does everyone have to be a lawyer?"

"Why did you call, dear?"

"I don't know."

"You need money."

"I'm fine."

"The invitations didn't go out."

"Are you kidding? They were ready a month ago."

"That leaves only one thing."

Dara sighed. "Brady's mad at me because I want to seat his frat brothers in the corner, beside a ficus tree. They're lucky we even invited them. They want to build an ice luge for the reception."

"But the wedding's in October."

"It's a block of ice with a channel cut into it. Supposed to be for making frosted martinis. Except they use it to chug beer. You should see them down on all fours with their lips stuck to the bottom. They did naked bar slides at the last wedding we went to. Someone called the cops. Did I mention that?"

"We'll give every table a disposable camera. It'll be a Kodak moment. Don't you have to wait for the responses before you do the seating chart?"

"I know who's coming. Half the Greeks in Syracuse, a dozen WASPs from Greenwich, and the cast from *Animal House*. He doesn't even like them, Dad."

There was a knock at Nicky's open door. A woman stood in pearls, sheer stockings, and a silk blouse. Nicky half expected her to be cradling a lap dog. One of those with beady black eyes and a high-pitched yelp. The woman checked her diamond-studded wristwatch.

"Where's Marty?"

"Excuse me, dear," Nicky said and lowered the phone. "Hi, Tiffany. I don't know. I think he's still in court, with Lottie."

"He's supposed to meet me here."

"If you want, I can leave a message with his secretary, Laurel."

"As if that'll do any good. We've spent thirty grand in fertility treatments, not to mention an ovulation kit and a downtown hotel room, and he can't even get five minutes off."

"I'm sorry." Nicky tried to erase the mental image of Martin tearing off his clothes as Tiffany lay on the bed wearing only a stopwatch.

"You should be."

Nicky studied the woman's face, which was free of wrinkles but reminded him of a carved pumpkin two weeks after Halloween. She wasn't much older than his own daughter, the same medium build and dark hair—straight and shoulder-length. But she was different somehow. More mature? No, *tougher*—the angles of her cheeks and jaw more severe, her mouth a permanent frown.

"Dad?" Dara said from Nicky's lap.

"Just a moment, dear," he said. Storm clouds were gathering over Tiffany land. What could he say to make them go away? "You must be frustrated."

"I'm fucking pissed. And don't pull that empathy shit with

me. You make my husband work nights and weekends. He leaves at dawn and comes home so late he just falls into bed. I have to pull off his shoes so he won't stain my satin sheets. I saw him more when he was in the Army, where he was on call twenty-four-seven."

"He's been working a lot with Lottie—"

"So? He works for you, too, doesn't he? I mean, it's your firm when you get down to it, right?" Before Nicky could craft an answer, she said, "You're just like her, full of excuses."

"What I meant was I'll talk to her."

"Talk? Listen, if this last treatment doesn't work, we're going to have to adopt a Russian baby. Do you have any idea what those things cost? Not to mention the airfare."

Nicky couldn't help himself. He said, "Don't we have babies here?"

Tiffany blew out her breath, spun on her high heels, and clopped down the hall. Another satisfied customer. Nicky lifted the phone back to his ear.

"What was that?" Dara said.

"The urge to procreate."

"Sounds like an ad for birth control."

"Having children is very important to some people."

"Easy, Dad."

Dara knew he wanted to be a grandfather almost as much as he wanted another child of his own.

"I'm just saying," he said.

"And I'm just saying we're pretty far from there, okay?"

"You sound discouraged." He thought of Tiffany using the term *empathy shit*. No one had ever called him on that before. And what was it that Lottie had said back in court, when he had suggested a charitable contribution? *Don't give me your bullshit.* What was happening? Was he losing his touch? He tried hard to be sincere with his daughter. "Look, planning a wedding is difficult. In a way, it's good that it is. It's your first real test—can you plan a huge party for your family and friends?"

"I thought it was supposed to be for us."

"That's the honeymoon."

"Don't even get me started on that. He wants to go to the Ritz Carlton in Jamaica. You should hear him. 'It's got five thousand acres and four hundred rooms, right on the Caribbean. There's a spa that gives rose body wraps, cornmeal body scrubs, and deep-tissue massage therapy. And there's a new championship golf course, with caddies that will call in your lunch order so that it's ready at the turn. You can see Johnny Cash's old house from one of the holes.' "

"Sounds nice."

"That's the problem. It's too nice. Costs seven hundred a night. Five hundred bucks for a couples massage and fruit bath. He thinks we're made of money, just because his bonus is twice my salary."

"Is that right? I had no idea he made that much. I thought stockbrokers were struggling these days. You know, with Internet trading and fraud investigations."

"He manages cash reserves for corporations. It's a total racket. Gets an absurd commission for buying risk-free bonds. But that's not the point. We don't know he's going to be making that sort of money forever. We have to save for our future. Our retirement, or a home at least. Do you have any idea how much an apartment costs in the Upper West Side? Not to mention a house in the 'burbs."

"I thought you were thinking of moving back here. Cheap houses, good schools, nice people—"

"Rain, sleet, snow."

"You have to embrace the weather. Buy cross-country skis. Take up downhill again."

"You just like going to a mountain called Greek Peak."

Nicky didn't deny it. His mother's parents had come to central New York from Crete because of all the Greek names on the map. She had once offered him five dollars to memorize them all. There were the easy ones, like Syracuse, Greece, Ithaca, Athens, Sparta, Troy, Marathon, and Corinth. There were ones from literature, like Homer, Odessa, Hector, and Medusa. Then there were the hard ones, like Lysander, Ilion, Ionia, and Apulia. What had struck Nicky were the dozens of places named after Roman statesmen. The one he liked best was Cicero, in honor of the great orator, who after a brilliant legal career entered a political arena plagued by partisanship and conspiracy. It had always bothered Nicky that the man had been executed.

"We haven't ruled it out," Dara was saying.

"Ruled what out?"

"Moving back. When we have a family. Thing is he'd have to find a job. He could take one that pays less if we had enough money saved. But that's not going to happen if he doesn't change. Live within his means, as you put it."

"It takes courage to be cheap."

"That's what I tell him. He says, 'Then you're a very brave woman.' Besides, what are we going to do in Jamaica? Sit on the beach and get sunburned while men in bow ties bring us banana daiquiris?"

"What would you rather do?"

"Go to Greece. Climb the Acropolis, see the Roman baths, maybe check out an archeology dig."

"That sounds expensive, too." Nicky cringed at the thought of going somewhere that required shots so you wouldn't get sick. Not to mention the threat of terrorism. He wrote himself a note to check the distance between Greece and Iraq.

"Not if we backpack. Stay in youth hostels, campsites near the beach. We can stay in a hotel if we find a cool one that's not too expensive. There's this one in the Greek Islands, it's called a 'cave house,' built into the side of a cliff with volcanic rock for walls. Only eighty bucks a night. The air fare would be free with his frequent flyer miles. And it's not like we'd need to rent a car. Athens has a spotless new subway. Only seventy cents a ride. You can take a ferry between the islands, and a bus most other places."

"What does he say to that?"

"That he works hard all year and needs to veg out on his vacation."

"Does he have a point?"

"Maybe, but it's not his vacation, it's our honeymoon. This is going to set the tone for the rest of our relationship. I don't want our free time to be about vegetating. I want it to be about learning, facing challenges, growing as a couple."

He wondered when his daughter had become so serious. It seemed like only yesterday that her world revolved around dolls. Spending hours on Saturday mornings rearranging Care Bears and Pound Puppies on the shelves in her room, singing, *Monchhichi, Monchhichi, oh so soft and cuddly.* For a while, when he drove her anywhere, she would say, *Are we there yet, Papa Smurf?* Once, he picked up one of her Strawberry Shortcake dolls, wanting to know what the fuss was about, and was disappointed that it had lost its berry scent and smelled like BO. Still, he couldn't bring himself to throw it out, even after Dara had left for college. It was probably mildewing in a box in his basement at this very moment. He wanted to tell his little girl to lighten up, that she had her whole life to be stressed out, but he knew better than to criticize her.

He said, "I absolutely agree with you."

"You do?"

"You're a team, a partnership."

"So what do you think I should do?"

"I can't tell you that. Wouldn't be my place. All I can say is that in every partnership I've been in, I've agreed to things I didn't want to."

"What partnerships? You mean, like you and Scarlet? The one who loves me so much?"

"More like me and Lottie. We have our differences. Sometimes she wins, sometimes I win, but usually there's give and take."

"If I hear another person say that marriage is about compromise . . ."

"It's true. You can curse it but you can't change it. Like a law of nature."

"He can compromise my big fat Greek ass."

He wondered who had taught her to swear so much. Brady? Or maybe his raunchy frat brothers?

"Can, keister, caboose," she said. "Whatever."

"You don't have a big fat anything. You have a figure like your mother's."

Nicky fingered the two photos on his desk. One of Corin in a sky-blue prom dress, a white corsage on a spaghetti strap, head cocked to the side, and an obliging smirk on her lips, as if she were being offered a compliment she didn't quite buy. And the other photo, of Dara, also in a prom dress—this one navy blue, with a red corsage on the other strap. There had been something about it that had struck Nicky when she'd come downstairs. He'd told her to wait on the patio while he got his camera. Then he'd said something to her—he wished he could remember what—and it had caused the same reaction as in Corin.

Nicky recalled the day Corin had learned she was pregnant, how she'd told Nicky that if it was a girl they were naming her *Damara*. Nicky had sung, *Damara, Damara, I love ya, Damara, you're only a day away.* So Corin had suggested *Daria.* Then Nicky had pointed out that, if people pronounced the name like *Maria,* it would sound like a distressing bowel condition. Nicky had wanted something a little less ethnic. *Dara* sounded like

Sara. What could be more American? He wished now he'd given Corin what she'd wanted.

"Was she thin?" Dara said, after a respectful moment of silence.

"Don't you remember?"

"I can't really tell from the pictures."

"I carried her up an entire flight of stairs at the Brewster Inn on our wedding night."

"You knew you were going to get lucky."

"Honey."

"Sorry."

"She was like you, except—"

"What?"

"You wear those jeans—the tight bell-bottoms that hang low around your waist. They make your fanny seem flat."

"They're retro, Dad. Like Paris Hilton on *The Simple Life.*"

"She wears them so low they have to blur her fanny cleavage."

"But you look, don't you?"

"Are you bringing your retro fanny home this weekend?"

"Next."

"Put the frat boys closer to the wedding table and stick your cousins in the corner."

"Really?"

"I'll tell the waiter to give their table an extra bottle of ouzo—they won't know where they're sitting."

"Uncle Cosmo will smash his plate on the floor."

"We'll give him a paper one."

"He'll use a glass."

"Plastic then."

Dara seemed to think about this, then said, "You're the best."

Nicky knew she meant it, but unfortunately she wasn't registered to vote in Syracuse.

CHAPTER 5

"What did I miss?" Nicky said to his secretary.

Laurel Lewandowski was concentrating on her computer screen, which displayed an online forecast of the weather in Alexandria Bay. Behind her hung a framed needlepoint that read,

I Can Please Only One Person Per Day.
Today Is Not Your Day.
Tomorrow Is Not Looking Good Either.

She thrust a stack of pink slips at him. "Your orthopod's new out-of-court fee is three hundred an hour, two if he can tell the truth. Your process server says you spin a terrific tale of tragedy in your complaint but that you lost him on the last page, which is missing. And your publicist says to bring your cowboy hat and bathing suit to the shoot on Tuesday. I don't want to know."

"Where is everyone?"

"The kitchen. Lottie and Martin are back, and look happy. Well, as happy as Martin looks. Which reminds me, sorry about his bitter half. I thought of trying to stop her but I didn't want to spend the long weekend in the hospital."

"Don't kid yourself. It would've been a whole week."

"Without pay, I'm sure. By the way, Lottie snapped at *me* because she thought *I* told Tiffany where they were."

"Sorry."

"She called Tiffany a bitch, right in front of Martin. He didn't even wince. I guess Tiffany harassed them on their way back from court. Martin had to put a leash on her."

"That's a cat fight I'd like to see."

"I wonder who he'd root for."

"Both, if he was smart."

The firm's lunchroom was equipped with a half-fridge that smelled like spoiled milk, a small microwave whose door didn't shut all the way, and a plastic table whose vinyl top was peeling. Lottie had taken away the black-and-white TV after she'd learned that Laurel and her sister Marcy, the firm's second secretary, were watching soaps three hours a day. Nicky was outraged—he wanted to know if Nevada was going to wake from his coma and learn he was the father of Kelsey's baby.

Lottie and Martin stood near the sink, pouring themselves coffee. In front of the window was the rest of the R&M gang—"senior counsel" Wally McGuffin, paralegal Terence Thomas Jefferson, and co-tenant Dana Dzikowski who went by "Diz." Marcy had left early to prepare the family camp on the St. Lawrence River for the invasion of the in-laws. If the news was good, she would be sorry she missed the meeting, since it would probably be followed by free food and drinks at Lucky's.

"Let me guess," Wally said. "He reserved decision."

"You make him sound like a wimp," Terence said. "The man's circumspect is all."

"Take it easy. I'm not dissing a brother.' "

"He's WASPier than you, Walter."

"I'm Catholic."

"A fish eater, I know that. I'm talking about the way you dress, how you talk, your boloney and Wonder Bread sandwiches. You've got to loosen up, or else you're going to end up like Marty over there, a one iron up your butt."

"It's only a five iron," Martin said, "and it helps to keep my head still on short putts."

"Are you going to tell us what happened?" Diz said to Lottie, "or just stand there poker faced?" Diz stood with her hands locked behind her back, her shoulders about to pop out of their sockets. She was a six-foot-tall natural-blonde who did triathlons on the weekends and couldn't stand still during the week.

Lottie smiled. "Motion denied."

"He ruled from the bench?"

"While plaintiff didn't sustain a 'loss of multiple fingers,' she did sustain 'permanent and severe facial disfigurement.' "

Everyone cheered except Nicky, who was disheartened by this grim assessment of their client's condition.

"Onondaga stays in the case," Lottie said, "and we're gonna make them pay."

"Over Lord Vader's dead body," said Terence. He'd done three years of hard time at T&S before escaping a week after the Onondaga case was filed. Barth had threatened to file a motion to disqualify R&M, but in the end he'd let Terence work on the case.

"He grumbled something about an appeal, but after calling his client he took me aside and made me an offer."

The only sound in the kitchen was the clink of Lottie's spoon as she stirred in her third packet of Sweet'N Low. She took a sip and made a face like her brother.

"Is there a conspiracy around here against making a decent pot of coffee?"

"Well?" Diz asked.

"Six."

Wally's jaw dropped. "Million? That's a fee of two mil for the firm."

Nicky could almost see him calculate his year-end bonus in his head, this fifty-year-old man who'd come to work for the firm after being temporarily suspended for dipping into his client's escrow account.

"Judge must've scared him," Diz said. "Wasn't his last offer half that?"

"He's coming around," Lottie said.

The others grew silent, compelling Nicky to venture from the safety of his spot in the doorway. "Aren't you going to accept?"

"Don't even start with me." She turned to the group. "He violated the first rule of litigation back in court. Letting our opponent know what we're thinking."

"I thought the first rule of litigation is to get a good result. Besides, it's not like I told him you want to settle. Just the opposite. If anything, it improves your bargaining position. You're the bad cop who doesn't want to cut a deal. Counteroffer eight and tell him he's twisting your arm."

"It's too early to talk settlement, even if we're going to do it."

"Really?"

"This isn't one of your shakedowns, Nick. You don't know the nuances this case involves."

"I wonder what Martin thinks."

"Leave me out of this one," Martin said.

"Are you kidding?" Lottie said. "He agrees with me."

"I don't know about that," Diz said.

Martin said, "Shut up, Diz."

"What are you two talking about?" Lottie said.

"Nothing. I'm on board, whatever you decide."

"Whatever I decide? Christ, Marty, I've told you a thousand times, I don't want a yes man. I need to know what you think."

"I learned a long time ago not to think. Gets me in trouble."

"Once a grunt, always a grunt," Diz said.

"Actually, I learned that from my wife."

"Sounds like a no to me," Nicky said.

"I don't care," Lottie said. "I don't need people to tell me I'm right."

"So, you're just going to reject their offer?"

Finding no paper towels, Lottie shook her hands dry. "Hell, yeah! We're going to make them pay. They ruined that poor girl's life."

"Did they? I thought they just bought the products from the other defendants. Maybe failed to test them, okay, but it's the other defendants that are responsible, right? Onondaga's just the only one that can pay."

Nicky tried to ignore the others' confused looks. He was arguing the other side, and wasn't sure why.

"I don't sort 'em out," Lottie said. "I just sue 'em. Bottom line is six isn't enough. We asked for ten."

"But what's the difference between six million in satisfaction and ten million in satisfaction?"

"Umm, four million in satisfaction?"

There were nervous titters.

"Are you sure you don't mean one-third of four million?"

The tittering stopped.

"I can't believe this. Are *you* implying *I'm* greedy?"

Nicky lifted his chin. Deep down, in a place he would never admit, he hated arguing, believed it to be a giant waste of time. This was an unfortunate feeling to have in his line of work, he knew. But instead of switching to another area of the law, he'd come to think of his job as resolving arguments, making peace. This wasn't that hard for someone with a ready smile and half a brain. Listen to the other side, show them you understand their position, then throw them a bone. Maybe crack a few jokes, if you had to. And it worked, too, most the time. But he'd learned long ago there were some people you couldn't make go away. And everyone who practiced law in Syracuse knew that Lottie Magnarella was one of those people.

Wally was the first to leave the room, then Diz and Martin. Terence Jefferson stepped between Nicky and Lottie, and took their hands, which he pretended to examine.

"You know the rules. I want a clean fight. No low blows. No wrestling. And no hair pulling. You know how you white folks get."

Once Terence had left, Lottie said, "Since when did we start permitting racial jokes in the office?"

"Is it just me," Nicky said, "or have you been unusually touchy lately?"

"Why don't you ever just come out and say things?"

"What're you talking about? I can be direct."

"Only when you're talking politics. Not when it really matters, when you're in litigation."

"Some people might say that's when subtlety matters most."

"Some people have their heads up their ass. Out with it."

"Okay. How are you fixed for cash?"

"Is that what you think this is about?"

"You tell me."

"I've been trying to tell you for fifteen years—some things aren't about money."

"So you want to take cases to trial in order to get *smaller* judgments?"

"You see? I can't stand it. You undermine everything this firm stands for, everything I'm trying to do as a lawyer."

"By winning cases?"

"By settling them."

"What's the difference?"

"Honestly, it's like talking to a wall. I'm just going to say it. I'm quitting as your campaign chairperson."

Nicky had to force himself to swallow.

"I've had reservations for months, but your behavior this morning in the slip-and-fall case was the final straw. I just can't be associated with someone of your—someone like you. Don't worry, I'll come up with an official reason. My caseload is getting out of hand, I couldn't do your campaign justice, I'll think of something. But the truth is, I can't take it anymore. If you lose in November, we may have to dissolve the firm. I won't expect half of everything, just an amicable distribution of assets."

Nicky fumbled for a chair. In New York State, a judge's campaign committee wasn't a mere formality. Only the committee, not the judicial candidate, had the power to solicit campaign contributions. Nicky had a ton of money, it was true, but he had carefully budgeted his campaign so that he had enough to live on for the rest of his life, plus enough left over for a future campaign . . . one on a national scale. If his judicial campaign committee fell apart now, it might throw his plans into disarray.

She took the seat opposite him. "I'm sorry."

"We had a deal."

"Yes, we did."

"Not that naive pact we made fifteen years ago. I'm talking about your picking up the slack here and there so I can do charity work, attend fund-raisers, make connections in the party. Your agreeing to chair my campaign in exchange for all the firm's assets."

"What assets, that crappy coffeemaker?"

"We own everything in this office. And a half mil in accounts receivable."

"Take the money, I don't want it. I want the man I once knew. The man who was going to hold arrogant doctors and ruthless corporations accountable."

"Aww, Lottie. I just told you that stuff because you wanted to hear it."

"No, you meant it."

"Maybe I did, I don't remember."

"You changed, after Corin. I never understood why. Losing her—"

"Lot."

It stopped her for only a moment. "I'm sorry, but it would make most men mad."

"What use would getting mad do?"

"To make you get even."

"What can I do to the man? He's a paraplegic. I deliver his meals."

"Not mad at *him* so much, but others like him. No-good, lying, cheating bastards—they're all the same. But instead of stopping them, you help them, with that *I'm Smart* thing."

Nicky gazed out the window at the brick wall across the alley. He'd never thought he was *helping* drunks by driving their cars home, but disarming them, taking the weapons of mass destruction out of their hands. Besides, what was the point in punishing an addict?

"There's no getting even."

He knew this sounded like he was renouncing justice, an ideal that was Lottie's entire reason for living. But she didn't argue with him. Her pity irritated him.

"And why does it have to change my life, anyway? Because your husband's leaving you made you hate all men?"

"I'll ignore that, given the painful subject I raised. But, for the record, I left him."

"Tell that to his girlfriend."

"Don't bring that slut into this. And don't try to reframe the issue. You lose your wife and all you do is decide to make more money."

"I've told you—"

"I know, your call to public service. Your ability to bring people together, get things done. You're a Mediterranean Bill Clinton."

"And you're the only one who can have a dream? Representing only women? Risking a jury verdict and cutting your fee to 'make them whole'? Who're you, Erin Brockovich?"

"The difference between my calling and yours is mine is premised on integrity and honesty."

"Are you still mad at me for not leaving Scarlet?"

Lottie's face fell, and Nicky knew he'd gone too far. They could insult each other, raise the specter of each other's lost loves, trash each other's very missions on earth, but this scar was too tender to touch. Still, he didn't apologize.

"Get over yourself," she said.

As she rose to leave the kitchen, leave him, he felt anger wash over him for the first time in years, hot tears springing to his eyes, burning blood coursing through his veins.

"I brought you into this firm, trained you, gave you half of everything. All I asked for was some support, some loyalty. How can you do this to me?"

He found himself standing alone, fists balled, his voice ringing in his ears, like it belonged to a stranger.

"You think you can just walk out on me? I won't let you! Do you hear me?"

CHAPTER 6

"Greek in the house!" a young man shouted, pointing at Nicky.

Nicky had thought his day couldn't get any worse.

"Zeus chug!" the other young men shouted back. They started pounding on their picnic tables, rattling their plates and silverware.

A little guy in jeans and a T-shirt jogged to the center of the room, dropped his pants—boxers and all—and raised a cup of milk to his lips. At first Nicky thought this was the slowest chug he'd ever seen, the noise from the tables giving him a headache. Then he realized that was the point—the kid bare-assed and motionless, like a Greek statue.

The others chanted "Zeus! Zeus! Zeus!" as the milk slowly began to disappear.

Nicky wondered how he got himself into these things. At six o'clock, no one had answered his knock at the front door of a big, old house on the SU campus. Inside, wooden furniture and beer cans had littered a cavernous room, whose windows were covered by thick black shades. An old yellow lab had stood up in front of a dark fireplace, shaken himself awake, then led Nicky toward the rumble of voices and the clank of dishes. Nicky had found a roomful of guys in sweatshirts and baseball caps bearing the letters ΔTX. They'd looked up, put down their forks and fallen silent. Then they'd busted out laughing.

That's when Nicky realized there were no *Young Democrats for Nicky Rigopoulos.*

When the cup of milk was finally empty, the little guy wiped off his white moustache, pulled up his jeans and returned to his seat, where he was greeted by heavy slaps on the back.

"It looks like I'm not the only comedian here tonight," Nicky said. "The least you can do is let me do my routine."

There were whoops and hollers, then a kid with broad shoulders and curly red hair climbed onto the table and extended his arms, commanding silence. He was the same one who had pointed at Nicky. The kid said, "You going to give us a campaign speech?"

"Who're you? D-Day or Bluto?"

"Those names are retired. I'm Double-Down. The runt with the donkey schlong is Yoda, that bald one over there is Frazier, and that chubby one in the corner with the Drew Carey glasses is Two Beers. He's worrying about whether this is going to cut into his study time."

There were some jeers and jibes.

"It'll only take a minute. I thought I'd do something different tonight. Instead of telling you about myself, I thought I'd tell you about yourselves."

"Cool, a psychic."

More chuckling.

"Let me give it a try, see if I'm right. What're there, fifty of you? Only a dozen minorities, right in line with the University average. Can't pledge until you're a sophomore, and a few of you are probably on the five-year plan, so you're ages nineteen to twenty-two. Statistically, that means half of you call yourselves independent, and only a fifth of you vote. Most of you are probably from New York State—central New York, Buffalo, Long Island."

"Go Giants!" someone shouted.

"Giants suck!" someone shouted back, throwing a handful of peas.

That prompted a volley of dinner rolls, followed by some hand-to-hand combat, and eventually a truce.

When Nicky had the boys' attention again, he said, "The Giants do suck, and so do the Jets, but only because I'm a Bills fan. Where was I? About a quarter of you come from private high schools, more than able to pay SU's forty-grand-a-year tuition, room, and board. The rest of you need some sort of financial aid. As far as majors go, most of you have already changed once, and half of those will do it again. But the one thing you all have in common, you want to have a little fun before you have to go out and find a job. And you hate the University's administration—what they're doing to the Greek system. How am I doing?"

"This sucks," someone shouted. "Worst stand-up routine I've ever seen."

"I thought we ordered a stripper," shouted someone else. "Show us your tits!"

When the chorus of catcalls died down, Double-Down said, "You could've gotten that stuff from the catalog."

"Then let me tell you what I think. The guys on the Sunday morning talk shows—the shows you sleep through because you're hung over—they'll say you're Generation Y. That you're skeptical and disconnected. You don't care about drilling for oil in Alaska, or the cost of prescription drugs, or the impact of the Patriot Act on public libraries. You're more likely to vote for the next American Idol than for president. And the only political issue that galvanizes you is maybe the war in Iraq. But I don't buy that."

"You don't, huh?"

"I see something else. You don't like war, but who does? What keeps you up at night, except for Zeus chugs and naked bar slides—"

"Bar slides," someone shouted.

"What keeps you up is the future."

"You mean like next weekend?" Double-Down said.

"What you're going to do when the party's over. After you graduate with a degree in I-don't-know-what-I-want-to-do-with-my-life and a boatload of debt. What's it up to? Fifty grand in student loans, five in credit card debt, and if you've traded in that piece of junk your old man gave you for a new piece of junk to impress some girl, another fifteen in car loans? What's that, seventy grand?"

"Per year."

"You want to know the worst part?"

"Hey, fellas, it gets worse."

"The job market sucks, despite what the White House tells you. Some people are getting jobs, sure, but are the jobs the ones they want? Forget whether they like the work, which is a whole other issue, but do they have the right pay and benefits? Can you imagine having to take a second job at the mall just to pay your Visa bill? Plus, the unemployment rate among kids is twice that of everyone else. Your résumés will be buried in a pile of others just as impressive. Face it, in the back of your mind, you know that, when you get out of here, you might be moving back home for a while. Have to pick up your room and empty the garbage again."

"So, what can you do for us? Get us all jobs?"

"I'm not going to blow smoke up your ass. Say read my lips, no new taxes. I'm not running for Congress anyway, just Supreme Court. You probably don't even know what that is, do you? It's not the highest court in the state. In New York, we call that the 'Court of Appeals.' No, in New York, the Supreme Court is the state-wide trial court of general jurisdiction. Its jurisdiction is greater than other state trial courts like county courts, city courts, or town courts. It hears civil cases in which more than twenty-five thousand dollars is at stake. It has exclusive jurisdiction over matrimonial actions, declaratory judgments, and what are called 'Article 78' proceedings—actions brought most typically when a governmental body or officer has exceeded his jurisdiction or has failed to do something required of him. In upstate, criminal trials are handled by county courts and smaller local courts, depending on whether the crime is a felony or misdemeanor. Bottom line is you probably won't see me but some city court judge if you have a lead foot, or maybe you get caught doing whip-its in the cookie aisle at Price Chopper at two a.m."

Two of the kids high-fived each other.

"But I think it's only fair to warn you, if you did show up in my court for drunk driving, I probably wouldn't let you go on your own recognizance. I would probably detain you until trial or require a few years' tuition in bail, because you would probably be screwing up your life and would need some time alone to think. And that's the sort of no-nonsense attitude that I would apply in my civil cases, regardless of whether you are the plaintiff or defendant."

"That's your campaign promise?" said Double-Down. "To throw the book at us?"

"Hey, if you want someone who'll hold your hand and tell you sweet lies, then don't vote for me. I'm not running for *Dad of the Year*. I'm running for judge. Judges make decisions. Almost every decision is both fair and unfair, depending on which perspective you have. I can't promise what my decision will be, but I can promise how I'll make it. By applying the law to the facts, fair and square. Without playing favorites, and without crying crocodile tears as I reach for a knife. I'll just look you in the eye and tell it like it is. And you know why? Not because I love America, or I feel your pain, or any of that crap. It's just because I respect you, and because I believe everybody deserves the same chance. It's as simple as that. And if that doesn't matter to you, if you're too cynical or stupid to see that, then I guess you're right—I don't want your vote."

Nicky soaked up the room's serenity. No pants dropping. No smart-ass remarks. He might have even reached the one student registered to vote in Syracuse.

"You can all close your hymnals. I see that green table folded up over there. Who thinks he can beat an old man in Ping-Pong?"

Nicky received a few apologies as the dishes were carried to the kitchen and the picnic tables were pushed aside. The Ping-Pong table was pulled out, and the kid known as Frazier slid aside a framed composite of fraternity photos, and lowered a beer tap from a hole in the wall. Double-Down explained how the beer was pumped up from a keg in the basement, Frazier's future engineering degree hard at work. How the house was officially dry this semester because of some overzealous pledging last spring. If the University found a can of beer in their dumpster, it was bye-bye Delta Tau Chi.

"You're not going to blow us in," Double-Down said, "are you?"

"As long as none of you get behind the wheel."

"We all live within walking distance of the house, and the bars. And by the way, we don't call it Ping-Pong anymore. It's beer pong or smash pong."

Double-Down set a cup of beer on either end of the table, a paddle's length from the edge. He explained how the object of the game was to hit your opponent's cup with the ball. For every hit he had to take a sip, and for every slam dunk he had to chug. Hits were worth one point, dunks were worth five. First person to twenty-one was the winner.

"A warm up before hitting the bars," Double-Down said.

Nicky realized that in a few short months he was going to have a son-in-law who was not so far from this mentality. Maybe he should reverse his decision to move Brady's buddies to the middle of the ballroom.

It took Nicky only a few volleys to get back in the swing, remembering what it was like to play his little brother Alex in the basement growing up. By the end of the game, which Nicky lost by one point, he'd suffered two chugs and inflicted one. When he retook his place among the spectators, the brother known as Two Beers offered him a fresh beer, which he turned down.

"I have to greet people at the Fair at seven-thirty. I don't want to smell like a brewery."

Two Beers handed the cup to someone else. "I'm sorry, Mr. Rigopoulos. I feel kind of responsible for all this."

"Why? You the one who called?"

"Double-Down did it to bust on me. He found out I'm in the College Democrats."

This got Nicky's attention.

"No big deal," Two Beers said. "I just help students register to vote in Onondaga County, you know, before October tenth."

Voter registration? Nicky clapped Two Beers on the back, two believers in a room full of atheists. "Don't worry about it. Why aren't you drinking?"

"I have a date tonight, and my girlfriend's kind of uptight."

"Why do they call you Two Beers?"

"Freshman year, that's how many it took me to get drunk."

"Probably saved a lot of money." Still, Nicky felt sorry for the kid, with his nerdy interest in politics and his uptight girlfriend. He reminded Nicky of himself.

"You got a real name?"

"Todd Grossman."

"What do you have, scoliosis?"

"Spina bifida."

"That was my next guess. Occulta?"

The boy nodded. "Usually people ask if it's MS."

"No, your muscle tone's too good. You lift weights?"

"Since I was in eighth grade. Not that it shows."

"It makes a difference. Keeps the disease from running your life, right?"

"You know someone with it?"

Nicky shook his head. "I used to be on the Board of the March of Dimes." And he stopped himself. He didn't want to get into it—being a plaintiff's attorney, having handled med mal cases involving spina bifida. Next thing the kid would be asking, *What for? Failure to diagnose the disease, so that the mom could abort the fetus? No,* Nicky would explain. *Failure to advise the mother of the need for folic acid.* But it wouldn't matter—they would be talking about the disease like it was a life-ruining condition . . . which it was for some, but not others. Nicky was contemplating a subtle change of subject when the boy let him off the hook, saying, "Listen, you've been pretty cool about all this. If you need someone to hang up signs around campus, I know the right spots."

"You mean it?" Nicky said.

"No prob."

"Thanks. I have some signs in my trunk."

But Nicky came back in carrying more than signs.

"You have enough stuff?" Todd said, opening the big box that Nicky had put down.

"I don't know, let's see," Nicky said. "Emery boards, cigarette lighters, and lapel pins for the ladies. Salons will put them up at the front desk if you ask them the right way."

"All with logos," Todd said. "Nice."

"Nothing but the best for my constituents. And for barber shops, we have combs, cigar clippers and Titleist golf balls. I was seriously debating using Nike balls. You know, for some sort of Nike-Nikomedes reference, but I wasn't sure I could pull it off without risking a trademark-infringement claim."

"Lawyers."

"For dry cleaners, we have cuff links, tie clips, and sewing kits. For bookstores, we have bookmarkers, pens, and plastic coffee mugs. For golf pro shops, we have tees, ball markers, and divot repairers. For bars, we have coasters, bottle openers, and bumper stickers. And for men's clubs, we have playing cards, baseball hats, even a dart board."

"That's your face on it."

"Aim for my big fat Greek nose. People say you can't miss it."

That got Nicky a big smile, the first time it seemed Todd was really warming up to him. And just like that Nicky knew he had just turned one vote into ten.

CHAPTER 7

"You wore that to book club?" Nicky said to his wife.

When he'd gotten home at midnight, his front door had been wide open. He'd locked it and stepped in front of the foyer mirror—the one with gilded edges that Scarlet had bought on a whim. He'd straightened his tie, run his fingers through his salt-and-pepper hair, then popped a breath mint. He'd found Scarlet in the billiards room by the bar, a bottle of Tanqueray at her elbow, a red silk cocktail dress clinging to her chest and hips.

"Sure," she said, "a three-thousand-dollar Oscar de la Renta. Except for some reason they didn't call it 'book club' tonight. Kept calling it 'The Barristers' Benefit.'"

"Oops." He grabbed the remote, sunk into the La-Z-Boy, and pretended to surf the news channels. "I was handing out palm cards at the Fair."

"Didn't you already do that twice this week?"

"You don't win an election by sitting around the house."

"When have you ever sat around the house?"

"When have you ever missed me?"

In the beginning, he'd welcomed Scarlet into his home, lounging with her in front of her new entertainment system, which included surround-sound speakers and a satellite dish. But then he'd started to notice little things about her, like the way she criticized celebrities' love interests or plastic surgeries with such venom that it made him wonder if she were on a first-name basis with them. He'd brushed this off as one of the

64

character flaws that makes a lover endearing, but then the objects of her criticism started to expand, spreading to the couch, the house, and ultimately himself.

He wasn't doing things right—setting the thermostat, loading the dishwasher, sorting the laundry. He'd wanted to say he'd done these things for decades, and Corin and Dara had never complained. But instead he'd shelled out three hundred bucks for a remote-controlled digital thermostat. He'd learned to scrub the dishes spotless, dry them so no water dripped on the way to the dishwasher, then load them her way. And he'd read all her labels so he knew which clothes to hand wash and hang dry, and which to machine wash (cold water, unscented detergent) and fold when the drier buzzed.

But his efforts to please her only made her more unhappy. She began focusing her criticism on his personality—his taste in music, which she'd said was stuck in the eighties. His personal habits, the annoying way he cut up his food into child-size morsels and chewed each one twenty times. His Syracuse accent, the nasally honking sound that made him say *Lah-tie's gunna Cape Cad.* Even his manhood itself, one winter morning in the frosty bathroom of a Lake Placid ski lodge.

He felt her scrutinize him now in the billiards room. She snubbed out her cigarette, weaved across the room, and leaned on the arm of his chair, her ice cubes rattling in his ear.

"Fair smells sweeter than I remember. No onions and fried dough." She sniffed. "I didn't know they sell liquor."

Nicky ducked under her glass and stood up. "Everything must smell like liquor to you by now. I have to get up early for the Farmers' Market. Lottie and Diz got me a booth."

"Shouldn't shit where you eat."

"Excuse me?"

"Not Diz. I know she plays for the other team. I meant Lilly. You know, the wife of the party chairman."

He ran through his list of plausible denials—he was at the Fair the entire evening, he left the Fair briefly to talk to the party chairman, Wesley Longacre, about the election, or he never went to the Fair because he had to ask Wes's wife, Lilly, if he could use her farm for a commercial. But for some reason his mind stuck on Lottie's insult about honesty.

He said, "I know what I'm doing."

She didn't flinch at this debut of candor. "I didn't know she was your type. Or you hers. Little miss goody-goody."

"She's not like that."

"She feeds the sick and the poor, doesn't she? Like Mother Teresa?"

"A lot of people do Meals on Wheels."

"Is that why you got into that?"

Nicky had been volunteering at MOW long before Lilly had started. He'd thought of it as a way to get to know senior citizens, learn their concerns. The only problem was that, if they were too frail to shop or cook, they were probably too frail to vote. But he'd fixed that by giving a list of their names and addresses to Wes, who'd promised to send over a van on Election Day.

"We share a common interest," he said.

"I bet that's not all you share. Beds, bathtubs, body fluids. Do you pray together afterward? 'Forgive me, father, for I have been a very, *very* bad girl.' "

"Cut it out. She's a good person. She loves kids."

He regretted the words as soon as they left his mouth.

"In that case, maybe she can give you two-point-three children. They could play with the two she already has."

He headed for the door.

She said, "Maybe if I wanted kids, you'd sneak off with me, too."

He stopped. "When we first met, you said you did."

And he had believed her. She had been a nanny for some friends of his at the time. He had watched the way the children ran to her, and clung to her, but at the same time obeyed her—surrendering at the count of three, dreading one of her time-outs. She had exuded maternal hormones, filling his head with images of crowded station wagons.

"I changed my mind when I got down to a size two," she said. "I don't want all of the rolls of fat and stretch marks. Sagging boobs and varicose veins."

"Come on, it's not like that's anything you wouldn't fix. A nip here, a tuck there."

She didn't deny it, this thirty-year-old woman with all new parts—saline breasts, a liposuctioned ass, a plastic nose, collagen lips, ceramic teeth, botox eyelids, green contacts, auburn-dyed hair, and a nuclear tan.

"You sure it's not because you don't want to give up the limelight? Have to skip your Junior League parties for PTA meetings? Trade in your Jaguar XK8 convertible for a Dodge Caravan?"

"First of all, serving on the boards of the Syracuse Symphony, Everson Museum, and Landmark Theatre is hardly an ego trip. And second, I wouldn't be caught dead behind the wheel of a minivan, much less a Dodge. It would have to be a BMW. That new SUV, the X5."

"Let's do it. We'll go to the dealer tomorrow."

"Then what? In nine months I get stuck with an eating-pooping-crying machine while you plan your next campaign? It's been twenty years since you've had to change a diaper, Nick. Read a bedtime story, give a bottle at two a.m. I know what crap comes with having a baby, I remember. God, how can I forget, listening to the girls bitch. Face it, you do what you want when you want. Besides, you already have a kid."

"I want another, I want a family again. We'll hire a nanny. We already have a maid."

"Oh, you'd like that. A little French hottie."

"A male nanny then. What do they call them? A manny."

Mischief danced in her eyes.

"A gay one," he said.

"That'd be a great role model for a child. He can teach our son to speak with a lisp and pick up boys in the locker room. They can stay up late getting fashion tips from *Queer Eye for the Straight Guy*. Besides, won't having an au pair blow your middle-class image?"

"We're hardly middle class, Scar."

"You clip coupons. Wear suits off the rack. You drive a Saturn."

Nicky admitted his choice of cars had been limited since he'd decided to run for office. The Saturn was American, owned by GM, and made entirely in Spring Hill, Tennessee, and he liked the no-hassle way they sold it to you. Besides, it ran fine, better than her English-made Jaguar, which he'd agreed to buy only because Ford owned the company, a fact he'd relied on to get the endorsement of a local labor union. And he wasn't ashamed of his clothes. He shopped at Christopher's, formerly Learbury, which had once made suits for Brooks Brothers. Good quality at a reasonable price. Sometimes he even shopped at that discount store, Marshall's. And what was wrong with off the rack? It's not like he had an odd body size—forty regular with a thirty-two waist. Maybe a thirty-three in the winter holiday season. At five-foot-eleven and a hundred seventy pounds, he'd always thought of himself as lucky.

"You won't even let us join Iroquois Country Club," she said.

"They don't let in Blacks or Jews."

"They have some Jews. They'd let you in, if you kissed some ass. Apologized for suing their members. Maybe shaved your moustache."

"That's the third time today someone mentioned it. What's wrong? I just trimmed it."

"You look like Saddam."

He let out his breath. "Anyway, whether I'd get in isn't the point."

"You mean they're too exclusive."

"They're racist."

"I heard they'd let Blacks in but none apply."

"Do you really believe that?"

Nicky had once asked Scarlet how she could be such a raging racist and still have married him. She'd told him she hadn't known how swarthy he was, just thought he was real tan. And as for his name, she'd said he'd acted white enough. Nicky had always wanted to ask what that had meant. Out of a sincere desire to communicate better, he'd re-read a dog-eared paperback called *How to Argue with a Conservative*. But this had only driven her to buy a signed hardcover of Ann Coulter's *How to Talk to a Liberal (If You Must)*.

"Whatever," Scarlet said, "but Drumlins? The women are boring, always going on about their husbands and their kids. And the pool is so crowded, teeming with the little monsters."

"That's why we have our own pool, if I remember correctly. Not to mention a tennis court."

"You won't play with me. Always campaigning, or doing commercials. Or whoever you do on nights and weekends."

"You had your own tennis pro up until this year. And I use the full meaning of the word 'had.' "

"Paolo," she said, losing herself in reverie.

"You could find someone to play with if you really tried. Form a league with your fellow board members. Play at their clubs some of the time—Cazenovia, Limestone, wherever they go—and here some of the time."

"Can you imagine those old stiffs trekking into the city in their tennis whites? We're six blocks from the ghetto."

"It's not that bad. It keeps things in perspective. Reminds us of what we have to be grateful for."

"We can afford to live anywhere we want. On the water in Caz or Skaneateles." She pronounced the word *skun-ee-at-uh-lis*, without a central New York twang. "Even a horse farm in Manlius would do. You can keep your perspective there. But no, you have to be a Syracuse resident. Why? It's not like you're running for City Court. What are there, six counties in the Fifth Judicial District? You can live in any of them, to run for Supreme Court. And you'd probably stand a better chance winning if you lived out in the 'burbs, with all the Republicans."

"I've told you a million times."

"Right, you would feel like a traitor, like you were abandoning your roots. This is where you grew up. Please, you didn't grow up on Robineau Road. You lived on the North Side, with all the Eye-talians. Do you think they would have a funeral if you left? Cry on their cannoli?"

"White flight is part of the reason the city is hurting for tax dollars."

"Then send them a check every April fifteenth. Besides, it's not like you're above selling out, screwing Peter to get paid by Paul."

He looked at her laser-smooth legs, diamond ankle bracelet and pedicured toes. "You'll never get it."

"Oh, screw you. You're going to judge *me?*"

"Do we have to do this now? I can't take all this arguing."

"We haven't even talked in six months. Ever since you threw your hat in the ring. Why do you even need to be a Supreme Court Judge? If Eliot's going to appoint you to the Court of Appeals, he'll just do it. That's what Pataki did with that one guy, right?"

Nicky had already explained to her the procedure for nominating a Court of Appeals Judge. How seven candidates had to be recommended and ranked based on their credentials and experience. How then the governor could pick one. And how the appointees and candidates are almost always judges, and appellate judges at that. He was too tired to go over it again.

"What do you want from me," he said, "a divorce?"

She didn't flinch. Obviously, she'd been thinking about it, too. Was it so awful for him to be thinking about it? They had had some good times together, mostly involving sex at fancy resorts, okay, but good times nonetheless.

"I know you won't consent to one," she said, "and I can't get one without grounds. You haven't moved out, even when I've changed the locks. You haven't shouted at me in public, even when I've pissed you off. And you've been too careful to give me any proof of adultery."

So she had even been doing some research. He wanted to commend her on her efforts of discretion, now that they were on the subject. The way she joined every garden club and nine-hole group she could find so she always had an alibi. But she was right, he wouldn't consent to a divorce . . . without certain concessions. He'd done the math and knew he wouldn't have enough money to run for governor someday if he gave her half of everything now.

She finished making herself another drink. He wondered if this was the time to get the divorce ball rolling, eight-and-a-half weeks before Election Day. He noticed the dopey look in her eyes, the sluggish way she squeezed behind the coffee table and sunk into the couch. He decided it was as good a time as any to make his initial settlement offer.

"Here's the deal. You ready?"

She shimmied to an upright position.

"We stay married through the election, then you get a four-bedroom house on a lake, a Stickley furniture shopping spree, a nineteen-foot motor boat, a new BMW, a membership at two country clubs, and enough support so you won't ever have to work."

He waited for a reaction, wondering if he could have gotten away with a three-bedroom condo and a one-club membership.

She said, "If you think you can buy me off like one of your—"

Then she stopped, her attention grabbed by someone else's voice, her eyes fixing over his shoulder. He followed her gaze to the TV, on which camera lights caught a green sheet covering a body. The body lay on a stretcher being wheeled out of a modest white colonial.

"What is it?" he said.

"Isn't that—"

She didn't have to finish. It was.

CHAPTER 8

"Any chance you can turn that thing off?" Nicky said, shading his eyes.

The light went off and he waited for his vision to return.

Lottie's street had been clogged with police cars and a TV news van, all bathed in flashing red lights. At the end of her driveway, sawhorses and police tape had held back a throng of onlookers, including more than a few carnivorous reporters, Nicky was sure. He had coasted by, circled the neighborhood, and parked on the next street over. There, he'd slipped between two houses, gotten down on all fours, and crawled into a wall of bushes. While he usually liked free press coverage, he hadn't been in the mood tonight; he'd been too worried something was wrong with Lottie. On the other side of the bushes, as he'd been brushing off his suit pants, he'd seen his loafers light up.

Now he saw a silver badge, large eyes, and a slender neck. A woman said, "Returning to the scene of the crime?"

Nicky was confused. "What do you mean? What's going on here?"

"That's what I'm trying to find out."

He introduced himself and extended his hand.

She took his wrist. "I know who you are. Detective wants to talk to you. And don't give me any trouble."

"I wouldn't dream of it. They showed a body on TV but didn't give a name. I could tell it was Lottie's house. But it wasn't her, was it? Please tell me it was someone else."

Nicky knew that didn't sound right. His arm was jerked along, his feet stumbling over the lawn. It all gave him a sinking feeling. Everything below the exterior house lights was the way he remembered—the flower garden he'd watched Lottie plant, the peeling shingles he'd promised to paint, the cheap patio furniture he'd convinced her to buy. What if something terrible had happened inside? What if that body under the green sheet *had* been Lottie's?

On the back deck stood two uniformed cops talking in hushed tones. Nicky tugged his hand free and lagged behind his escort to hear the first ask the second a question. The second said something about blunt trauma.

"Whose blunt trauma?" Nicky said. "Who died?"

The cops stared at Nicky like he was speaking Chinese.

"Come on," the lady cop said.

She let him go in the kitchen, where a crime tech dusted for prints and a police photographer took pictures. A voice crackled over a walkie-talkie. Nicky grew angry, seeing all these people in Lottie's house. He'd spent countless hours here, sometimes working, sometimes hanging out. A cutting block lay on the counter beside a butcher knife. Had there been some sort of break-in, maybe a struggle?

"Don't move."

Nicky watched the cop walk down the hallway to the living room. Then he stepped into the office adjoining the kitchen, craning his neck to see if anything seemed out of place—the papers on the desk, the books on the shelf. A taped silhouette lay on the hardwood floor, beside her chair. A man stepped in front of him and said, "Curiosity killed the cat."

Nicky tried to hide his alarm. He said, "That's a fine attitude for a cop."

"What gave me away? My square jaw or the steely look in my eyes?"

"The badge on your belt."

"Name's Halliday."

"You the one they call Doc?"

"By the same ones who call you Tricky Nick. Slick Nicky, the Greek Sheik, the Middle-East Mouthpiece. I can't remember 'em all. You look a lot bigger on TV."

"What happened, Detective? Where's Lottie?"

"We'll get to that. First, I have a few questions."

"For me? Hold on."

"Don't worry. Routine stuff."

Nicky didn't like where this was going. Lottie was Lord knew where—detained in some squad car, dying in some ambulance, dead in some morgue—and he was going to stand here and give an interview? He wanted to walk away but the man had a gun on his hip. Everyone had guns on their hips. There had to be another way out of this.

"Bellevue?" said Nicky, nodding at the green golf pencil the man had removed from a small spiral notepad.

"This? Swiped it from the pro shop. Can't afford the dues. Don't get all clubby on me. What were you doing in the bushes?"

"I didn't mean anything by it. You look like you do pretty well for yourself. Nice jacket, nice tie. What's that, a Rolex?"

"Lolex, from Chinatown. Five dollar, run long time."

"Aren't knockoffs against the law?"

"I wouldn't know, I'm not a lawyer. Now about those bushes."

"I was trying to get in. What did you think?"

"I didn't know. Maybe you were trying to get away."

"Get away? From what?"

"Where were you earlier tonight?"

"Where was I?"

"Don't answer that," Diz said, appearing in the doorway.

Nicky would have bristled if he wasn't so grateful. She was a member of the book club. She would know what happened to

Lottie. He reached out and pulled her close with a desperation that surprised himself.

"Where's Lottie?" he said into her ear.

Diz pushed away and turned to Halliday. "I step away to take a call, and you're already violating my client's rights."

"Your client?" Nicky said.

"First of all," Halliday said, "I didn't know he was your client."

"I'm not," Nicky said.

"And second of all," Halliday said, "you can't be his lawyer, because you may be a witness."

"A witness?" Nicky said. "To what?"

"What're you talking about?" Diz said to Halliday. "Your guys put the time of death between seven-forty-five and eight-fifteen."

"Time of death," Nicky said. "That's exactly what I want to know—whose death?"

"Nick, please. Let me handle this." She turned back to Halliday. "I was at a SkyChiefs game with Marty at that time."

Newburg? Diz went to a game with *Newburg?* What was going on?

"You may be a witness to the motive of the perpetrator," Halliday said.

"I may be a witness," Diz said, "but not to anything relevant. Besides, there are three or four other people who can testify to the same things I can."

Nicky felt his chest tighten. He couldn't help it any longer. "Are you two talking about what I think you're talking about?"

"That's for a jury to decide, Ms. Dzikowski."

"No," she said, "that's for me to decide. If you don't like it, you can ask the DA to try to stop me. File a motion to disqualify. A complaint with the Grievance Committee."

"Whatever you're talking about," Nicky said, "don't I have

any say in it?"

"No," Diz and Halliday said in unison.

Diz clamped a hand on Nicky's bicep. "We're outta here."

"Hold on," Nicky said.

"Yeah," Halliday said. "We're getting off on the wrong foot. Why don't you and your *client* come down to the PSB to talk?"

"The Public Safety Building?" Nicky said. "There's press out there. Can't we talk here?"

"I can always bring you down in cuffs."

"So much for getting off on the right foot," Diz said. "Why don't you lay off the idle threats, Doc? We both know you don't have probable cause yet. But go ahead and arrest him—if you want his statements suppressed."

"Maybe you don't know everything I know. Maybe I do have probable cause. Maybe I want to let him go and watch him for a while."

"Maybe he's not talking to you."

Probable cause, arrest, handcuffs? Now Nicky didn't want to know what was going on. Whatever it was, he knew three things—Lottie was not okay, Halliday wasn't going to let him go until he asked his questions, and it wasn't smart to answer them.

Halliday looked up at Diz and sighed. "I didn't see any windows in the basement. We can do it there. Wipe off that shit-eating grin, Counselor. I've got two conditions. One, you don't touch anything. Last thing I want is a suspect contaminating the crime scene."

"And two?"

"He doesn't take five."

"Are you kidding? You just called him a suspect. I can't let him give up his right against self-incrimination."

"Take it or leave it. But I think your client should know it's his call, not yours."

"Fine."

"Well?" Halliday said to Nicky.

Nicky was glad somebody was finally asking what he thought. He wasn't going to waste the opportunity. Things were moving too fast. He needed to catch his breath. He put a palm on his fingertips. "Time out. Detective, stay. Diz, come."

As Nicky marched out onto the deck, Halliday said, "Sergeant, keep an eye on him. Guy likes to run for things."

Diz used her elbow to slide the glass door shut, then she followed Nicky to the corner of the deck.

As Nicky listened to her tell him about Lottie, he felt himself grow numb. Long ago he'd learned to gauge how big a loss he'd suffered by how long it took him to feel it. For his fifth birthday, he got a cat with seven toes, who he called Lucky. On Christmas Eve, Lucky crawled into the car engine to get warm. As the family left for mass Lucky lost two legs, and then later, in Nicky's arms, her life. It wasn't until New Year's morning that Nicky realized Lucky would never again jump onto his bed. He'd pulled the covers over his head and felt tears roll down his cheeks. But now he felt, what? Nothing.

"You're getting that look in your eyes," Diz said. "Are you listening?"

He was wondering who was going to handle Lottie's cases, write her clients, chair his campaign committee. Martin? The guy had the touch of a sledge hammer. And who was going to mow her lawn, feed her fish, water her plants? Sal? He would put the whole thing up for sale. What did any of it matter? He knew he still wasn't getting it. He tried to picture Lottie's face— her sneer, the curl of her lip, the flash of a fang. *The better to eat you with,* she used to say in bed. It worked—he began to feel her presence. The slap of her hand as he reached for a lunch check. The screech of her voice when she caught him talking to her bosom. The stench of the hair spray that held back her mane of black hair. God, he would miss her.

Diz had her hands on his shoulders, not so much to comfort him as to brace him. When she seemed sure he wasn't going to faint, she grabbed his lapels and shook him silly.

"I don't care if you don't hire me. I don't care if you don't like me. I don't care if you never speak to me again. But you are not, I repeat, you are not waiving the Fifth Amendment."

He brushed away her hands and straightened his suit. "I appreciate the advice, Diz. I really do. But did you see the press out front?"

"The same vultures that show up at any sign of carnage."

"But this is different," Nicky said. "They're not here for Lottie."

"You mean you? You don't know that."

"Are you kidding? Did you see how many people there were? I'm waiting for *Court TV* to show up. They're probably sharpening their claws."

"I hate to break it to you, but you're not that important. Besides, you can handle it."

"I don't know. This isn't someone else's skin at stake."

"Just keep your mouth shut."

"But they'll expect me to say something, and if I can convince them I didn't do anything . . ."

"No," she said, "we're not trying this thing in the press."

"Forget a trial, I'm in the middle of a campaign. I've been waiting too long for this. And so had Lottie. She wanted it, too."

At least until yesterday, he wanted to say. But he couldn't think about that right now. He tipped back his head and drew a deep breath, watching an avalanche of clouds bury the moon. He remembered a line from the end of a short story by James Joyce he'd read in college, something about the waves of despair crashing in about a young girl's heart. His Catholic professors at Le Moyne had always pushed Irish things on him—literature, philosophy, politics. Like ancient Greece had been a cultural wasteland. Diz was looking back into the kitchen at the redheaded sergeant standing with her thumbs hooked under her utility belt.

"Please tell me you have an alibi," Diz said.

"I don't even know when she died."

"I already told you that. They think about eight o'clock based on a couple things. A grocery store receipt in her purse, an electronic time stamp on her computer, and preliminary medical examiner stuff—body temperature, skin color."

"How did it happen?"

"Hit on the back of the head with a blunt object. Only once, but hard enough to splatter the ceiling."

Nicky sat on a wet chair. *Jesus.*

Diz said, "Maria D'Angelo rang the bell when she showed up for book club at eight-thirty. Martin's wife Tiffany had been right behind her. The door was unlocked so they let themselves in. After they stopped screaming, they called the ambulance. The EMTs took one look and called the cops."

"They have any leads?"

"There was no forced entry. Nothing stolen that they can tell. They're checking if she was, you know, raped."

"So that makes me a suspect?"

"They're talking to everyone. Wally, Terence, Marty. That was him on the phone when I found you. They'd called him to come down to the PSB but he wanted to stay home, be with Tiffany. They even talked to me."

"What did you say?"

"What do you think? It's a criminal investigation."

"You think I did it?"

"I didn't tell them that."

"But you think I did."

"Frankly, I don't care if you did or not."

"I forgot, you're a criminal defense lawyer."

"No, I'm a former employee."

"Is that what this is about? I hired you because you're good. And you worked for me for only three years."

"Then I believe you. Does it matter what I think?"

There was a rap on the glass door to the kitchen. The redhead was brandishing a five-battery metal flashlight.

"They love those things," Nicky said.

"I thought you'd think it makes her look hot."

Nicky was offended by the suggestion he could be attracted to a woman at a time like this. Did people think he was depraved? He rose and ran a hand over the sopping seat of his pants.

"Where's Sal?" he said.

"They can't find him. Called his bar, his house, his cell phone."

"Aren't they moving kind of fast?"

"He's next of kin. They have to notify him before they release her name. It's funny. No, not funny."

"What?"

"They asked me if Lottie had recently lent him some money. Do you know anything about that?"

Nicky balked, then said, "No."

Diz eyed him. "Where were you earlier?"

"With a friend."

"Don't tell me you don't have a confirmable alibi."

"Okay."

"You've got to let me represent you."

"I thought you said you don't care if I hire you."

"I'll do it for free."

"I can pay you."

"Sounds like deal."

"No."

"You know I can do it. I was an assistant DA for five years, and I've defended two murder cases. Even won one of them."

"Don't blame yourself about DeShante. They had his prints on the gun."

"Still, I'm batting five hundred. Not bad."

"If I were going to hire someone, it'd be you. But I can take care of myself. I am a lawyer, contrary to popular belief."

"You know what they say, he who is his own lawyer—"

"Has a client who will listen."

"They have it out for you."

"For what?"

"Running for judge, suing them, just being you."

"You were the one who sued them for brutality. Lottie let you do it. I never liked the idea. My parents raised me to trust cops."

"The cops don't know that. It was the firm's name on the briefs. Besides, you sued her ex-husband, that cop. What was his name?"

"Tony Donatella, and it was just an order of protection."

"Oh, you just told him where he could and couldn't go? What happened, anyway?"

"Didn't Lottie tell you all that stuff?"

"It was before we started bonding. Before you dumped her and she needed a shoulder to cry on."

Nicky felt a pang of guilt. Why had Diz made the dig? Was it a lame attempt at a joke, or was she was trying to distract him, weaken his resolve to defend himself?

"He'd started paying Lottie little visits when he found out we were together. Poured maple syrup into her hard drive. Ran sandpaper over her CDs. Hid open cans of tuna fish in her attic. Put rat poison in her cat food dish."

"Good clean fun."

"We got the order and the visits stopped. But then there were phone calls."

"You ever find out from who?"

"We knew from who."

"But could you prove it?"

"Terence helped us put a trap down on her phone, but the phone company couldn't trace the number. We decided to tape some of the calls using an answering machine. But then he masked his voice, used one of those synthesizers. She had to change her number."

"Couldn't the cops do anything?"

Nicky shrugged, then it hit him.

"What's wrong?" Diz said.

"I just remembered who Tony Donatella's partner used to be."

CHAPTER 9

Halliday said, "You know anyone who would want to kill Ms. Magnarella?"

"Half the lawyers in Syracuse," Nicky said, "plus a few judges."

Halliday chewed on his pencil eraser.

Behind them rattled an air handler, whose maze of steel ducts hummed over their heads. The basement did have windows, little grimy ones. Outside Nicky could make out curved pieces of corrugated metal topped by grass. He didn't think anyone could see inside, even nosy reporters, but he stepped behind the furnace just in case. Diz stood between him and Halliday, like a referee, which made Nicky think of Terence Jefferson before yesterday's argument. Nicky had always admired the kid's spunk. What did he say this time? *No hair pulling. You know how you white folks get.* Then he realized the others had probably heard Terence say it, too, maybe even heard Nicky shout at Lottie.

"Anyone specific?" Halliday said.

"Who?"

"The defense counsel and judges who wanted Lottie dead."

Nicky couldn't believe it. The guy was writing that down.

"No."

"Anyone else?"

"Just cops."

Halliday smiled. "What sort of cases did she work on?"

"A third personal injury, third med mal, third workers' comp. All plaintiff's work. Represented only women."

"Why?"

"Said she identified with them. Wanted to help them."

"Any of these women not happy with the way she handled their case?"

Nicky pretended to think about it, wondering if this guy was just busting his chops. "No."

"Any particularly contentious disputes with other lawyers in the past year?"

"I told you, they all were contentious."

"I thought you said 'half the lawyers.' "

"She gave everyone a hard time. It was her style."

"She ever say she was afraid for her life?"

"As a matter of fact, she did, just yesterday. Said someone was going to kill her in her house."

Diz put a hand on Nicky's arm. Halliday stopped writing.

"I'm sorry," Nicky said. "This isn't easy."

"You know when Ms. Magnarella left work last night?"

"No."

"You know where she went?"

"I guess she—"

"Don't guess," Diz said. "Only what you know."

"It's all right if he guesses," Halliday said.

"Not with me, it's not."

"Wherever she went," Nicky said, "it wasn't for long."

"How do you know?" Halliday said.

"Because last night was Friday—girls' night."

"As in hitting the bars?"

"More like staying home, drinking wine and talking about stuff. Oprah, Doctor Phil, the Atkins diet."

"She tell you about that?"

"The low-carb thing? They're all on it."

"No, what they do on girls' night."

"They call it book club. My wife goes sometimes." Nicky could hardly believe it, his wife and his ex-girlfriend hanging out together, until he figured out they had something in common: their dislike of him.

"Your wife Scarlet?" Halliday said.

Nicky nodded, wondering how Halliday knew her name.

"She come last night?"

"She was at a benefit."

"Which one?"

Nicky told him.

"You with her?"

"No."

Halliday seemed to consider something. "What time did this book club start?"

"Usually? Eight-thirty. Would end at eleven or so."

"How long had it been going on?"

"Couple years."

"Was it always held here?"

"Far as I know."

"You know why?"

Did he know why a bunch of women had picked one house over another? He wanted to say, *You'll have to ask Lottie.* But he just shook his head.

"Who else was in book club?"

"I don't know all of them."

"Who do you know?"

"I already told you all of this," Diz said to Halliday.

"I want to hear it from him."

"Why? To harass him?"

"Maybe he knows something you don't."

"I was in book club. He doesn't even read."

"That's a lie," Nicky said. "I just need books with a lot of pictures."

"It's my interview," Halliday said to Diz. "Are you going to let me do it or not?"

"Why don't you quiz him on the mating habits of South Pacific seahorses while you're at it?"

"Aren't those the ones that reverse their sex roles?"

"So?"

"It's just interesting you picked that particular animal."

Now Nicky felt like he was the referee. He said, "There was Lottie, Scarlet, Diz, Maria—"

"Maria D'Angelo?"

"Yes."

"Who else?"

"The others weren't regulars. I can't remember all their names. My secretaries Laurel and Marcy were in it for a while but dropped out."

"Why?"

"They said they didn't have time for it. Said they were the only women there who had kids. I think they felt intimidated."

Halliday flipped through his notepad. "I have Laurel and Marcy's last names and addresses, as I'm sure defense counsel would remind me. One thing I forgot to ask, they have husbands?"

Nicky told Halliday about his secretaries' families, his firm's other employees, and their families.

Halliday said, "How much you pay them?"

There it was again, that left hook, catching Nicky off guard.

"Each of them? I don't know, offhand. I'd have to check. Is that even relevant?"

"I'll tell you after I find out."

"Maybe you could ask them that question," Diz said. "He said he doesn't know."

"Is that what he said?" Halliday said. "Or did he say he'd have to check?" Then he chuckled. "Getting back to Ms. D'Angelo, she was one of Ms. Magnarella's clients, wasn't she?"

"Lottie had a couple clients in the club over the years," Nicky said. "Whoever's cause she was fighting at the time."

"Any clients in particular you didn't like?"

"What do you mean?"

"You said, 'Whoever's cause she was fighting.'"

"I liked them fine. Not enough to cut my fee for them."

"Was that an issue between you and Ms. Magnarella, cutting fees?"

Nicky thought about this one. "She could do what she wanted with a client. It's just not the particular way I preferred to handle things."

"And she preferred to include her clients in book club?"

"No more than one at a time. She didn't want them to outnumber her."

"Why?"

"I don't know." Nicky rubbed his eyes. What was he doing there? How had all this happened? Was there something he could've done to protect Lottie? Why hadn't she confided in him?

"Why don't you ask him something he has personal knowledge of?" Diz said.

But then Nicky heard himself say, "Control was important to her." Surprising himself, like the day before, in the kitchen.

Halliday said, "And it wasn't to you?"

"Don't answer that, either," Diz said.

Nicky held out an arm, touching her sleeve. "I suppose it is, in a way."

"I get a sense there was some tension between you and Ms. Magnarella," Halliday said. "Were you two ever involved?"

Nicky ignored Diz's objection. "Briefly."

"It ended?"

"About a year ago. Lasted a few months."

"Who ended it?"

"It was a mutual decision."

"Your wife—you said she was in this book club with Ms. Magnarella."

"So?"

"Did she know about you and Ms. Magnarella?"

"Detective—" Diz said.

Nicky felt his temper flare.

"Forget it," Halliday said. "I withdraw the question, as you lawyers say. Moving back to your relationship, your friendship, with Ms. Magnarella, how would you characterize it?"

Nicky folded his arms and waited until he'd regained control of himself. He said, "Close."

"Even recently?"

"Maybe professional is a better word."

"Maybe it's a completely different word. Ever have any fights with her?"

"We've had our fair share of disagreements."

"About what? Cutting fees?"

"Sometimes."

"What else?"

"Standing here, I can't remember any that were important."

"You remember a disagreement yesterday at work?"

Nicky just stared at the man, trying to see if his answers even mattered.

"Was it about her blowing up your firm?"

"It was about certain business differences."

"She wanted out."

"As my campaign chairman."

"Not your partner?"

"That came up as a possibility."

"Is that why you two argued twice in open court yesterday? And once at your firm?"

"You seem to know as much about it as I do. What's your point?"

"What were you were doing last night if you weren't at the Barristers' Benefit?"

There it is, Nicky thought. Good thing he had an answer ready, or at least half a one.

"I was at a Young Democrats meeting."

"Where?"

Nicky told him.

"Any witnesses?"

"Only fifty."

"When did this meeting end?"

"Seven-thirty. I had to get to the Fair to hand out palm cards—fliers."

Halliday chewed his eraser again. "I didn't know the State allows that sort of thing. Partisan politics and all."

"A union lets me stand on its property. It's by the front gate."

"So that's where you were?"

Nicky shrugged.

"Let me try it another way. If I were to ask the State Troopers, who have a post at the Fair, if they saw you out front, what do you suppose they'd say?"

Diz wasn't objecting, just eying Nicky coolly, like she wanted to know the answer, too. Nicky felt the walls of the basement close in around him. "I didn't make it. I was with a friend."

"Who?"

"I'm not at liberty to say at this time."

Halliday smirked at Diz, who was shaking her head at her sandals. "Where?" he said.

"On the other side of the city."

"Where, Nick?"

"Skaneateles."

"When?"

"From eight 'til eleven."

"What were you doing?"

Nicky shook his head. No way was he answering that one. He looked at a clothesline stretched from wall to wall, sagging under Lottie's black bras and red panties. When he'd known her, she'd only had white ones. When had she switched? Would it have made a difference to their sex life? Was he that shallow? Looking at them now made him feel like he was invading her privacy, like he was dirty.

"Eight 'til eleven, huh?" Halliday said. "Must be some friend."

"That's it," Diz said. "This interview's over."

"He hasn't told me anything."

"Over, Detective."

Halliday closed his notepad. "Have it your way, Counselor. But 'over' isn't the word I'd use. More like, 'interrupted.' The Trickster and I will be talking again."

Nicky had just about had it, Lottie lying dead somewhere and him having to explain their relationship. He didn't like that nickname, either. And he didn't like threats. He'd tried to keep things professional, cutting Halliday some slack. There was no need for insults. He felt strange, standing there with his fists balled, heart pounding. He hadn't lost his temper since before Corin had died and now he was going to do it twice in two days, like his father when he drank too much or his crazy uncle. But he couldn't stop himself.

"Your ex-partner Tony Donuts was stalking Lottie. She got a restraining order against him. You know that?"

Halliday laughed. "I just made fifty bucks off Sergeant Hard-body upstairs. She thought you had too much self-respect to play that card."

"So you did know?"

"I've already talked to him."

"What was his alibi?"

"We'll check it out."

"The department will check it out or you'll check it out?"

"Now you're the one making a point."

"I'm just wondering why you aren't grilling him."

"You want the truth, man to man?" Halliday put his arm on Nicky's back and wheeled him around, away from Diz. He leaned in close and lowered his voice. "I think you did it, I got what you call a sixth sense. And you know what the best part is, Nick?"

"What, Doc?"

"I'm gonna prove it."

CHAPTER 10

"You're not up yet?" Diz said the next morning. "I've already run five miles, swum two, and hurdled a reporter."

Nicky sat up and yawned as she kicked the front door shut. She wore black biking shorts and a grey sports bra. He was under a comforter in his boxers and T-shirt.

He said, "I hope you're not expecting a relay."

"It's how I react to stress. I did the Las Vegas marathon while studying for the bar."

He laid back down on her futon and worked a pillow under his neck. She set a cup of coffee and bag of bagels in front of him, on a glass-and-steel table that went perfectly with the torture rack he was on. She wore the biggest sports watch he'd ever seen, complete with compass, heart monitor, and something that belonged in a cockpit.

"A marathon in the summer? Wasn't that hot?"

"End of January. I took the bar in February. Graduated a semester early."

"Why doesn't that surprise me?"

"Because you believe in your lawyer, you trust your lawyer, you listen to your lawyer."

"I don't like where this is going."

"I get the sense you see this as a power struggle. Mano versus lesbo. You have to get over that. Like that scene from *Jerry McGuire*. 'Help me help you.' "

Nicky knew she was right. What he couldn't get over was this woman—this girl—going a mile a minute, trying so hard to help him because of a lousy job.

"You know," he said, "it's okay to just stop and be sad sometimes."

That did it. She stiffened. "You think I'm the one in denial? You talk about Lottie like she moved to California. Your pea brain can't even grasp what's happened."

His *pea brain?* Is that what she thought of him?

"Maybe you're right," he said.

She took a gulp of coffee then started her stretching routine—hamstrings, quads, calves. He watched, admiring her flexibility.

After they had shaken Detective Halliday, Nicky had followed Diz to the front door. When he'd asked what she was doing, she'd said, *Running the gauntlet. You want to stay here all night?* That's when he'd taken her hand and led her back down the hall. *Didn't I teach you anything?* he'd said. *Never stand and fight if you can crawl in the other direction.* She'd shrugged and followed him through the bushes. Her car was parked in the eye of the storm, so he'd driven her home. Then he'd followed her in, wanting to talk about Lottie and knowing Scarlet would be no help. Little did he know that, after an hour of talking, Diz would go on a three-hour cleaning spree, which evidently required blaring Aerosmith, slamming cupboard doors, and running the vacuum.

Now she was rolling her head and slowly blowing out her breath. "Let's call a truce. I'll stop manhandling you and you stop being a pussy. Have a bagel. When I get back, the only thing I want to talk about is this alibi of yours."

She closed the bathroom door and started the shower.

"Incredible," he said. "Woman's a force of nature."

He bit into a whole wheat bagel, wishing for butter instead of veggie cream cheese. The apartment had an old industrial feel, with brick walls, twelve-foot ceilings, exposed wood beams, a loft, and oversized windows. He knew the building was over a hundred years old, home to the Nettleton shoe factory before its facelift in the mid-eighties. Diz's furniture was Spartan— steel chairs, some cacti, and a canary-yellow mountain bike hanging from a hook in the ceiling. Roller blades rested in the corner, next to some kickboxing gear. The few books on the shelves were about women or sports. The one that caught Nicky's attention was *Storm Tactics Handbook: Modern Methods of Heaving-to for Survival in Extreme Conditions.* That's how he'd always thought of Diz, the kind you could push out of a plane above a rain forest with a stick of chewing gum and a ballpoint pen and expect at work on Monday morning. A female MacGyver.

On an end table, between her car keys and cell phone, lay a flat, square object—black plastic with a grey screen. His heart quickened. He picked it up, remembering Diz's insistence on representing him, and the fact that she'd talked to the police about him. He'd asked her, *What did you tell them?* and she'd said, *What do you think? It's a criminal investigation.* He turned on the PDA then scrolled through its calendar. Spinning classes, discovery deadlines, court appearances. Then he saw it, identical notes on the previous Monday and Wednesday: *LUNCH W/ CMM.* Carlotta Maria Magnarella. People grabbed lunch with each other all the time at R&M, but it was a pop-your-head-in-at-noon sort of thing. Not by appointment. Unless maybe it was a birthday, or a business meeting.

The shower was off. He switched on the TV as Diz emerged wearing a bathrobe.

"Speak of the devil," she said.

"What do you mean?"

"That reporter on TV, Trace Lipp. The one I ran into on my way into the building. Asked all about you—whether you had any idea who did it, where you were last night, when you'd last seen Lottie. He lives on the first floor. Name used to be Tracy Lipowitz, back when he was doing SU games on the radio. Before he had his teeth capped. This place is home to all the rich and famous. Bachelors and bachelorettes."

"Is that why you moved here?"

"To meet a nice girl and settle down? Fat chance. I just like it. People are young, educated, fairly hip. They don't pass judgment."

"Is that important to you?"

She worked the towel through her short blonde hair, the light from the bathroom making it look Andy Warhol–white. "You got cream cheese on my Palm Pilot."

"Huh?"

"You heard me."

"Oh, that. I was looking for Martin's number. Let him know he still has a job."

"Uh-huh. What about Wally?"

"I'm not worried about him. Martin's got a wife, trying to have a family."

"There's a phone book in the drawer."

"There was no answer at his home. I wanted his cell. You don't believe me, pick up the cordless and press redial."

For a second, he thought she would do it. But instead she picked up her Palm Pilot and starting pushing buttons. What was he doing? Bluffing wasn't his strong suit. It was too close to gambling, which was against his personal philosophy. The way to solve problems was to be honest, direct. And, of course, a little schmoozing didn't hurt.

He scanned the photos on her book-shelf for a new topic of conversation. There was a half dozen of them. One of her crossing a finish line with a number pinned to her chest. One of her spiking a volleyball wearing a SUNY Buffalo Bills jersey. And one of a girl wearing a blue-and-white plaid uniform and a pout, holding a pair of ballet slippers.

"No offense, but I can't picture you doing pirouettes."

"That makes two of us." She didn't look up from her Palm Pilot. "I used to skip it to shoplift cigarettes. Got me suspended."

"Can't picture you doing that, either."

"I was different then. I was the last of six kids, my mom barefoot in the kitchen as my dad hunted for food. It was all very *Leave It to Beaver*. It wasn't until college that I felt okay with myself."

"You mean came out of the closet." He had to divert her attention from the Palm Pilot.

She looked up at him. "That was a part of it, yes."

"That when you got into sports?"

"You mean, am I a dyke because I'm a jock or vice versa?"

"Hey, I'm just trying to bond with my new lawyer."

She handed him the Palm Pilot, which showed Martin's cell phone number. "How did my therapist put it? It was a healthier outlet for my energy."

"So that's why you stopped smoking? Because of what your therapist told you?"

"That, plus the chicks didn't dig the smell. What about you?"

"I tried out for the girls' volleyball team in middle school but they said my back was too hairy."

"I meant, what were you like in school?"

"Few less pounds, few less wrinkles."

"You're pretty good at putting other people under the microscope."

"You mean I can dish it out but I can't take it? Now we're getting to know each other."

"Diagnosing your problems isn't the same as solving your problems."

"Your therapist tell you that, too?"

"What my therapist would say is you're being hostile."

"No, just having a bad day. Can we keep talking about you? I'm not big into the subject of Nicky Rigopoulos at the moment."

"It's your nickel."

"You billing me for this? I thought you said it was free."

"I thought you said you could pay."

He picked up a black-and-white photo. A rolling river winding below a cloud-capped mountain, light slanting across a flock of birds.

"You take this?"

"In the Adirondacks."

"Pretty good. I could never do photography. It's funny—I buy the best disposable cameras I can find."

"You need the right equipment, and some patience. But the developing's the tricky part."

"I know, I always forget to pick them up at the store."

He found another photo, this one showing a young woman with long, dark hair, sunglasses around her neck, and a sunburned nose.

"Is this her?"

"Lisa."

"I'd almost forgotten."

"Not me."

"No, you probably think about her every day. It was a sailing accident, right?"

"Yes."

"What was it, ten years ago?" He waited. "If you don't want to talk about it—"

"It's all right." She sat on the futon, her tone flat, like she was telling the story for the second time that day, which maybe she was, considering Halliday's fondness for interrogation. "She was teaching me how to sail on Lake Ontario. There was a storm."

He nodded, recalling the details, wanting to help her. He said, "The boom came about."

"She was trying to get out of my way."

"She didn't have her life jacket on?"

"She was a good swimmer." Diz reached for the photo. "I can still see her in the wake, waving her arms. 'You're going to have to turn the boat around,' she said. Just like that, real calm. I tried."

"I'm sure you did."

"The Coast Guard searched for two days."

Nicky hated himself at times like this, when he had to play lawyer. Of course, that never stopped him. He sat down next to her and put his hand on her knee.

"Look, I'm sorry for telling you how to be sad. I know this must be hard on you, too. You and Lottie had your differences once, sure—her suing wife beaters and you defending them—but you'd become friends. Everyone could see that. Girls' night out, lunch once in a while, even handling some cases together."

When she didn't deny it, he said, "Were you working much with her lately?"

"What're you doing?" she said. "Trying to see if I had a motive to kill her?"

Nicky took his hand from Diz's knee and gave her a hurt look.

She rolled her eyes. "All right, what do you want to know?"

"What kind of stuff were you working on together? Maybe you know something but don't realize it."

"A year ago, one of her clients was stopped going fifty in a twenty-five. Few months ago, another was 'weaving in her lane'—I love that excuse for pulling someone over. She blew a point oh nine. I took care of both. No points."

There had been a time, before Corin, when Nicky would have congratulated a lawyer who had saved the license of a drunk driver.

"That's it. We practiced different sorts of law, Lottie and me. She'd gotten out of police brutality cases, and I'd quit ambulance chasing."

Nicky mulled over his next question, like in a deposition, when he knew the answer and was deciding whether it was worth it to show his cards. If he asked her whether Lottie had invited her to join the new firm, he would be showing he didn't trust her, maybe even that he'd checked her digital calendar, if she hadn't already guessed that. No, he wasn't ready to put her on the stand yet.

"You've got on your thinking cap," she said. "You're wondering what my alibi is. Or, at least, why I was at the SkyChiefs game with Marty."

"It is a first."

"Lottie asked me to bring him. Said he's been working hard and needed to blow off some steam. I asked her, 'What about book club?' She said no one had finished *A Million Little Pieces*. They were just going to watch *Desperate Housewives* on her TiVo and eat low-carb fondue."

"She liked *Desperate Housewives*?"

"She *hated* it. It was kind of fun to sit through, watching her bite her tongue, just dying to lay into the characters. Everyone else liked it. I swear, those women are so vapid. They're worse than you—they don't read anything, even the crappy stuff. She thought I was different because I'm not a *domestic slave*. That's what she called them behind their backs. She thought I'd have fun at the game because I'm *so sportsy* and the SkyChiefs were playing the Buffalo Bisons. What a name, the *SkyChiefs*. Political correctness gone awry. And the team emblem—that baseball bat with the little airplane wings. Anyway, I told her that watching baseball is like waiting for grass to grow while people analyze it with statistics. It's the only way to make it remotely interesting."

"So I shouldn't bother to ask how you liked the game."

"No, but you probably want to know why we left so early. It started at six, and we were out of there by seven-thirty because Marty's sphincter was wound so tight—what was that line from *Ferris Bueller*?—'if you stuck a lump of coal up his ass in two weeks you'd have a diamond.' "

"He can be a tad retentive."

"He wouldn't even have a beer, just kept answering phone calls from his wife. Something about missing a two-hour window before book club. But how do you know I'm not lying? Let's see, Alvarez hit a homer in the second after almost beaning us with a foul ball behind third base. We didn't see anyone there who would recognize us. But I can get the ticket stub from my jeans pocket, if you want it. Probably has the ticket handler's prints on it, if you want to send it to the FBI lab in Quantico."

Nicky considered the woman beside him. The one who read books like *East of Eden* and hated shows like *Leave It to Beaver*, but quoted movies like *Ferris Bueller* and *Jerry McGuire*. The one who used to prosecute felons, and now saw a therapist. She seemed like a bulldog one second and a puppy dog the next. But was she capable of murder?

"So you dropped off Martin at work."

"At his car, about quarter of eight. Give him fifteen minutes to get home, and fifteen more to spend with his blushing bride before she had to leave for book club."

"Enough time for you to make it to book club, too."

"You mean, did I go, and if not, why? The answer's no, and the reason is ESPN Classic had a special on at eight about ultra-distance triathlons. Sylvia Andonie, this Mexican, did twenty Ironmans in a row in 1998. Took her six hundred forty-three hours. It was totally awesome. This woman doing twenty times what only a fraction of men can do even once. It made me want to go climb a mountain or swim a lake. I felt like Marty in the morning when he first got out of the Army—you know, when you'd ask him how he was doing?"

"He'd say, 'Sir, I'm so motivated, there should be two of me.' "

"I was getting ready for a run when the cops called."

Nicky tried to stretch his arms behind his back, like Diz. Maybe he should renew his membership at the Y. "The witness may step down. The court would like to thank her for her time and note that it appreciates her candor."

"I know you trust me. You're just being safe. Now that we got that over, we can get down to business."

She stood up, circled the coffee table, and paced back and forth.

Nicky braced himself. "Like my alibi?"

"That's one thing. I want the where, when and who. The what we can leave to the imagination. Then I want you to have a serious talk to this woman who won't cover for you, or whose honor you won't sully."

"Anything else?"

"If we want to prove you're innocent, our best bet is not vouching for your whereabouts, but finding the animal who did this."

"Like talking to Tony Donuts?"

"He wasn't at the top of my list, actually. No, what I want to know is why Trace Lipp asked me a little while ago if I knew that Sal's bar was in the dumps, and that he was taking money from Lottie. And, if that's true, why didn't you know it? And, if so, why didn't you tell me?"

Nicky kept his mouth shut.

But this didn't stop the bulldog, who said, "Because if you're covering for him, then you're a sucker and a loser in November, and I can't help you, no matter how much money you don't pay me. If you're not covering for him, and you want to save your ass, then I suggest you have a serious talk with him, too."

CHAPTER 11

"I told you afternoons are bad," said Lilly Longacre. "I had to find a sitter and get rid of the barn hands."

Nicky watched Lilly's britches tug against her hips as she led a horse into a wash stall. She secured the animal in cross-ties, turned on a hose, and ran a soapy sponge over his sides. He snorted, sounding to Nicky like a satisfied sigh.

"What's his name?" Nicky said.

"Aer Lingus. He's an Irish jumper. Three-quarters Thoroughbred and one-quarter Irish Draught. Can clear a fence taller than you then turn on a dime and leave you a nickel change."

"What do you use him for? Show jumping?"

"That and eventing. Show jumping plus cross-country and dressage. Have you seen it? It's like asking someone to figure skate, then run a marathon, then high jump. This guy's a stud. Do you see an ounce of fat on him?"

Nicky was embarrassed, but he actually felt jealous of the horse, the big muscular dope. If he was a person, his name would be Buck or Bo or something, in his senior year of college, on his way to the NFL as a linebacker. No, linebackers were too smart. Still, Lilly didn't look at Nicky that way. Should he be working out more? Maybe doing the low-carb thing? Or at least cutting down on the baklava? He decided he would talk to Diz when this was all over, have her recommend a workout routine and diet. Nothing extreme, like that Mexican triathlete. Just walking and stretching, maybe some light weights.

He sucked in his gut and said, "What about that fat one over there?"

"Big Mac? He's for beginners. Like riding a couch."

"He's the size of a pickup. How many do you have here?"

"What you see, plus another dozen in the lower barn."

"That building down the hill?"

"That's the arena. The lower barn's on the other side of the riding ring. We've been there. Remember the time with the leather straps?"

"In the stall next to the Arabian."

"He's not there anymore. That one wasn't ours."

"What does boarding them involve?"

"Grooming, exercising, schooling. We keep a jumper here for your friend, Martin. I teach his wife Tiffany how to lay off the riding crop and stirrups, and land on her shoulder instead of her head. She's as stubborn as the horse. Plus we breed, buy, and sell."

"How many people does all that take?"

"Four full-time, three part-time."

"Including you?"

"I'm just the owner. Help out a few hours a week."

"Still, that's the size of my law office."

"We barely break even."

Nicky had never asked her this stuff before, and hoped he wasn't being transparent, but he wanted to loosen her up. "Couldn't you tell them it's because of the holiday weekend?"

"Wes never lets them take Saturdays off. The work needs to get done. I'm going to be taking horses out on hacks and mucking stalls until dark."

Nicky wanted to know what *hacks* and *mucking* were, but he didn't have all day. "I couldn't wait until Monday night."

"I don't know if I could've made even that. I'm running out of excuses. There's only so much colic a horse can get."

"I'm sorry to inconvenience you."

"No, I'm sorry. I know how close you were to Lottie. So, what happened? They were so vague on the news, like they didn't want to get sued or something."

He gave her a sanitized synopsis of the night before, as she resumed working, running a towel over the horse and leading him back to his stall.

She said, "Who do the police think did it?"

He flicked his fingers, a gesture he'd intended to be dismissive but that came off like he was shooing one of the barn's flies. "They don't know what they're doing. You know what I kept thinking when I was there, watching the crime techs work?"

She shook her head and brushed golden bangs out of sapphire eyes.

"How lucky I am. How lucky we are, you know, to have found each other. Life's too short, Lil. You can't wait for things to come to you. You have to go get them."

They held each other and kissed, Nicky smelling shampoo and leather, and feeling the firmness of Lilly's body. He put his mouth to her ear and told her how sweet she was, how much he needed her.

"I love you," she said, pulling away from him and taking his face in her hands. "It's funny, when I first saw you on TV, you seemed, I don't know, vain."

He stepped back.

"I'm not saying you are, just that you look like that on TV. You know, plaintiff's attorney—smooth, confident, self-centered."

"I thought I looked like Saddam Hussein."

"What, your moustache? I think it's exotic. Reminds me of that Greek count from *The Sun Also Rises*. You know the one with the long name who drinks absinthe with Jake and Lady Brett?"

"I'll have to recommend that one for book club."

"Don't be mad. All I meant was you seemed a certain way before I met you. But really you're generous and caring. I watch you at the shelter. You have a good heart. And the funny thing is, Wes is the opposite. Publicly he's all service and duty, but once you get to know him he's cold and selfish. Did I tell you what my therapist called him? 'Emotionally unavailable.' "

Nicky wondered if everyone was seeing a therapist. Maybe he should be, too, a female one that could help him understand the women in his life, maybe even confirm his alibis. "I'm not sorry you had to send the barn hands away. I'm sick of meeting at night, out here in the middle of nowhere. I feel like silly teenagers."

"Prisoners."

"You know what I've been thinking about? Pulling the trigger."

Her eyes showed hope and a bit of fear. "Filing for divorce? You mean it?"

"Don't you still want to?"

She threw her arms around him and kissed him again. There was more hugging and kissing, and hugging again. Then they fumbled with each other's clothes until their fingers found skin. Finally, they lay in a stall, picking straw from each other's hair. Nicky wanted to ask if she was going to answer his question. But she just leaned back and studied him. Then she narrowed her eyes, like she'd put two and two together. He had to beat her to the punch.

He said, "I need you to confirm my alibi."

She sat up and tucked in her shirt. "I knew it."

"Lil, please."

"I don't know."

"I'm begging you, this isn't just my career on the line."

"I'm not ready. Things were going so well. Why can't we just keep them the same?"

"Because they're not the same."

"Well, I'm not ready."

"You keep saying that."

"You don't have to be mean."

"You didn't think about this before?"

"Theoretically, but Hunter and Cassy aren't even in middle school yet. Do you have any idea what it's like when your parents get divorced? Mine sent me to prep school, all the way down to Middleburg."

Nicky wanted to tell her that Foxcroft sounded more like a country club than a penal colony. With its horses and pastures, and exclusive inmate population. This woman had a strange idea of hard times. "And that's the only reason?"

"Are you asking me if I'm having second thoughts about leaving Wes? I'm not going to lie, I still hope he might change, yes. I can't help it. I sit in church and hear the minister talk about commitment and fidelity."

"Love and companionship are pretty good, too."

"I know they are, honey, but then Wes will do something for me—a little thing, like buy me a horse, or have a portrait painted of me, or take me to Paris."

A little thing? Nicky thought.

"It'll remind me of the way he used to be, before we were married, when he would take me sailing on Cape Cod in the summer. Or fly down to visit me on weekends at Sweet Briar . . ."

As Nicky listened to her go on about her husband, about what her kids' lives would be apart from their dad, Nicky realized what he, this Greek count–lookalike, really was to her. A hobby, like a charity or horse.

"Don't you see?" she said. "I can't help but pray he changes. Or that I change, I don't know. I have my own little Serenity

Prayer. 'Lord, give me the strength to change the things I can, the courage to accept the things I can't, and the wisdom to take my Zanax.' "

Nicky wondered where she was getting this Lord stuff. Was it a way of trying to shroud her marriage in impenetrable holiness?

"It just would be so much easier if Wes and I stayed together. In a perfect world."

"I understand that. You've invested a lot of years in your marriage and you don't want to throw them away. And you have kids who you don't want to subject to the same hell you went through. I have a daughter, too, and I'd feel the same way. But don't you understand? I'm suspected of a murder I didn't commit. That could mean scandal, bankruptcy, prison. A cramped cell with a three-hundred-pound boyfriend. And the only person who can save me is you."

He waited for her to respond, then felt insulted. "I don't need your permission, Lil."

"I'm not worried. I know you won't tell them about us, not before the election. Wes would never forgive you."

Never forgive you was an understatement. Maybe Wes Longacre couldn't officially take the Democratic endorsement away, but he could still hold back his personal endorsement, not to mention campaign funds and volunteers. It would probably mean the election.

"Besides," she said, "he'd believe me, not you."

"Don't tell me, you've actually lined up someone who'll say you *weren't* with me. Who is it? Some barn hand?"

She ran her fingers through her hair and brushed straw off her britches.

He turned to go. It was the way he preferred to end his affairs, not with a bang but a whimper. Outside the barn door, the waning afternoon light silhouetted a cloud of mosquitoes.

Beyond them lay the long dirt path that led through the maple trees to his car. This was their routine—him leaving first, while she waited. This time, he stopped at the door.

"I forgot to tell you," he said, "Trace Lipp's out there."

"The reporter?"

He was hurt that she seemed more concerned with the press than with the demise of their relationship. Like their breakup had been a foregone conclusion she'd reached before he arrived. Was she smarter than he'd thought?

"He followed me here. He's probably parked out back. You might want to take the front way out when you leave."

Her expression of confusion gave way to pity. "Oh, honey," she said. "I always take the front way."

Nicky reached the end of Lilly's driveway in his Saturn, and saw parked across the road a dark blue sedan. He hesitated, then pulled up behind it, got out, and tapped on the driver's window.

The glass came down.

"License and registration, please," Nicky said.

Halliday smiled. "Don't got none, Officer. Car's stolen."

"Why do cops do surveillance in Crown Victorias?" Nicky said. "You might as well be in a red Gran Torino with a white racing stripe down the side."

"Like from *Starsky & Hutch?* I tried to get one of them from the motor pool but they were all out. You're a different man without your mouthpiece around."

"Diz? She's all right."

Nicky felt comfortable talking to the man. No, not comfortable—he still had to watch his words—it was something else. He felt . . . grateful. Was he crazy? Maybe, but he felt like he could finally be himself, the man seeing through his bullshit, seeing him for who he was, but not caring. Not quite the way it was with Sal. With Sal, Nicky always felt like he had to prove himself, show that he was down to earth, not snotty. A guy's guy. The thing with Halliday, he didn't seem to care. Of course, maybe that was because he was intent on throwing Nicky in jail.

"I remember her from the DA's office," Halliday said. "Real sanctimonious. Once accused a cop of knocking a perp's head on the hood of a car. You should've seen her, lecturing the guys in the squad room."

"Did he do it?"

"As I recall, police report said the guy turned to flee and ran into a telephone pole."

"Like a cartoon."

"I've seen stranger things. This one time, when I was still on patrol, I stopped at a 7-Eleven for some coffee. This kid comes up to me. Jeans way down his ass, tattoo on his chest, do-rag on his head, two-hundred-dollar hightops, gold tooth—you get the picture. He reaches into his pocket and pulls out a bag of coke. Says, 'I just bought this on the corner. I want you to arrest the guy sold it to me.' True story, scout's honor. Kid thought he could get rid of his competition."

Nicky wanted to ask what happened, but then Halliday was saying, "Anyway, a perp hits his head on a car hood or a telephone pole, what's the difference? You're missing the point. She wasn't a team player, Diz, making a big deal of nothing. Like we were the enemy."

"But she delivered the verdicts, right?"

"Still does, in her own way. I waited outside her apartment all morning, until you came out. Then I had to wait some more as that Tracy guy jumped into his Hummer. Not exactly undercover reporting. I came this close to pulling the prick over for speeding, just to see his face. Have him step out of the car and do a sobriety test in front of all his viewers. But then we got out of the city. I figured you spotted him out back of the farm, so I came around here to wait."

"You must really be gunning for your guy."

"Not gunning, just zeroed in. There's a difference. One's a vindictive abuse of authority; the other's sound investigative technique."

"Isn't it sound investigative technique to wait for the facts to come in before you pick your target?"

"That's just the rigamarole for judges and juries. I like to cut to the chase. Here's my theory; now I come up with the evidence."

"What if your theory's wrong?"

"Then I guess I'd try another one."

"You're funny, how you asked so many questions back at the house, like you were checking every lead, but how your mind's made up once we're alone. Like that part with Diz was just a show."

"Not a show, just the way I operate. First, pick the most likely suspect. Then, get all the facts about him, even the answers to the stupid home-run questions, like did you do it?"

"You haven't asked me that yet."

"Did you do it?"

"No."

"I don't believe you, but doesn't it make you feel better that I asked?"

"Not really."

"Anyway, get all the info, then apply it to your theory. See if it fits. You waste too much time just dangling out in the wind, changing directions with every fact comes along. I learned that from my old man. He was a science teacher, always working with hypotheses, trying to disprove them."

"What if it doesn't all fit?"

"It doesn't all have to fit, not in the real world. Just enough."

"How much is enough?"

"You'll know as soon as I do. Open the door one day to find me holding a warrant."

"This is very enlightening, in a Keystone Cops sort of way."

"You think we're unprofessional? You should see some of the departments in small towns around here. Like *Reno 911*. You ever watch that show? Cracks me up."

"Do the guys downtown know you work like this? Your police chief?"

"I've personally caught six murderers so far this year. And there have only been a dozen homicides."

"But what if they didn't do it?"

"They'll all be convicted."

"On evidence that you developed. What about the leads you didn't bother tracking down?"

"What you're forgetting, these are bad guys. Dealers, dope fiends, gang bangers. If they weren't in prison, they'd be starting fights down at the Dinosaur Bar-B-Que, pulling knives on SU students."

"In other words, who cares?"

"All I'm saying, I'm not going to lose sleep over it. They're innocent, that's what appeals are for."

"Why are you telling me all this?"

"I don't know. Guess I can relate to you somehow. Except for the fact that you're a killer. Besides, what're you going to do? Stand up in court after the DA rests his case and say, 'Detective Halliday was biased.' "

"So you admit it."

"I admit you think it."

Nicky let out his breath. "Did you even check out Tony's alibi?"

"He was on the other side of town playing cards, a game called Hearts. Know it? He shot the moon five times. Guy always did have balls."

"Who was he playing with?"

"His partner and their girlfriends."

"You believe him?"

"Why wouldn't I?"

Nicky wanted to repeat some of the stories Lottie had told him about her ex. Payoffs, complaints, internal investigations. "Tony's been known to be a stranger to the truth."

"Nothing's ever stuck."

"But he never made it off the beat, while his partner did."

"I had more ambition."

"I heard it was because you weren't on the take."

"Don't believe it—I'm as crooked as the next cop."

"Can you say that a little louder?" Nicky lifted his lapel.

Halliday smiled. Maybe that was why Nicky felt like he could talk to the man, when the man wasn't threatening him.

"How about you?" Halliday said. "What're you doing out here in God's country? You're a long way from your dad's restaurant on Salina Street."

Nicky was flattered the guy knew his family. "Can't a kid from Skunk City ride horses?"

"I bet you don't even know the difference between a hock and a fetlock."

"Maybe not, but I know a horse's ass when I see one."

Halliday laughed at that one. "This is a big farm, stretches all the way up that hill to the left, all the way down to that stream to the right, and all the way over to that forest in back."

"You telling me or asking me?"

"I had plenty of time to check it out. Owned by the Long-acres. Maybe I'll just have to ask the missus what you're doing here."

"She's pretty busy. Short handed. Doesn't want to be bothered."

"In that case, maybe I'll just talk to Mr. Longacre."

Nicky smiled, trying to be like John McCain—the man who'd mastered misery in a POW camp.

"I want to ask him," Halliday said, "what he's doing with a farm way out here on the other side of Skaneateles. Know what I think? I think he doesn't like to ride, probably doesn't even like horses. To him, this is probably just a few rows on a spreadsheet. A tax write-off. Something for his wife to do, to shut her up. She's happy because she can get away. He's happy because she's happy. Except he'd be pissed if he knew what was really going on out here. What do you think?"

"Maybe I'll win the election, anyway. Ever think of that? And then where will you be, when you show up in my court to testify in a case?"

Nicky wasn't used to threatening people, and it made his voice tremble.

"I'll take my chances," Halliday said. "Can I give *you* some friendly advice?"

"No."

"You want a deal? Come down to the PSB without your lawyer, and give me a statement."

"You mean a confession."

"That's the idea."

"But I'm innocent," Nicky said. He kept his voice even, but he wondered if his tone was whiny. Like his daughter's when he would ground her for smoking cigarettes. *It's not like I'm hurting anybody,* she would say. *I don't even drink.*

"We went over this," Halliday said. "Let's leave the legal mumbo jumbo out of it. You say you didn't do it, I say you did. Where does that leave us? All we have is the facts. Is there motive? Check. Is there opportunity? I have to talk to your girlfriend, but we both know what she'll say. Young gal like that with a rich husband and two shiny kids. She ain't gonna lie for you, even if you are banging her. All that leaves is the weapon, and that'll turn up. Why don't you save yourself a headache and plead, while the price is right?"

Nicky recognized the tactic—he'd used it many times before in a more civilized setting, as he sat behind a mission-oak desk and his clients sat in leather-backed chairs that were an inch shorter than his. He would explain the weaknesses of their cases and the risks of litigation, and then mention settlement in an offhand way. For the first time, he understood why his clients hated him.

Halliday was holding out his business card. "Offer's good only until we arrest you. After that, DA's gonna throw the book at you."

CHAPTER 12

A silver BMW coupe blocked Nicky's side of the garage. Its bumper sticker read,

> For a Little Heaven on Earth
> Vote DeVine

Nicky didn't recognize the car, but Scarlet's girlfriends were always parking in his way. Once, he'd actually heard her tell one of them to park at an angle. When he'd later called her on it, she'd said it was so her friend could turn her car around. How could you argue with someone like that? But what really bothered Nicky was the way, like now, she left the front door open. Bugs coming in, air-conditioning going out. The joys of marriage. Should he tell Dara about this stuff before she took the plunge?

In the foyer, he flipped through the mail on the table—bills, financial statements, women's magazines. Then he headed for the billiards room to make himself a drink, and dropped his suit jacket on the floor.

He would need a double.

The living room was a mess. Not a mess, a shambles. He'd never known the difference before. Couch and chairs over-turned, fabric undersides removed. Cushions ripped out of their covers. Credenza tipped over, drawers pulled out, contents everywhere. It was worse than Dara's bedroom after a sleepover. The dining room, the study, and the billiards room were no better. He considered the possibility that he'd been robbed, but nothing seemed to be missing, or even broken. Like someone had been looking for something.

He called out for Scarlet. She wasn't in the kitchen or backyard. No sounds from the pool or basement. He felt a twinge of panic. Had she been here when someone broke in?

He climbed the spiral staircase. Down the hall, light spilled from his bedroom. His mattress creaked. Scarlet was known to take naps in the middle of the day, especially after a three-martini lunch. But what about the car in the driveway? In the doorway, Nicky found the answer. He felt his face flush, but he forced himself to fold his arms and lean against the doorjamb.

"Honey, I'm home," he said in a falsetto voice.

Scarlet rolled over and pulled the sheets up to her neck. "Hello, dear. Dinner's on the stove, and the kids are at soccer practice. How was your day?"

"Traffic was hell. Hey, Randy."

Randy DeVine propped himself up on his elbows. "Hey, Nick."

"How's the divorce business?"

"Booming," Randy said, glancing at Scarlet.

Nicky didn't want to go there just yet. He said, "Your goons having fun tearing down my signs?"

"You have enough of 'em—lawn signs, bus signs, even that big one on the warehouse off West Street. By the way, how did you get that billboard on 690?"

Nicky had been showing Scarlet how unflappable he was. But now his interest was piqued. "Hasn't your party told you all that stuff?"

"They won't return my calls. I think they're obsessed with next year's mayor's race."

"They should cut their losses and gun for more seats on the

City Common Council. Then you could push through whatever sketchy development projects you want."

"I forgot how you feel about DestiNY USA. How can you still be against it when it was awarded all of those 'green bonds'? They're going to clean up the lake, you know. That should make even the Indians happy."

This was too insulting to Nicky to warrant a response, the idea that any of the city's financial, social and environmental problems could be solved with the mirage of a six-billion-dollar mega-resort resembling the Mall of America on steroids, especially when it came with a thirty-year tax break.

"What's your problem with the city handing out tax incentives anyway?" Randy said.

"I admit, some of them work. But too many shoulder a small number of property owners with a disproportionate tax burden."

"So you're against high taxes *and* government subsidies? You think that the market should solve all our problems? Be careful or you'll become one of us conservatives."

"The city has a forty-five-million-dollar budget deficit," Nicky said.

"And some of the highest property taxes in the nation," Randy said. "You know what I think is hurting you in the polls? Not this Lottie thing, but the fact that people don't know you. I mean *really* know you. They know your face and name from all those TV commercials. But they don't know what you're thinking. Or at least they don't *feel* like they know what you're thinking, which is the same thing. You're too—what's the word?— aloof. Like, what I want to know, what do you think the city should do with Interstate 81, rebuild it or raze it and replace it with a street-level boulevard?"

"I don't know, Randy."

"Me, neither. See, on the one hand, I understand how putting in a nice landscaped boulevard might, you know, unify the city, seeing as the route cuts right through it. It might also create more taxable properties that could be used by businesses. On the other hand, a boulevard would lead to more congestion down there. People want to get home after a day of work, not go shopping downtown. Of course, you would say that's the problem—home to people is the suburbs, not the city." Scarlet yawned dramatically, catching Randy's eye. "But, hey," Randy said, "we could go on like this all day."

Please, no, Nicky thought.

Apparently realizing all of a sudden that he was naked under Nicky's six-hundred-count Frette linen, Randy filled the awkward silence. "By the way, congrats on getting the Working Families endorsement."

Nicky felt his eyelids grow even heavier. "Same to you about the Veterans Party."

"First time being in the National Guard helped me. My staff told me not to bring it up, thought you'd throw it in my face, like Kerry did to Bush. You know, say everyone else was over there humping it through the rice paddies."

"I'd never do that," Nicky said. Not even to a schmuck.

Randy was in his early fifties, with a dark, even tan that matched Lottie's, and no grey hair on his chest. An Armani suit hung neatly folded on the back of a chair, in front of a white silk dress on a hanger. The passion must have been overwhelming.

"That's what I told them," Randy said. "Anyone who's ever had a case against you knows that. Like the way you didn't mention my three exes in our radio debate. Not that you needed to anyway."

"No, it wasn't your best performance. But I doubt anyone was listening."

Scarlet looked from Randy to Nicky, and back to Randy again. "I don't mean to interrupt. Do you want me to leave you two alone? I was going to tell Nick something. What was it? The pool guy can't come until next weekend. No, that wasn't it. The cleaning lady came this morning."

"I noticed. She the one who took apart the home entertainment center, cords everywhere? Tipped over the armoire and rifled through my first editions?"

"No, she came before the mess. Oh, that was it—the cops came by, said something about a warrant."

"Thanks for calling me."

"I didn't want to bother you at work."

"Did they even have to knock or were you waiting at the door with open arms?"

She reached for what he guessed was a vodka tonic, ice cubes and a lime at the bottom of the glass. He could picture her lighting a cigarette if she had one.

"They left a list somewhere of the things they took. All of it yours."

This got his attention. "Where is it?"

She finished her glass.

He said, "When did this happen?"

"This afternoon, probably when you were out in Skaneateles."

Nicky was stunned.

"Hey," Randy said, "Scar told me about that. Lilly's a total babe." Like they were on a golf course, shooting the breeze about their conquests. Saying, *I got laid in that sand trap one night back in high school.*

Scarlet shot Randy an evil look, which Randy didn't appear to catch. "What about her husband?" Randy said.

"Nick doesn't respect him," Scarlet said. "Thinks the guy's a lightweight. What do you call him, Nick? A 'limousine liberal'?"

"Can't argue with him there. But, hell, that applies to half the Dems in the country."

"Nick doesn't respect the party, at least in central New York. He agrees with its ideals but thinks it's weak, putting up lame candidates, who don't get their message across."

"No kidding?" Randy said to Nicky. "Why aren't you a Republican? You'd go farther. They wouldn't even need me. It'd be easier for everyone."

Nicky was still wondering how Scarlet knew he'd been in Skaneateles. "Isn't tonight that trustees award shindig? I thought you'd be the one in Skaneateles all day, neck deep in mud with cucumbers over your eyes at that spa, Mirbeau."

"I decided to stay home," she said, snuggling with Randy. "Curl up with a good book."

"How long you been reading trashy romances?"

Randy said, "Come on, Nick, it's not like that. We really like each other. This could be something real."

Scarlet crinkled her nose. "Isn't he cute? We met at the Barristers' Benefit. I saw him pull up in his limited-edition BMW 850 Ci, a few dings in it but six figures when it was new, and I said to myself, now here is a man who appreciates the finer things. This is our first date."

"Hope you made him buy you dinner," Nicky said. "Or did you skip right to dessert?" He turned to Randy. "You know, you should watch what you eat."

That did it, Nicky hitting his mark. The color rose in Scarlet's cheeks. "We went to L'Adour. Had roast duck, crème brulé, and an obscenely expensive Châteauneuf-du-Pape in front of everyone. When the bill came, I put down your Am Ex."

"What good is money if you can't spend it?"

"Such a brave boy, trying to be strong. I know it's killing you."

Nicky shrugged.

"I was waiting for you to do something stupid," Scarlet said. "Now I have grounds for divorce. The DA will prove infidelity in its case against you, at least by—what's it called?—a preponderance of the evidence. Plus you'll probably go away for more than three years, which itself is grounds."

He wanted to ask where she'd learned the term *preponderance of the evidence.* "And you think that gives you the right to take half of everything?"

"My lawyer does."

Randy shrugged. "Sorry, Nick."

"Don't apologize, you ass," she said. Then she turned back to Nicky. "Have you read what they're saying about you in the paper?"

Nicky didn't want to know.

"According to an 'unnamed source' in the police department," Scarlet said, "they suspect you and Lottie of having an affair. It's only a matter of time until other women come out of the woodwork. Pretty soon, it'll all be right there, in black and white."

Nicky should have known Halliday would talk to the press. But he kept his chin up—infidelity wasn't fatal in a Supreme Court election, unlike a murder charge.

"Can I ask you a question?" Randy said.

Scarlet and Nicky looked at him.

"You really kill her?"

His forehead was creased, his hands twisting the bed sheet.

"I'm serious. I want to know how it's going to affect this election thing. I wouldn't have run if I knew I was going to win. I just did it on a lark. You know, like in that movie, the one with Robert Redford?"

"The Candidate," Nicky said, wanting a whole bottle of scotch now.

"That's the one. What happened was, I got a call from the Republican Chairman. He said, 'Remember all those clients I've been referring to you? Now's your chance to return the favor.' There were candidates who wanted to run, but he thought I was stronger. What was I going to say? I couldn't blow the man off. So I told myself it'd be free advertising. Get my name on all those bus signs, meet some future clients like Scarlet here, and enjoy the rush of business after the election. But look what's going to happen—I'm going to have to quit my job and take a huge pay cut to do something I know nothing about." Randy shook his head. "Funny how things turn out, isn't it? You actually wanting to win this Mickey Mouse race, and me going to do it. Hey, where you going?"

Nicky walked down the hall, and said through gritted teeth, "I'm going to lose to this jackass?"

CHAPTER 13

"People grieve in different ways," said Sal. "Me, I'm all dead inside. Like I've lost the will to live." He shook his fist at the track. "Run for your life, Seven, or you're dog food!"

Nicky covered his head with his racing program, imagining how many people from Syracuse were around.

"What?" Sal said. "There a pigeon in the rafters?"

Nicky glowered. "Remind me again why you're my best friend."

"Would you cut it out?" Sal said. "I took care of the funeral home, the church, even the florist. There's nothing else to do but sit with my aunts and eat biscotti."

"We could've postponed this."

"How can you even say that? You know Sheldon gives the box to another client on Monday. Season is over by Tuesday."

Sheldon Sheinbaum, Sal's bookie, always went to Vegas for Labor Day weekend while his wife and kids went to the Jersey Shore with a babysitter and five grand in fun money. Now there was a couple who knew the value of compromise, Nicky decided.

"Besides, Lot would've wanted us to come. We had a lot of good times here."

Nearby a woman in a sundress fanned herself with a straw hat. Next to her a man in a blazer and sunglasses accepted two Bloody Marys from a waiter without a thank you. Nicky had always felt nervous in the Saratoga clubhouse, like he'd crashed a party thrown by the Great Gatsby. Like someone in a morning suit was going to tap him on the shoulder at any moment. Detective Halliday was right—places like this were a long way from Spanakopita on Salina Street, where he and his brother used to slave away—first scrubbing pots and pans, then busing tables, and eventually being promoted to taking orders. He could still see his father behind the bar in a white dress shirt drying wineglasses, and his mother in the kitchen making dolmades, meat and rice rolled into grape leaves. He'd loved the smell of the place—lamb, feta cheese, garlic. He looked around now at the people with their fair skin and straight teeth, their trust funds and Mayflower pedigrees. He knew this was one club that would never accept him.

He said, "We had too much to drink and lost too much money is all."

"Come on," Sal said, "this box should have our name on it. Lottie was sitting in this very chair when she flipped off the governor. And you were sitting there when I first realized you weren't a stiff. Lent me a C-note for a trifecta in the last race, remember? My three horses came in dead last—bing, bang, bong. I was so schnockered I got sick in the ladies' room."

"I don't remember you paying me back."

"Why do you think I invited you again the next year? Hey, remember that box over there, where you met that vixen, what was her name?"

"Carmen."

"With that miniskirt and pierced belly button. Disappeared with her in the sixth, back at the ninth. Where did you go is what I want to know."

"I told you, we had lunch at the Turf Terrace."

"That's what you call it, huh? Lottie was so jealous. That's when I knew the writing was on the wall with Tony."

This got Nicky going. "I had nothing to do with her and Tony."

"Would you ease up? I'm just saying she was hot for you."

"Well, that's not why I made her my partner."

"Christ, are you uptight. What's wrong with you?"

Nicky hesitated, then told Sal about Scarlet, ending with the part about having to spend the night in a hotel.

Sal shook his head. "I hope that Daisy chick is worth it."

"Lilly."

"Who?"

"Her name is Lilly and she's not."

"Not what?"

"I can't take it."

"I'm messing with you, trying to lighten you up. Listen, let me give you some advice on how to forget your troubles at the track. First, order a real drink. None of this club-soda-with-lime shit. Second, bet on a goddamn race. Not much—say, sixty or eighty bucks—but spread it out over three horses, and bet one to show. That way, you'll win something and feel better. It'll build your confidence. Then you can take the rubber bands off your wallet and start really having fun."

Fun? Lottie was dead. Nothing was going to get Nicky to forget that. As for the gambling, he wanted to point out all the people behind them, up above in the mezzanine, waiting in line to punch some buttons on a computer screen, and transfer their Social Security check straight from their bank to the track. It was sad. He'd already lost forty bucks, winning only once—a lousy buck seventy-five on a two-dollar bet. But Sal wouldn't understand, saying something stupid like, *It's the price of the ride.* There was no reasoning with the man. Nicky watched him take out a mini-TV and extend its antenna.

Nicky thought the TV clashed with the track's old-timey feel—wood everywhere, ceiling fans whirring, ducks flapping across a pond in the infield. But then he noticed the other invasions of technology—the JumboTron next to the scoreboard, the little closed-circuit TVs in the corner of each box. He admired the track's compromise of old and new, rich and poor. Men in tank tops and cutoffs standing down by the rail holding tallboys, while women in pearls and diamonds sat up in box seats being served gin-and-tonics.

"What're you doing?" Sal said, adjusting a dial. "Checking out the talent? All those honeys with fake racks, hanging onto their sugar daddies. My favorite is those waitresses in white shirts and bow ties. Triggers my chambermaid fantasy. Remind me to tell Monique. You know Sheldon was going to get one of those new luxury suites down at the end? I told him I'd been in one—glass wall between you and the track, air conditioner spewing at you, zillion channels on cable—it's like you're not even here. You know sometimes it gets up to a hundred here in the boxes, but they won't let you take off your jacket?"

The mini-TV emitted a roar, drawing Sal back to a fuzzy baseball game.

Nicky sat there, feeling his heart ache about Lottie. His life was going down the drain. He kept thinking about Randy De-Vine. Not the part about him and Scarlet, but what the putz had said before Nicky had left. What he'd called their race—*Mickey Mouse*. Had he been right? Nicky knew running for Supreme Court was, what? Not beneath him in any sense, but . . . conservative, noncontroversial, safe. So what if he won? It wasn't like he could change the world. There would be 345 other judges in the state, just like you. And, if you made it to the Appellate Division, there would be fifty-four other judges just like you. And, if the stars aligned and you made it to the Court of Appeals, there would be six other judges just like you. That's what people had implied when he'd bounced the idea around last winter. Lottie, Scarlet, even Lilly. *You've waited so long and saved up all this money. Why don't you spend it on running for something that matters more, like Mayor, or state senator, or even state assemblyman?* Nicky had shrugged, resenting the snub of Supreme Court Judges, saying he knew what he was doing. Wes Longacre was the only one who understood.

Some people say you're doing it because you just want to win your first race, Wes had told him after a fund-raiser, while Nicky was helping straighten some tables, like he was back in his parents' restaurant. *That, instead of the word "loser" linked to your name, you want the title "judge," for when you run the next time. For some office that's a stepping-stone to the big time. State attorney general, lieutenant governor, maybe even governor. Hell, we've already had one Greek in Albany. But I know better. I know how much money you gave to Democratic campaigns in 2006—the max. Fifty grand to Spitzer, fifty grand to Cuomo, and fifty grand to the State Democratic Party. And a hundred grand to Hillary, other federal candidates, the DNC, and a slew of PACS. And that was just in 2006. So what happens when you win this election and become a Supreme Court Judge and that spot opens up on the Appellate Division because what's-his-name is facing mandatory retirement at age seventy? Why, Eliot picks his pal, Nicky. Boom, no election, no Senate confirmation, as long as Nicky is a Supreme Court Judge, which he is. And then what happens when that spot opens up on the Court of Appeals? Same thing, although there are a few more jumps to go through. Maybe a few people have figured that much, okay, but what they don't know is it doesn't end there.*

At this point Wes had put a hand on Nicky's shoulder, stopping him from his clean-up work and leaning in close, like the two were sharing a crude joke. *Think of all the former state court judges who've made the transition to the federal side,* Wes had said. *Senator John Cornyn, Congressman Ted Poe, Attorney General Alberto Gonzalez. And what if you're appointed to the federal bench first? Director of Homeland Security Michael Chertoff, FBI Director Louis Freeh, Solicitor General Ken Starr. Shit, even Roy Bernardi became Deputy Secretary of HUD after being mayor. But the key is winning this first race. You'll have to shell out the dough to even have a chance as a Dem in the Fifth Judicial District. Hick counties like Herkimer, Jefferson, Oswego, Oneida. You could take all the people in Lewis County, stick them in the Dome, and still have room for all the bratty students at SU.*

Nicky appreciated Wes's understanding, the uncanny insight that made him such a good party chairman, but wondered how the man could be a devout Democrat, the way he hated people so much. He really was a limousine liberal.

Sal swore at the Yankees, then switched off the TV.

He looked at Nicky. "You still here? You only have three more races after this one. What's the point in coming?"

Nicky lifted the program. "I've never gotten the hang of using this thing."

"That's why you have to go down to the paddock. Hang on the fence, watch them go by. See their muscle tone, their eyes. Then go with your gut."

"Please don't tell me you whisper to them."

"Sometimes the jockey's more important than the horse. Take that one who just went by, Jerry Lee Davis."

The rider was almost at the gate, his emerald jersey luminescent against the dry dirt track.

"You know the man's middle name?"

"He's in the hall of fame. Began riding quarter horses when he was ten, racing thoroughbreds when he was sixteen. Won his first mount in '76. Next race he was thrown. Broke his nose, jaw, and six ribs. Had to sip his meals through a straw for three months. Ran in, I don't know, probably thirty thousand races since then. Know how many he won? Twenty percent. Know how many he finished in the money? Fifty percent. You could put the guy on a mule and it would pay."

"Does the term 'gambling problem' mean anything to you? Vernon Downs, Turning Stone, Powerball. I can't even play nine holes with you without taking out a second mortgage. Nassaus, skins, sandies. It took me an entire summer to figure out how a press works. Half the time I don't even know what's going on. I want to give you fifty bucks on the first tee and tell you to leave me alone."

"What do you want from me? Cut off my 'nads and enroll in the seminary? You sound like my sister. I have a few simple pleasures. Strippers, steaks, cigars. I stopped drinking, I pay my alimony, and I visit my kid three times a year. Who says I have to give this up?"

Nicky waited for the last of the horses to walk by.

"All I'm saying, I don't know why you do it. Most of the time, it's like throwing your money away. My father used to say, 'Only bet what you can afford to lose.' "

"Let me tell you something. My old man was a cop, sat behind a desk, but was straight as six o'clock. Never made much money, or had much fun, if you ask me. But Lottie worshiped him, probably why she married shit-bird. And my mom, the librarian, she made my dad look like a jewel thief. Still, she had spunk, in her own card-cataloging way, gave Lottie her ambition. It's why she went to law school. So here they are, Mr. and Mrs. Middle America, working their whole life, squirreling away their nickels and dimes. Finally, they take their pensions and move to Miami, not far from where your parents used to be before you moved them into that ritzy condo north of West Palm. Anyway, then what happens? He has a heart attack from all that fried fish and she gets skin cancer. I'm telling you, it ain't worth it."

Nicky thought of his own mother, who had discovered a lump in her breast shortly after moving to West Palm. He remembered the speech he'd given to Lilly at her horse farm, about life being too short. He'd just been trying to get her to cover his ass, but deep down he must have thought there was something to it.

Why, because Lottie was gone? Or was it because he'd missed his chance with her?

"You know," Nicky said, "you and Lottie are a lot alike."

"Were, and I know. Looked alike, too. Except no one called me 'Sal the Body.' Don't look surprised. I know what guys said about my sister."

"I never said it."

"That's because you loved her. We all knew that. Almost left your trophy wife, the one who was just dying to have kids. Until Lottie started busting your balls. I told her to lay off, but she never listened."

Nicky bit his tongue, not wanting to defame the dead.

"But I know what you mean," Sal said, "about the similarity. She had as much sack as any guy I know."

Certainly more than me, Nicky thought. The horses filed into the gate. One backed out, causing a half dozen men to converge on it.

"By the way," Sal said, "I know you didn't do it. I don't even need to hear your alibi."

"I appreciate that." Nicky wanted to remind Sal about Lilly, the reason they had fought. Did the man even listen to him?

All the horses were in the gate.

Sal leaned over, not taking his eyes from the track. "If you need my help, just say the word."

Before Nicky could ask what Sal meant, there was a ring.

"And they're off! It's Ptarmigan, Vamanos, and WhoWants-ToBeAMillionaire!"

The horses flew past Nicky's box, their necks stretched, their hooves sending up clumps of dirt. At the back of the field was a horse Nicky sympathized with, a dark one named Notorious Liar. Behind that, Jerry Davis was struggling on a yellow mare named Gold Rush. Nicky wondered what the horses were thinking. Did they know they were merely pawns in someone else's game? Or did Nicky maybe have it all wrong? Were the horses the rock stars, and people the mindless groupies?

Nicky leaned in close to Sal. "You saying what I think you're saying?"

"If I know you didn't do it, what's the harm? You and me were at the bar, upstairs having cigars and planning your next fund-raiser."

Nicky listened to the pounding of the horses' hooves and saw the jockeys' heads low against the horses' necks. Their bright jerseys shrank as they rounded the first turn, leaving the shadows and entering the light, which spilled across the track and over the neat hedge of the infield. He didn't want to admit it but Sal was getting to him with this racing stuff. He had the feeling he was watching something pure, exactly as it would've looked a hundred years before, and maybe the way it would look a hundred years from now. He watched the pack tighten up, and he found himself rooting for Notorious Liar. A horse with a cruel name like that had to have at least one fan.

"Thanks, Sal, really," Nicky said. "But apart from not wanting to drag you into my own personal nightmare, I don't know if us linking our stories would be all that convincing to the cops."

"What's that supposed to mean?"

"You sure you were at Niagara Casino the night of the murder?" Nicky said, feeling his stomach tighten.

"I told you, with Monique. Our six-month anniversary. She wanted to see the Falls and catch a show. Look at that, how tight they are, only three lengths separating them. Go, baby, make your move! Hey, why are you asking me that stuff again?"

"Cops think Lottie lent you money recently. A lot of money."

Out of the corner of his eye, Nicky could see Sal's jaw muscles ripple. "Setting aside the fact that Lottie was my sister," Sal said, "my blood for Christ's sake, she never gave me that money. Changed her mind. Besides, if she gave it to me, why would I fucking whack her?" He shouted the expletive so loud that a woman looked up from her racing program.

"I didn't say 'gave' but 'lent.' Cops seem to think you did it so you wouldn't have to pay her back."

The horses came around toward the final bend, changing positions, Notorious Liar appearing near the front of the pack now.

"Let me tell you something," Sal said, still shouting above the cheer of the crowd. "I pay my debts. You want someone to cross-examine? Look at that Amazon attorney you have. Lottie told me all about her."

"Told you what?"

"Lottie wasn't the first friend she lost under, what you call, mysterious circumstances."

"What do you mean?" Nicky said, but he knew.

Sal had turned his attention back to the horses, who were coming down the final furlong.

"And here comes Gold Rush on the outside! It's Notorious Liar and Gold Rush! Gold Rush and Notorious Liar! And it's Gold Rush by a nose, followed by Notorious Liar and Millionaire!"

As the horses went past, Nicky was sad for Notorious Liar, now a notorious loser. But Sal was on his feet, waving a ticket, and before Nicky knew it, Sal was pulling him close, lifting him off his feet and shouting in his ear.

"Exacta! Exacta, motherfucker! Exacta!"

Then, over Sal's shoulder, down in the grandstand, Nicky saw him, the man with perfect hair and gleaming teeth. He stood beside a guy with a scraggly beard and a camcorder, its eye black and cold.

CHAPTER 14

When did Tracy Lipowitz become an undercover reporter? What are the apartments like at Nettleton Commons? Does Diz know if Lottie was seeing anyone lately? Are you upset that you and Lottie didn't make up before she died? Why do they call that detective "Doc"? Does he know about Lottie's ex-husband? Can't you go over his head? What's the point in having political connections if you won't use them?

Nicky rested his head on his desk, Dara was making him so tired. She'd missed her calling as a lawyer.

He was at the office, using the Labor Day stillness to think. He'd stared at his caller ID for six rings before picking up. He'd learned long ago that it was easier to take Dara's questions head-on than try to dodge them. And if you cried foul, she would rehuddle, then rush at you again with a fury. It reminded him of a line from a Star Trek movie Brady had rented for them once—an alien staring into the camera, half her face a machine: *Resistance is futile.* Nicky hoped Brady had learned that lesson. If not, maybe it was time for their first father–son talk.

Not that it was easy to answer Dara's questions, some of which were downright insulting. *Do you have an alibi? How long have you been seeing that one? Do you think it's smart to boff the party chairman's wife? When are you ever going to learn?*

Some of her questions threw him off guard. *How much is Diz's retainer? What's her defense strategy? How did she do in the Empire State Games last summer? Are you attracted to her?*

135

Some of the questions came from watching too much TV. *Are they doing an autopsy? Did they do a rape test yet? Did they at least check under her nails? Did that detective read your Miranda rights before asking you questions?*

Some of the questions were off-topic. *Are you going to give Scarlet the house? Is the Hawthorne Suites the one with a fireplace in each room? Do they have anything available the weekend of the wedding? Do you have clean underwear?*

And some of the questions weren't questions at all, but statements. *Your best friend gets murdered and you don't even call me? You were going to wait for my bridesmaid to tell me it's on CNN? Have you called Uncle Alex yet? You think you can handle this by yourself?*

Dara said, "That's it. I'm postponing the wedding."

"Now there's an idea," Nicky said.

"It's no big deal. I'll just make everything a year later. I'll get the church the weekend I want this time. When do you think the case will be over?"

"What case? There is no case."

"It might be good to not have caterers and florists on your mind."

"Actually, I was looking forward to having caterers and florists on my mind."

"If you need a distraction, maybe I'll move back home for a while—you know, take a leave of absence."

Bells and whistles went off in Nicky's head. The last thing he needed was to derail his daughter's dreams, too.

"Why are you so eager to put your life on hold? Are you and Brady still arguing?"

"I don't want to talk about that."

"Really? Because I'm here to listen. I think he did something totally unfair and you need to vent."

He went to his window and opened his blinds, waiting for

her to bite. Below, the streets were empty, everyone having flocked to the Finger Lakes or the Saint Lawrence River or the Adirondacks. No, not everyone, just the people who could afford it. The rest went to Green Lakes or the Fair or down the street to the above-ground pool. Above, the contrail of a jet split the deep blue sky in two.

"Now it's the ceremony," she said.

"Let me guess. It's about having to pick me as his best man."

"No, he thinks you're cool, and he knows he has to have a religious sponsor. He refuses to pronounce Koumbaro right, though. He keeps calling it Kumbaya."

"Does his family not like that it has to be on a Sunday?"

"It's not that, either. He says they do that sometimes in the Episcopal Church. He prefers it, says that way he and his frat brothers can party for two nights before the wedding, instead of one."

"Is it the way he has to do everything three times, or wear the ring on his right hand, or that flowered crown?"

"You sound like you don't like the ceremony yourself."

"I'm just aware how it looks to others."

"He understands the emphasis on the Holy Trinity, that he can switch the ring to his left hand after the reception. Says he wants to be king for a day. It's the ceremony that's the problem—what's included and who does what."

"I thought Father Benedictos and Reverend Graham hammered all that out."

"They did and it was nice—tasteful. But Brady saw the program and he's decided Reverend Graham isn't getting enough 'playing time.' "

"What does he want, to change the lineup?"

"So that it basically converts the Greek Orthodox wedding ceremony into an Episcopal mass."

"I think only Catholics have mass."

"Brady calls Episcopalianism 'Catholic Lite.' I'm telling you, he has no respect for religion. He's trying to highjack my wedding."

"If all he's asking for is his reverend to have a bigger role—"

"I didn't tell you about the Service of Betrothal," she said, talking over him like her mother used to do, "you know, the part where we exchange rings. He wants to have a lecture about marriage, a formal declaration of consent, then a gospel and homily."

"Sounds kind of nice." Nicky hoped the *declaration of consent* involved Brady asking him if he could marry Dara, which he'd never done.

"During the Ceremony of the Sacrament, he wants to have vows exchanged. I explained that we treat marriage as a union not a contract. Know what he said? 'I read on the Internet that sometimes Greek couples do take vows and that, when the bride vows to obey, the groom gets to step on her feet.' He wants to stomp on my hundred-twenty-dollar bridal slippers."

"Your shoes cost that much?"

"They were on sale, down from two hundred. Of course, he's not changing the part about the wine. He likes that. Says he's going to do a few shots with his buddies in the pub across the street before the ceremony."

"Sounds like he's joking around."

"After the Ceremony of the Sacrament, he wants Reverend Graham to say another prayer and then declare us man and wife. The way he and Father Benedictos are alternating, it's going to look like they're a comedy routine. This is all just a giant power struggle. Brady doesn't care about the ceremony."

"He doesn't?"

"Suddenly he's a devout Episcopalian? He's never darkened the doorway of a church since I've known him except for Christmas and maybe Easter. And even then he cuts out after communion, just keeps walking to the car. To beat the rush, he says."

"Maybe his church just doesn't do it for him. Have you taken him to an Orthodox service?"

"Once, down here. He still talks about it. How he had to stand the whole time, as people lit candles and kissed things. How he had to cross himself backwards, touching his right shoulder first instead of his left. How he had to kneel down and bow his head like a Muslim, lifting it to face a sea of butts. He says we can raise our kids Orthodox as long as he doesn't have to go anymore."

"It sounds like you've worked out a happy medium."

"Are you kidding? Every time I give in, another argument pops up. I moved his frat brothers to table four and told him we can go to Jamaica, but now he wants six more invitations for his cousins, because his mother got a nasty phone call from her sister. Who knew cousin Carmilla wanted to hang out with a bunch of ethnic-types?"

"Cost isn't a problem, if that's what you're worried about."

"What about the space? How are all of these people supposed to fit in the church?"

"I'll have Father Benedictos arrange a simulcast in the lobby. Closed-circuit TV for the late arrivals."

"Very funny, and don't change the subject."

"You know, I think that's what this is really about—Brady and your fear of commitment. What does your therapist say?"

"Nice try. I'm putting in for a sub and coming home tomorrow. We'll talk more about it then."

"I'll see you this weekend."

"You need me now."

"I don't need you."

"I forgot, this is what you do."

"What do I do?"

"Shut people out. Do you have any idea how it makes us feel?"

As he formulated a response to this unprovoked personal attack, she said, "You know, when mom died, everyone was there for you. Grandma and grandpa, Aunt Athena, even Lottie—bringing you casseroles, sitting with you at night, inviting you over on weekends. But you just turned us down. At first, I thought it was a phase. What was the word that doctor used? Catatonia. But you never pulled out of it. Just went on about your business, like someone who'd had a lobotomy. I wouldn't be surprised if you never shed a tear."

He was hurt. "Dara, I don't want to get into this."

"Because you're going to have to open up to someone?"

He decided to treat that question as rhetorical. He knew that, on a certain level, she was right—he had trouble dealing with Lottie's death because it reminded him of Corin's, which he still hadn't gotten over. This embarrassed him, especially since he knew Dara had as much reason to miss Corin as he did. But he also knew that Dara was stronger than him. She'd reacted to the whole thing by facing adversity head-on, talking about painful subjects matter-of-factly. Disease, depression, despair. She'd look you in the eye, shrug then go back to making dinner. Nicky had reacted by, what? Easing up on his morals and rekindling his childhood dream of being a politician. Helping people, he called it, because he could. Was Dara right that it was just a cop-out?

"Fine," Dara said, "but I'm coming home for the funeral. Ask the hotel for a fold-up bed. Not one of those cheap ones that hurt your back. If that's all they have, tell them I'd rather sleep on the floor."

Nicky closed his eyes. "Why do you do this to me?"

"Do what?"

"You know I don't like you telling me what to do. I'm the

father, not one of your students."

"Maybe when you start acting like an adult," she said, "I'll start treating you like one."

CHAPTER 15

"You're early," Nicky said.

Diz walked over to the window in black biking shorts and another sports bra—this one neon-yellow. "Who wants to be outside on a gorgeous day like this?"

He clicked *PRINT* on his computer and logged off.

"What were you doing?" she said. "Following the news? I'm glad to see you're finally facing reality."

He snatched the article from the printer and slid it into a manila folder.

She pulled a video from her gym bag and popped it into the TV in the corner of his office. "In case you missed the latest."

He leaned back and laced his fingers behind his head, feeling his heart pound. The picture was snowy at first, then clear—a sea of straw hats and fists, the roar of a crowd.

"You and Sal grieving. Whoa, there he goes, unable to contain himself, throwing his arms around you. Wait, this is my favorite part, the way he puts you down to check out the piece of ass walking by. I feel so bad about the public invading this intimate moment of mourning."

Nicky found the remote control inside his desk and pressed *OFF.*

"I pounded on Trace's door and told him he'd gotten it all wrong. You two loved Lottie so much that you would do anything to escape your crippling grief. Know what he said? Same thing a prosecutor is going to say to a jury. 'The camera

142

doesn't lie.' Know what I said? Absolutely nothing. Know why? Because he's right."

"You told me to talk to him."

"Come on, Nick. You ever heard of being discreet? Meeting at his house? Upstairs at his bar? Or maybe you want to wait until Lottie's six feet under so you can do a little Greek dance on her grave."

"Diz—"

"Don't. You can't dodge this bullet with some lame excuse or some stupid joke. You know what the problem is? It hasn't sunk in yet. Halliday is going to arrest you and charge you with murder. The DA is going to find witnesses to testify against you. Then you're going to jail. Make office furniture at Auburn Correctional. Maybe if you're lucky you can score a job in the law library. But don't bend down to get the soap. Your prints are all over Lottie's home office."

"I helped her remodel. Stain that bookshelf, install those hardwood floors, even set up her computer."

"Fine, I'll just put you on the stand and have you explain that. Open you up to cross-examination on how you didn't have an affair with her and how your partnership wasn't about to dissolve. Not that it would matter—they're going to convict you in the press long before a jury is picked, not to mention before the election is held. Why are you helping them?"

"Don't worry. Juries love me."

"Is that so? Even the eighty percent who think personal injury attorneys take too much of their clients' winnings?"

"Not Greek personal injury attorneys, not in New York State. We've got the largest Greek population in America."

"We've also got the most tort cases."

"But folks in Syracuse love Greeks. Rony Seikaly, George Pataki—"

"Lee Alexander," Diz said, referring to the former Syracuse

mayor who had been convicted of taking kickbacks.

Nicky decided not to mention Yanni, gyros, and the Olympics. Katie and Matt over in Athens with that fat weatherman who wasn't so fat anymore.

Diz's eyes remained fixed on him. She drew a deep breath and rolled her shoulders, like she was about to throw a barrage of karate kicks. Except instead she exhaled, sat down, and put her running shoes on his desk. Showing him she was as cool as he was, in control. "Did you find out anything from Sal, at least?"

"No luck."

"Why, because he had an alibi?"

"He was with his girlfriend in Buffalo."

"And did you talk to this girlfriend?"

"He didn't do it, Diz."

"Did you even get a name?"

"Monique somebody."

"Bleached-blonde hair, supermodel breasts? Stripper-turned-aerobics instructor?"

"She's a bartender now. You know her?"

"From the gym. Lives upstairs from me. I'll talk to her."

"No, you won't. Jeez, who doesn't live in your building?"

"How long they been dating?"

"Six months."

"Why haven't I seen him around?"

"He's got a bachelor pad. Jacuzzi inside, hot tub outside. Calls it his 'swingle.' Short for swinging single."

"Bear rug in front of the fireplace and mirrors on the ceiling? Gee, I'm so sorry I'm gay. What did he say about the money?"

"Said she never gave it to him, changed her mind. He got really upset when I mentioned it, in fact."

"I bet he did."

"I believe him."

"Oh, if you believe him we can all kick back and relax. Fire up the grill and have him over for some burgers. Did he explain why Lottie withdrew ten grand on the day of the murder?"

"Where'd you hear that?"

"Did you ask him?"

"How could I ask him if I didn't know? Maybe it was a deposit on the new office space."

"Cash?"

"Maybe the landlord has tax issues."

"Did she ever do anything that anyone could blackmail her for?"

"Are you serious? You've been talking to Halliday too much."

"What about clients? She ever give money to them? You said before that sometimes she would cut her contingency fee if their recovery wasn't enough."

He couldn't deny this. Lottie would have said that cutting fees and giving cash refunds were the same thing, but deep down he didn't believe they were—that's why he'd argued with her when he'd found out she was doing it. "I don't know. It could've happened, I guess."

"But who did she give it to?"

He couldn't think, things were coming at him so fast. The news story, Monique living in the building, Lottie paying someone ten grand.

"I suppose I can try to look into that, too," Diz said, "although I'm not sure how. She have a list of her clients?"

"On the computer."

As he logged back on and opened the firm's billing program, she came around his desk and leaned on the back of his chair, breathing down his neck. He wondered if this was how Lottie's murderer had struck, from behind as she was looking at her computer.

He clicked *PRINT* again. "Her cases are the ones with her

initials in the far column."

"I know how to read a spreadsheet." She took the list and flipped through it. "Sal was a client?"

"He's having some problems with a creditor. Lottie was representing him in a collection matter. Don't start on that again."

"It wasn't one creditor but three. See, there are different matter numbers."

"So?"

She put the list in her bag. "You're a piece of work. Sticking your head in the sand won't make this go away. Speaking of creditors, I need money for expenses."

"What for?"

"To hire an investigator. Help me talk to Lottie's clients."

He took out his checkbook and wrote a blank check, his second in a week. He tried to imagine Diz and Sal taking off together for the Caymans.

"What was the last check for?" she said. "The one without an entry in the log there?"

"A loan. I told you Sal's having problems. It's why Lottie was helping him."

"The guy was on the dole from both of you? I wish I had his problems. The investigator should take a look at him."

"No."

"He's hiding something. I can feel it."

"Counselor, your client said no."

"What's the matter with you? Do you *want* to go to jail?"

He had to admit, he didn't want to go to prison, have to think of ways to avoid becoming someone's boyfriend. Maybe Diz was right—he could get a job in the prison law library, where he could offer to help the bullies with their criminal appeals and civil rights lawsuits. A job with leverage.

Diz said, "What about your alibi?"

He shook his head.

"You talked to her face to face?"

"I tried my best."

"Would it help if I talked to her?"

"Only if you want to scare her to death."

"We'll have to use her anyway."

"That may not be such a good idea."

"Why not? Has she got an alibi for your alibi? Where do you find these women?"

He debated telling her about his little run-in with Halliday, and how he was tailed by Trace Lipp, but he didn't want to pour fuel on the fire.

He said, "How'd your investigation go?"

"I talked to everyone from the office. They all had alibis. Wally was at Coleman's having a pint with—get this—his priest. The two were altar boys together back at Most Holy Rosary. Terence was coaching Mitey-Mite football. I love those little guys, with football helmets half the size of their bodies."

"On the Friday before Labor Day?"

"Parents weren't happy about it, so Terence made it optional. Only half the kids showed. He bought them Frosties from Wendy's afterward. The guy is amazing. Do you know he plays dodgeball on Tuesday nights? There's a league. Grown men dressing up in short shorts, headbands, and goggles, like they're back in grade school. They go to a bar before so they don't feel the hits. Marty joined for a few weeks until Tiffany found out. Anyway, Marcy was at her camp eating s'mores and playing Pictionary with her husband and kids. And Laurel was on the way there, refereeing World War Three between her two sons in the backseat. Seems they need two GameBoys to keep the peace."

"What about Martin?"

"He says he went straight home from here, after I dropped

him at his car at about quarter of. Says he got home at eight, in time to get yelled at by his wife for five or ten minutes before she left for book club."

"I want to talk to them. Assure them the firm will survive, that they still have jobs."

"Don't make campaign promises you can't keep. Besides, some of them have already made up their minds."

"About what?"

Then Nicky saw Martin pass by his open door, carrying an empty box.

CHAPTER 16

"Where are you going?" Nicky said.

Martin didn't answer, just kept stacking textbooks in a cardboard box.

Nicky had never noticed how small Martin's office was, or how jammed with military stuff. A snowshoe with a plaque on it from the 10th Mountain Division. A sand-colored combat helmet balanced on the tip of a commando knife fixed to a hunk of Humvee. A gold saber from an Iraqi soldier, traded for a pack of smokes. Nicky recalled that Martin had switched to reserve status after Desert Storm to go to college, just missing tours of duty in Somalia and Haiti. Still, the kid had seen action—a gaping hole in his combat helmet. Did he have a steel plate in his head? Had he ever killed anyone?

"This isn't easy for me," Martin said. "I consider myself a loyal person. Headhunters calling me every week for the past year, hiring partners from other firms offering to take me to lunch. Don't ask me who. I wouldn't feel comfortable saying. Point is I wouldn't talk to them, wouldn't even update my résumé. Tiff thought I was crazy. I guess she was right. You just can't trust some people."

Nicky wanted to ask which people, but he'd learned long ago not to take angry people head-on. *Go with the flow* was his motto, see where it takes you. Then, when the person was tired out and confused, lead him home. "You have to look out for yourself."

"Roger that. Can't afford to be idealistic. Got a two-hundred-grand mortgage, fifty in student loans, twenty in car loans, ten in credit card debt, even two in overdue country club dues. Do you know what it's like to have your name posted on a bulletin board like a deadbeat? At least student loan companies send their late notices in unmarked envelopes."

Nicky wanted to suggest that if Martin quit Iroquois and joined Drumlins he could save three grand a year, four before taxes, but it wasn't time for that. Martin still had some fight left in him.

"Not to mention the new baby," Nicky said.

"How'd you know about that? Oh, Tiff. I'm going to have to knock down her security clearance, the way she leaks sensitive info."

"Hey, kids are a big deal. It's hard to keep that stuff quiet. I don't think I'd be breaching any husband–wife confidences if I told you Scarlet and I talk about it. Actually, 'talk about it' is an understatement. She promised me a family, now she's changed her mind—same old story."

Nicky was trying to be nonchalant, but it was hard for him to talk about this. No, just strange. Like exercising a muscle that had spent the winter in a cast. But he knew he would have to open up if he was going to get what he wanted.

"I guess deep down I knew she would. My friends told me I was robbing the cradle, marrying on the rebound. Just to fill the house after Dara left for college. Hard to listen to people when you're lonely and in love. Or think you are."

"I'm not backing down on any promises, just postponing one until we get things a little more under control financially."

Nicky couldn't believe how uptight this guy was, catching the word *promise* on his radar and throwing up artillery.

"I've done everything I said I would," Martin said. "Said I'd propose, go to law school, buy a house near her parents, then join their stupid country club. Even get her a horse from that fancy farm in Skaneateles. That was a lot for a corporal from Fort Drum, standing in his army boots in a snotty sorority house at Saint Lawrence. I had to bust my ass at SUNY Plattsburg, going summers to finish early. Then the fun really started in law school. Cornell's full of cutthroat psychos."

Summer classes? Why was everyone in such a hurry these days to get through school? When Nicky went, college was a good time. Reading books you liked in an oversized chair in the library all day, going to parties late into the night, maybe playing some tennis or golf on the weekend. Only a few times a month would he have to cover a shift at his parents' restaurant.

"The stuff never came easy to me," Martin said. "I barely made *Law Review*. I swear, I don't know how I passed the bar my first time. I had to work twenty-hour days in the JAG Corps just to keep up with the work. But it was okay; I knew I would cash out someday. Become a rich plaintiff's attorney. Don't get me wrong, I'm not complaining about my pay. I'm just saying I've fought for every penny. Like our commercials used to say."

"You're an excellent attorney." Nicky thought of Dale Pardy's dig about the firm's commercials in the courtroom a few days before. He would have to check Dale out.

"You'd think it'd be enough. Do you know how much I hate getting my bank statement each month? When I open my Visa bill, I have to close the door and take deep breaths."

"It's enough to drive a guy to a big firm. Make partner and knock down a buck thirty-five to start. That may not be a lot in the big city, but it goes a long way around here."

"Negative, I'm not going to sell out and do defense work. Going to try plaintiff's work on my own for a while."

Nicky pushed aside the box and sat on the corner of Martin's desk. Under the glass, he saw a cutout of a cartoon—a lawyer saying to a client, *Justice costs $200 an hour. Obstruction is a bit more.*

"That's cool, I remember when I struck out on my own. That was an exciting time. I ever tell you about that?"

"Would it stop you if you had?"

Look at this kid, showing some attitude.

"I was a young buck at Trollop, Butterman & Heist, the predecessor of Trollop & Secore. That may surprise you—me and Barth being first-year associates together—taking crap from partners, defending cheap insurance companies, getting drunk together after work."

This made Martin look up, at least.

"This one time, I had a case against a local plaintiff's attorney, who shall remain nameless. Somehow he'd convinced his client to take my initial lowball offer. You know, the kind of number you feel ashamed to put on the table? So, we're in the judge's chambers before our final settlement conference, waiting for His Honor to get off the phone, or finish a putting lesson or whatever they do behind closed doors—hopefully I'll find out soon—and this guy, he tells me why he's dumping the case. Says he has another case, a big one, products liability, going to get him a new Porsche. No kidding, that's what he said, a—what's it called?—Cabrera Terra."

"Carrera Targa. A 9-11."

"Right. All the Yuppies were getting them back then. He says he just fired off the complaint and had to get ready for discovery. Tells me the case's strong points—you know the way lawyers do, like they're describing their kids' first steps—and I sit there listening, trying to be polite. Then he starts telling me the case's drawbacks, how one of his doctors isn't on board, thinks the guy's going to regain ninety percent of his eyesight, and how the guy is still a ten handicap. And I'm looking at him, thinking this is the way sole practitioners work? Screwing one client to help another, then breaching the other's confidences? So, we settle the case, and the next week, a partner comes into my office and dumps a pile of papers on my desk. 'A reward for settling that last one,' he says. I pick it up and guess what?"

"It's the schmuck's complaint."

"The defendant was a client of the firm's business department. They'd handled the patent of the product that was alleged to be defective—an industrial eye washer, for when chemists get stuff in their eyes. The company had been served with a summons a few days before."

"Did you call him or do it by letter?"

"Neither, I wanted to see his face."

"Nice."

"So he's in his office with his feet on his desk when I walk in. He's got a cigar going, the hot secretary bringing him coffee, the whole thing. The model of the eye washer was sitting on his bookshelf. 'You must be the only TB&W lawyer who ever comes down from that ivory tower,' he says. 'We have a case together,' I say. 'We settled it,' he says. 'No, another one,' I say, and drop my client's answer on his desk. He picks it up and reads the caption, and there's this moment, you know, as his mind struggles to catch up. Like, wait a minute, somebody broke an ethical rule here. Was it Nicky? No, he only has a duty to the court and his client. So that leaves—no, could it be?"

"So what'd he say?"

"Something innocuous like 'Great,' or 'Thanks,' but his voice was hollow. I don't know if it ever really registered."

Martin was shaking his head.

"Guys like that," Nicky said, "they don't get it. Just keep hacking through the weeds, never seeing the fairway. That's when it hit me. I remember, I was leaving his office, walking past all the people waiting to see him—construction workers, welfare recipients, pensioners. I stopped in the parking lot to look at his new Porsche. And I realized, 'Hey, if this jerk can do it alone, so can I.'"

"So I'm smart to go out on my own. What is this, reverse psychology?"

"Nothing like that, I don't hold it against you. Don't get me wrong, we have our differences. Our politics, for example. You hate the Dixie Chicks, what they said about Bush, and I respect them for having balls. You think Michael Moore is a big fat idiot and I think he's a blue-collar genius. And our litigation style. You like to pick a fight, I like to avoid one. Even the way we dress. I bet you haven't worn anything to work but a grey suit, a white Oxford and a rep tie since you started here. You wouldn't be caught dead in a glen plaid shirt with an Ainsley collar and French cuffs."

"If you're trying to piss me off, it's working."

"Hear me out. We have our differences, but we have our similarities, too. The fact that we're both thrifty. Our wives would say 'cheap' but that's because they're spenders. I see you driving that beat-up Chevy Cavalier while Tiffany drives a new Honda Pilot. Wouldn't settle for a CR-V. I even heard you tell Wally that she already wants something bigger. What was it?"

"A BMW X5. Got the idea from your wife, thank you very much."

"That's right, Scarlet made us test drive one of those. With the walnut console and the heated seats that put your ass to sleep. Thing's got everything. A stereo that shows you what song's playing on the radio. A computer that talks to you, tells you to turn left in two blocks. Even a phone number to call to open your door by satellite if you lock your keys inside. She tried to convince me she couldn't live without it. Where was I?"

"How we're long-lost twins."

"There's also the fact that we're both self-made, putting ourselves through school. It doesn't matter that you served weekends and summers running through muck while I waited tables at my parents' restaurant. We're both self-starters, motivated, and—all modesty aside—leaders, in our own way. People looking to us for guidance. Sure, Lottie was a control freak when it came to certain things, but I saw the way she asked your advice on the Onondaga case. She valued your judgment, told me so. You didn't wear those captain's bars for nothing. But the thing about being a leader, you have to be part of a team."

"So what's your point?"

Nicky took a bowling trophy out of Martin's box.

"You remember when we won this? How slim our chances were with Wally on the roster? Thank God for Terence."

"Kid's good at everything. Softball, basketball, golf. I was more surprised at you. Bet Terence five bucks you wouldn't know the difference between a headpin and a kingpin."

Finally, the guy was loosening up.

"My brother's a pro bowler," Nicky said. "Gave me a few pointers."

"Serious?"

Nicky nodded, unsure why he'd never mentioned it before. Maybe he was—what was that term Lilly used to describe her husband?—*emotionally unavailable.*

"Competed on the Midwest Tour for ten years. Lived in Toledo, sold Amway on the side. Now he's Assistant VP of Tournament Operations for the PBA at its headquarters in Seattle. Says the rain reminds him of home. Bunch of ex–Microsoft execs bought the organization a few years ago and are trying to turn bowling into the next worldwide sport. Which isn't so crazy when you consider it's supposedly a ten-billion-dollar industry in the US. Fifty-five million bowlers, ten thousand bowling centers. You're wondering what my point is again."

"My wife is expecting me home before Christmas."

"You need four guys to bowl on a team. You, me, Terence—we're all about average, right? But that season, we were on fire. Even Wally was hot—had a turkey in the last game, remember?"

"I know, I know—on our own we're good, but together we're great. Heard the speech a thousand times from my light infantry commander. Problem is he was there when the shrapnel started flying. You're bugging out in January."

"But the firm will still be here. Wally would be a good man to team up with."

"McMuffin? That cheeseball?"

"Why is he cheesy?"

"Are you kidding? The shirts with a shamrock on the pockets? The plaid wool cap? The lilt in his voice when he runs into one of his 'people'? Riverdancing, Pope-worshiping IRA-sympathizers. Filling the bars on St. Patrick's Day in their plastic green bowler hats, so drunk they have to use two hands to hold their Guinness."

Nicky was speechless. Where had all the kid's anger come from? "I didn't know you hated the Irish so much."

"I have nothing against real Irish, only Irish-Americans who think Ireland is a Norman Rockwell painting. John Wayne and Maureen O'Hara exchanging quips before they go off and have a litter of redheads."

"You mean *The Quiet Man?* I love that movie."

"Except Ireland isn't anything like that. I hitchhiked through it once on a thirty-day leave. Made Italy look like an industrial superpower. Poverty, alcoholism, mental illness. Grown men sitting in pubs talking to themselves in the middle of the week. Probably still living with their mothers, letting their farm rot. One turns to me this one time and takes a cigarette out of his mouth, burned down to the filter, and says to me, 'I like the feeling of pissing me pants.' I look down and his leg is all black."

"I know unemployment was high a few years back, but didn't they have a high-tech boom in the nineties? The whole Celtic Tiger thing. Or did I read somewhere that it was just a myth? You know, some nice stats driven by a fragment of the industry?"

"I don't know, Nick. We're not on *Crossfire*. My point is Wally isn't in touch with reality. Steal from your client then go say five Hail Marys and everything's hunky-dory. My father-in-law says the only reason someone would want to be your partner is to steal from you."

"What does he do?"

"Plays golf, flies his plane, sails his boat. He's rich."

"Good for him. Why doesn't he wave his magic wand and solve your money problems?"

"He's got alligator arms. You know," Martin said, turning down his hands at his armpits and wiggling his fingers, "oh, I'd like to pay but I can't reach my wallet."

"So don't make Wally your partner, just keep him as an employee. He's a scrappy lawyer, been around the block. He could teach you a few tricks. Which CPLR sections to follow and which to forget. How to work certain judges, how to negotiate a settlement. He could be a gold mine."

"Just keep an eye on the escrow accounts."

"Terence is trained, and the girls are good secretaries. Especially, Laurel, even though I know you don't like her. She's a little outspoken is all. She's been through hell with that ex-husband of hers. Anyway, you bring in a junior associate and you could make a nice living. So why go out on your own and reinvent the wheel?"

"You're assuming everyone wants to keep their jobs."

"What do you mean?"

"Come on, you have to know they all hate it."

"The firm?" Nicky wondered why he was always last to hear this stuff.

"Not the firm so much as you."

"Me?" Now he felt hurt.

"You haven't noticed the way their significant others give you the cold shoulder at office parties?"

"I don't know why they would. I pay them well. Let them do what they want."

"You pay them what you want, and make them do what you want. That's why Lottie rebelled, carved out her own niche."

"Huh." Nicky sat down, feeling like he'd been kicked in the stomach. His kids didn't really love him.

As Martin took out his desk drawers and started sorting through them, Nicky began thinking about snide remarks made by drunk spouses at past holiday parties. About lunch invitations he never got. About the times Lottie would come in his office, slam the door, and demand they restructure the compensation system. She wanted to keep more of what she earned and less of what she earned. At the end of the day, he'd given in. What did it matter to him? He'd tried to explain that they would each be making the same either way. He hadn't understood until now her real complaint—she'd wanted more control. More of herself in her work and less of him. Is that what they all wanted?

"I don't even know what more they want," Nicky said. "More flexible work assignments, longer vacations, bigger bonuses? Anyway, if you can figure it out, you can fix it."

"Thanks anyway, but I want a clean slate."

"Well, it's a big change. Have you talked to Tiffany?"

"Not that it's any of your business, but she's on board. In fact, it was her idea."

As Martin put the bowling trophy back in the box, Nicky felt his heart sink. He didn't know why he cared so much. Martin was a square. He couldn't provide the campaign support Lottie had, not knowing the players in the party. He wasn't even a

Democrat. The guy probably had a deer hanging from the rafters in his garage, bleeding out into a garbage can. But there was something about Martin's leaving that was different than Wally's leaving—if Diz was right that Wally was in fact leaving. Wally had been set in his ways when he came to R&M, but Martin had been impressionable. Nicky had—at the beginning, at least—taken Martin under his wing, shown him the ropes. This effort, coupled with Martin's work ethic, had resulted in Martin's bringing real money into the firm. Nicky knew that if Martin left, the firm—Nicky's baby—would die. It was time to take off the gloves.

"Do you understand what you're doing, how risky is it out there? For the first three years, my wife Corin typed letters and answered phones. We ate cereal for breakfast, peanut butter for lunch, and mac and cheese for dinner. The only reason I didn't have to close up shop is because I won a med mal case. I could finally afford a secretary. Do you know how many costs there are in running a law office? Rent and payroll, those are the big two, they'll kill you. They don't go away just because the money's not coming in. Another biggie is furniture and equipment—the computer, copier and fax always breaking down. Then there's the little stuff like supplies, library materials, and malpractice insurance."

"I'll get by."

"I don't mean to insult you, but how? If you're expecting overnight success at client development, think again. That takes years of work. I was active in the bar association my whole career. Worked my way up from handing out name tags at CLEs to serving as director. I've been a volunteer in the attorney-referral program, an arbitrator in Small Claims Court, and an adjunct at the law school—teaching courses in legal research and writing, mediation, negotiation. That's why other lawyers think of me when referring cases."

Nicky could feel a bead of sweat drop under his arm, but it was too late to stop.

"Even my little foray into politics isn't spontaneous. I've been active in the party for years—donating money, organizing political campaigns, holding up signs on street corners. I even graduated from the Leadership Greater Syracuse Program. It was worth it, but do you know how much time that took?"

He had to come up for air.

Martin said, "I shouldn't have a problem getting clients. After I get a verdict against Onondaga Furniture, I'll have plenty of money to advertise."

"Maria D'Angelo is the firm's client."

"Tell her that. She wants me."

Nicky watched the kid continue to pack up firm property. His chest as deep as a keg of beer, his shoulders as wide as a door, his biceps as heavy as thighs, stretching a T-shirt that said *ARMY OF ONE.* He could kick Nicky's ass, there was no doubt about that. But Nicky could take him in a battle of wits. Nicky's firm would have a legal right to any fee recovered in the Onondaga case, a lien he could enforce in court. Still, what was the point in fighting? Nicky didn't really need the money, and he had to admit he'd always liked Martin, with his boyish round face and crew cut. It was no time to be petty.

"Congrats," Nicky said. "No, really. I'm happy for you. By the way, in case you were wondering, you should settle it. I know you want to, from what Diz said."

"Thanks, but she guessed wrong about me. I thought Lottie should've been more aggressive in the case, not less. As you said, I like to pick a fight while you like to run away from it."

"I didn't say 'run away.' I said 'avoid.' There's a difference."

"Whatever you call it, you compromise too much. You just let me take a client."

"I graciously agreed to waive my firm's lien on any fee. As a severance package."

"More like an overdue bonus. Anyway, I don't need your charity, or your advice. I'm taking the ball to the hoop."

Who was this kid with his sudden cockiness? When he'd first come to the firm, he would ask Nicky if he could *speak freely* before offering his legal opinion, like he was going to be court-martialed for insubordination. Maybe Lottie's death, and financial pressures at home, had pushed Martin over the edge. Had he really thought things through? Did he really think he could get the fee with only Nicky's permission? The firm worked on an accrual basis, so the fee belonged to both him and Lottie, which meant, to get it, Martin would have to also get the permission of Lottie's heir. Good luck getting Sal to give up a couple million dollars. Plus, wasn't the kid smart enough to ask for the assignment in writing? Hadn't Nicky taught him anything? Still, Nicky knew Martin was no dummy—he would figure it out sooner or later. Nicky knew he had only one card left to play.

"If you stay, the firm is yours. I'm serious, the whole thing. The office space, the equipment, the clients. I'll give it to you, as long as you try to keep it together. Things aren't working out after a year, you can do whatever you want with it. What do you say?"

Martin kept packing.

"Well?"

"Don't you get it? I don't want my name linked to a murderer."

Nicky felt his Mediterranean blood flowing again. "You seem awful sure I did it."

"You had the motive, you had the opportunity, you had . . ."

"I had what?"

Martin put a lid on the banker's box, wrapped his big arms around it, and bumped Nicky's shoulder on his way to the door, where he stopped.

"Tiff called Scarlet yesterday. The police found the murder weapon. At your house."

CHAPTER 17

"Martin isn't here," Tiffany said.

"I just left him at the office," Nicky said. "I was calling you."

"Lucky me."

Nicky had raced through the empty streets of Syracuse in his sluggish Saturn, frantically punching numbers on his cell phone. Trying Tiffany had been a last resort for just this reason. He knew he should be careful what he said to her, that she was opinionated and moody, but he didn't have time to walk on eggshells.

"He said you talked to Scarlet yesterday, something about a receipt from the police. Do you know where it is, or at least what it said?"

"Why don't you ask her yourself?"

"She's not picking up her cell, and she's not at home, which is strange because her car is in the garage."

There had been no reply when he'd shouted from the foyer. She hadn't been in the billiards room or basement, and he hadn't seen anyone out back by the pool, the sun bouncing off its serene surface. It'd occurred to him that maybe she was upstairs napping, taking a break from her rigorous shopping schedule. He'd taken the stairs two at a time only to find their bed made, their clothes put away, and the towels in the bathroom neatly folded—which only aroused his suspicion further.

"Why would I know where she is?" Tiffany said. "Maybe one

of the girls from the nine-hole group picked her up on the way to the course."

"I thought of that, but there's no tee time on her calendar."

"Maybe someone else then."

Nicky waited for Tiffany to elaborate, but she just let the comment linger.

"You mean Randy?" he said. "The two of them at Turning Stone maxing out on my credit cards?"

Nicky wasn't above calling his wife's lover at home, but he drew the line at calling around to fancy restaurants and resorts.

"I wouldn't know anything about that," she said, "but aren't they her credit cards, too?"

"I don't want to argue. I just want to know what you and Scarlet talked about yesterday."

"Tell me why I should help you, and not just hang up."

"Because you know I'll only call back. And if you take the phone off the hook, I'll just come over and ring the doorbell."

"I'll call the police."

"Then all your neighbors will come out to watch. I'll tell them I'm your father, come to make up for lost time. I'll cry and beg you not to forsake your Greek heritage."

Tiffany blew out her breath. "I called her to see if I could do anything. Not for you, I could care less about that, but for her, the poor thing. Bake her a casserole, take her shopping, I don't know what people are supposed to do. Emily Post doesn't have a chapter on death of a friend's spouse's ex-lover. Maybe I'm supposed to throw her a party. She wanted to know what it was like, when I found Lottie on Friday. We talked about other stuff, too—your run-in with Randy, whether the DA is going to put you in the pokey, and what a mess your place was after the police left. She had to call your cleaning lady again, what's her name?"

"Anna. Is she the one who put everything away?"

In the living room, the couch was upright again, the cushions back in their covers, and the credenza drawers replaced. What would Anna do with a receipt of evidence seized by the police? Put it by the phone? On the refrigerator? On his desk? His feet and fingers couldn't work fast enough, like he was trapped in a nightmare.

"What is she, Mexican?" Tiffany said.

"Who?"

"Hello."

"She's from Puerto Rico. Her husband is a landscape architect and her daughter is an interpreter in Family Court."

"She any good?"

"Her daughter?"

"Yes, her daughter. I want to know if she can tell me what's happening on the Spanish soap opera channel, if Pepé made it across the Rio Grande without being nabbed by Border Patrol."

"Anna's great."

"Figures. Hispanics get a bad rap. They work hard, unlike certain other minorities, who shall remain nameless. Nothing like the Orientals, though. Wouldn't it be great if they cleaned houses liked they cleaned clothes? I swear, those people don't smell. I heard they have smaller sweat glands than us."

It was hard for Nicky to talk to racists. He was always afraid what they thought about Greeks. He'd learned to ignore Scarlet. But Tiffany made Scarlet look like a card-carrying member of the NAACP. He felt particularly guilty listening to Tiffany talk this way about Anna, a sweet woman who would show him her gap-toothed smile whenever he fumbled with his Spanish. He remembered that the plaintiff in the trip-and-fall motion on Friday had been a cleaning woman, too. What was her name? Darlene somebody. No, Doreen. He walked by the bathroom and imagined scrubbing soap scum off shower tile, or kneeling in front of a toilet for twenty bucks an hour. Not bad pay, cash under the table, but he vowed to knock ten percent off the firm's fee on Doreen's case, if he ever got out of this.

He asked, "Did she say anything about the police listing something suspicious on the receipt they left?"

"You mean like the murder weapon?"

"Do you know what it is?"

"You're pathetic."

"Tiffany, please. I don't want to have to beg."

"This is crazy. You want to know whether the cops found the weapon you used to murder Lottie?"

"I didn't murder Lottie. I just want to know what they took from my house."

"Why?"

"If I can find the list, I can see which of the items wasn't there before Friday. Then I'll know the mistake they made. Or what they put in my house."

"Who, the cops? Sure, the Syracuse Police Department is in the evidence-planting business. You're the one who put it there. Tried to hide it, from what I hear."

"Now we're getting somewhere. Hide what, where? What did you hear?"

"You know, I could tell you. I mean, I'm this close, hearing the desperation in your voice. But I don't think I will, not after the way you've treated Marty."

"How have I treated him? Lottie was the one cracking the whip."

"So you wouldn't have to. And what did you do with all that money he made you? Don't think we can't do the math. You bill him out at a buck seventy, he bills twenty-four hundred hours a year, minus the seventy-five grand you pay him. That's more than three hundred twenty grand. All profit."

"We rarely bill him out at anything. Usually we work on a contingency fee. That means there are risks—we have to pay him whether or not we win. Plus, there's overhead—rent, secretaries, liability insurance."

"Not to mention long lunches, three-day weekends, and two-week vacations to Saint Croix."

"Is that what this is about, money? I'll give it to you. We'll call it back pay, an overdue bonus. I already gave Martin a big case, earlier today, but this will be cash."

"Excuse me?"

"Don't be embarrassed. I know you need it. Martin told me about the financial pressures you're under. Happens to every young couple that's starting a family. Tell me what Scarlet said about the list I'll give you five thousand dollars. Tell me where the list is and I'll give you ten."

"Ha."

"What's the matter?"

"Even if I believed you, I'd never take it."

"Why? I know you need it."

"I don't need a money trail to a killer," she said, sounding like Martin. *I don't want my name linked to a murderer.* Why was everyone so convinced he did it?

He stood in the kitchen, feeling waves of fear crash about his heart, thinking again of that short story by James Joyce. He had to concentrate. Would Scarlet have taken the receipt with her, put it in her purse for safekeeping? Or maybe given it to her new lawyer-boyfriend? No, she wouldn't care that much, as long as it didn't implicate her. Then it hit him—someone else could've taken the receipt, like the murderer—especially the way Scarlet always left the front door open. And why was he so sure the cops had planted the weapon? That could've been the murderer, too. He would have had plenty of time. The front door had been wide open on Saturday night. Had it been open today?

Then he saw it and gasped.

"What's wrong?" Tiffany said.

"The door to the patio. It's open but the screen is shut."

"So?"

"Scarlet never remembers to shut it, a catalog in one hand and a bottle in the other. Lets in mosquitoes every time she goes out back."

He descended the steps from the deck, a pit forming in his stomach.

"Is she there?" Tiffany said.

"She was. Tanqueray on the patio, flies buzzing around a glass. Beach towel and suntan lotion on the chaise lounge."

He stepped closer to the water, his heart pounding, his mouth dry. The phone clacked on the stone tile.

"Hello?" Tiffany said, her voice small.

There she was, in her red bikini, halfway between top and bottom, facedown, arms and legs out, not moving, like the way his brother would do it when they were kids, joking around.

He dove into the pool, the cold water blocking out all sound, a bubble forming on the back of his shirt, the chlorine stinging his eyes. He kicked with slow feet until he reached her, her skin cool to the touch, her arms stiff, like she was a flesh-covered mannequin. Her eyes were open, telling him to stay away. His lungs began to burn. He hooked an arm around her torso, trying to remember the last time he hugged her, and kicked to the surface. The sky was blue and scattered with birds. He treaded to the other end of the pool, knowing that it was no use, that she was far away from here. He pulled her up the cascading steps, water sloshing, his clothes heavy.

He rested her head gently on the patio and tried to catch his breath. Her eyes were bloodshot, her lips purple, her cheeks swollen. Her whole body was bloated. It reminded him of a photo from a wrongful death case he'd once tried—a two-year-old boy, a neighbor's pool, it'd been so horrible that he'd tried to block it out, telling himself, *The boy's family will be okay* or at least *It will never happen to you*. Still, bits and pieces came back to him, the way the boy's parents had put up pictures all over the house, telling their next child, *That's your brother. He's in heaven*. And now, looking at Scarlet, Nicky saw his expert witness on the stand, testifying about gas forming in tissue when a body starts to decompose, bringing it to the surface. *A floater*, the man had said.

Nicky stood there, casting a shadow over his second wife, his pants dripping into a puddle around her. It was all so surreal. He didn't know what he was supposed to do, how he was supposed to react. He thought of Tiffany's comment about Emily Post. He thought of Corin's casket being lowered into that hole. He thought of Dara telling him he was out of touch with his emotions. She was right. What were they? Sadness, seeing this girl he'd once loved? Guilt, knowing that somehow her death was connected to Lottie's? No, most of all, what he felt was—he couldn't help it—fear.

He imagined running back to the phone like a man who'd just lost his wife, and dialing nine-one-one. But what would he say? They would ask him his name and address. They would ask him if he'd checked for a pulse and tried CPR. His answers and tone would be recorded, ready to be played back to a jury. They would think, *He sounds like he's faking it, like he did it*. On either side of the yard towered tall hedges that Scarlet had hired a crew of muscle-bound men to plant, telling them to take off their shirts as she watched from the pool. Now the hedges blocked everything but their neighbors' roofs. No one had seen it happen. No one could help him.

He looked out over the back edge of the lawn, over Onondaga Park, and onto the valley below—the dying neighborhoods that he'd once dreamed of resuscitating, the half-vacant office buildings that pierced the skyline to the north, the watchful

University that sat on the hill to the east. A strange calmness came over him. His wife was dead and there was nothing he could do. His law partner was dead and there was nothing he could do. Somewhere out there was the man who had killed them, a man who was trying to frame him. He would have to find the man before he succeeded. The only question was how?

Then he heard it—the distant wail of a police siren.

CHAPTER 18

Diz pried Nicky's hand away from around her mouth. "Nick, is that you?"

"Get in here," he said, "and keep your voice down."

He pulled her into the shadows, between a thick sheet of canvas and a tall, vine-covered fence. He'd thought the darkness would shield him from recognition, but she leaned in close, so her nose was practically touching his, and chuckled.

"What happened to your hair? And moustache? Are those wraparound sunglasses? You look like Arnold Schwarzenegger. Can you even see in those things?"

He put a finger to his lips, stepped to the canvas's edge, and peered into the Fair's midway. A New York State Trooper strolled by, his flat-brimmed hat low over his eyes, his biceps stretching his grey short-sleeved shirt, a long black night stick hanging from his belt. Nicky turned around. "What took you so long?"

"Excuse me, but in case you didn't notice, this place is swarming with cops."

"And people. That's why I picked it. I didn't know that noise would drive me crazy."

"What, that Fast Ball game? I almost played it to give you a scare. Those baseballs sound like they're going to rip through the canvas."

"No, the other one, that Wac-a-Mole thing."

A man over a loudspeaker was shouting, "Whack that beaver!

Whack that mole! Whack that beaver when he comes out of the hole! Hit him in the head! Hit him 'til he's dead! Hit that beaver in the head 'til he's dead!"

She said, "We had one of those at the Erie County Fair, when I was a kid. Except it played that song from *Beverly Hills Cop*. What was it called? *The Heat Is On*. You remember it?"

She hummed a few notes.

"You're tone deaf," he said. "You going to eat that?"

She handed him a Gianelli sausage sandwich, its greasy sauce soaking through a paper plate. He went to work on it, telling himself to slow down, enjoy the peppers and onions, not get ketchup and mustard on his new T-shirt, but he was too hungry.

"Let me guess what's going on," she said, "while you clog your arteries. You found Scarlet but didn't want to wait around and chat with the cops. You took off without packing, then you stopped at the bank. No, a bank is too obvious. You stopped at a string of ATMs, taking out the limit at each one until you were cut off. Then you drove to some backwater city—Binghamton or maybe Watertown—where you traded your Saturn for a pickup, throwing in an extra hundred if the farmer would leave on the plates."

"Norwich," he said in between bites. "And it was a bike."

"A motorcycle? My, you really are playing *Terminator*. You probably went to an out-of-the-way mall to buy that jacket. Like Sangertown in New Hartford. They have that store, Forever Leather. I've seen the commercials. How is it?"

He extended his arms. "Two hundred bucks."

"You probably got your hair cut while you were there. May I?"

She ran her hand over the stubble on his head.

"I've always wanted one of those. I'd look like a bad ass."

"It makes me feel naked."

"Look on the bright side—at least you don't look like Saddam anymore."

"How do you know? Maybe he would have looked like me if he'd shaved his head."

He wiped his mouth with his coat sleeve and balled up the paper plate, tossing it against the fence. She bent down and picked it up with two fingers.

"Anyway," she said, "when you no longer recognized yourself in the mirror, that's when you called to meet me."

"If you're so smart, why didn't you buy a beer with that sandwich?"

"It wouldn't fit my jock persona. A girl in running shorts and a sports bra drinking a Bud?"

"But you got the sausage."

"Athletes need their protein. I was trying to be discreet like you told me."

"What did you discreetly find out?"

"I talked with my friend at the department. Halliday received a tip about Scarlet."

"In person?"

"Through nine-one-one. A woman. Didn't give her name, said she didn't want to get involved, but they have it on tape."

"Old or young?"

"I don't know. Haven't gotten a hold of it yet."

"When did she call?"

"A few minutes before the ambulance got there. They had to free one up. Hospitals are overflowing this weekend—car accidents, boating accidents, knuckleheads drinking and driving. What are you thinking about?"

"Whether it was Tiffany who made the call. If she hung up after I dropped the phone, I guess it could've been her, but I don't think much time passed before I heard the siren. It could've been a neighbor, but the timing's fishy—the call coming right after I got there. Are they doing an autopsy?"

"To see whether there was alcohol in her system."

"There always was. But I have a feeling that isn't what killed her. They should look for bruises on her head or neck. And whether there was any water in her lungs. If she died before she went in, she wouldn't have breathed it in."

"I'm sure the county medical examiner knows how to investigate a suspicious death."

Nicky wanted to say, *You ought to know,* thinking of the newspaper article he'd downloaded from Lexis/Nexis earlier that day. He said, "We should think about who would have a motive to kill her. Make a list or something."

"Was she seeing anyone?"

He decided whether he should be offended.

"The reason I ask," she said, "is statistically speaking, lovers are the most likely to commit murder other than, you know, spouses."

He took off his sunglasses and gave her a look. Then he thought about it and told her about Randy DeVine.

When he was done, she said, "Thanks a lot for the heads up."

"I didn't want to get into it. Didn't think it was important."

"Not important that a woman started having an affair the day before she was murdered?"

"What do you want me to say? The past few days my judgment's been impaired."

"So was hers. Isn't Randy the one with lifts and hair implants? I'll never understand heterosexual women."

He got a kick out of this, her human side. "You're assuming she found him attractive."

"You think she was just getting back at you? Did she know about your little friend in Skaneateles?"

"She guessed as much."

Diz mulled this over for a moment. "Did you tell anyone else about her and Randy?"

"Just Sal and Dara."

"What about Scarlet? She tell anybody?"

"Tiffany. Probably some girls at the club. Why?"

"It explains the warrant for your arrest."

Nicky couldn't believe it. No, he could believe it. He looked down at his new biker boots and shook his head.

Diz said, "A neighbor—not the person who called—he saw your car leave the driveway before the cops showed up."

A sense of urgency came over Nicky. "You've got to get Tiffany to explain everything to Halliday." Then he described Scarlet's conversation with Tiffany, Martin's conversation with him, and his conversation with Tiffany. "It'll show why I was there."

"She won't say you were acting?"

"Then find the murder weapon."

"How?"

"I don't know. Talk to Halliday. Get another receipt. Schmooze him."

" 'Schmooze' him? The man once kicked me out of a squad room because my blouse was too sheer and my hair too short. Said I was sending his men mixed signals. Even if he liked me, he's not going to give me something unless I give him something in return."

Nicky knew where she was going. "I'm not turning on Sal."

"I was thinking more about your girlfriend."

"Her? No."

"Aren't we the gentleman?"

"Tell him about Randy."

"You think he's going to believe that? Coming from the man's political opponent?"

She was right. He was tired—eyes burning, feet throbbing, back aching.

"How's the media treating my campaign?"

"I can't believe you're honestly asking that."

"Are we going to get into this again?"

"They pulled your commercials."

"Are they showing my picture on the news?"

"Your bar photo."

"Well, at least my face is still getting out there."

"Would you get serious? You've got to make a decision."

"You want me to turn myself in?"

"You know how hard it is to represent a fugitive? Partying it up at Saratoga is nothing compared to this. I've lost any credibility I had with the DA."

"Sorry to inconvenience you."

She balled her fists. "You say things like that, it makes me want to throttle you. I'm trying to help you, dumb ass. Slip down my fire escape, take a bus all the way out here, and wind my way through the poultry building—my clothes are going to stink for a week. I don't see anyone else trying to help a known fugitive."

"Sorry," he said, meaning it. Maybe Dara was right—there was something wrong with him.

"You want me to look at this from your perspective?" Diz said. "Fine. I'm Nicky Rigopoulos. I was born to help people. My law practice is merely a vehicle for financing my political career. I don't care about anything else, alienating my friends or being charged with murder, as long as I win an election for judge. Except—wait. Even if I do win the election, I won't be able to serve as judge because I'll be a convicted criminal."

He was surprised she knew him so well. Was he that transparent? Still, he tried to sound bored. "We've been thorough this. I get your point. I can be a tad myopic at times. Can we move on?"

"Myopic? You're downright blind. You want my advice? Stand and fight, for once in your life."

That was unfair. She didn't know him before Corin had died, before he'd hung up his boxing gloves. He pictured a new campaign commercial, one where he traded in his Reeboks for a pair of big, round gloves. It could show Terence taping his hands first, massaging his shoulders, holding a silk robe for him to step into. Or would that make Terence look too much like a servant? Maybe he should just put on a wide leather belt with two holsters. Pull down the brim of a cowboy hat over his eyes as a posse of drunk vigilantes rode into town holding shotguns and a rope with a noose. Nicky could stare them down, let his fingers hang loose as a tumbleweed rolled between them, right before he whipped out his two six shooters. *Bang! Bang!* Of course, that would make him look like a killer.

"You really think we could win?" he said.

"I really think you have to let me try. Cross-examine the DA's witnesses. Subpoena your alibi and the person who's covering for her. Put Sal on the stand to talk about Tony Donuts. Put up the guys from the office as character witnesses. Maybe I can raise a reasonable doubt. It's your best shot."

Nicky turned this over in his head, letting the idea sink in—the famous Nicky Rigopoulos on trial. The klieg lights, the packed galleries, the questions. "If I turn myself in, do you think they'll let me post bail?"

"You do have strong ties to the community, but that's up to the judge. The DA is going to oppose it, of course. Say you've proven yourself to be a flight risk through this little hide-and-seek thing you're doing."

He pondered the idea of being locked up in the Public Safety Building for a year with the sort of people Halliday had described—*dealers, dope fiends, and gang bangers.* He shook his head. "My best shot is staying free and finding the person who murdered Lottie and Scarlet."

"And just how are you going to do that?"

"I have a few leads."

"For example?"

"Dale Pardy."

"Who?"

Nicky told her about the motion argument the previous Friday.

"He threatened you?"

"It didn't seem like anything. But I've been thinking, maybe he came to see Lottie. Maybe that's why she withdrew the money. But maybe it wasn't enough."

"Jeez, Nick. Do you tell me anything? And why didn't you share this little detail with Halliday? It could be a motive."

"I didn't think of it at first. Then I decided I didn't want Halliday doing a half-assed job, sending some sergeant to ask Dale's alibi, then crossing Dale off the list."

"You're going to crack the case by yourself, is that it? With all your criminal investigative training? All those background checks you had Terence perform on witnesses?"

"If I find reason to believe he did it, I'll go to the police. I just want to talk to him."

"But why would he want to kill Scarlet?"

"Maybe he saw from the press that the cops thought I killed Lottie and he wanted to help pin it on me."

"And the fact that Scarlet was seeing Randy?"

"Just a coincidence."

Now she was the one thinking.

"Fine, I'll go with you."

"No way. This operation is going to require a scalpel, not a sledge hammer."

To his surprise, she didn't press the issue. Maybe they were coming to understand each other, or at least respect each other. She paced back and forth in front of the canvas. A baseball thudded against it.

"Strrrike!" said a man over a loudspeaker.

Nicky expected her to give him the old *help me help you* speech again. But she said, "I know we've never been close. Never really done anything out of the office. I don't even think we've been to lunch, just the two of us. I always wondered if it was because I'm gay."

"You think I'm homophobic?"

"I just meant, how many women friends do you have that you haven't slept with? Other than Lottie."

He let out his breath. How did everything turn into a psychoanalysis of him? He told himself to be reasonable, honest, direct. "It's not intentional, the romantic turn my relationships take. They just end up that way."

"But not with us."

"Are you saying you want to?"

"Would it make a difference?"

"Maybe, I don't know. You are attractive, in a pro-volleyball-player sort of way. Let me ask you a question. Have you ever slept with a man?"

"Once, as a matter of fact, in high school. My first time."

"I assume it didn't go well."

She didn't answer. He wondered if he should apologize. But she was just thinking. She said, "It went fine, I guess. I just knew I was missing something. That there must be more to it."

He felt his heart start to ache again. "I know what you mean."

"You mean Scarlet and Lottie and the rest of your conquests, compared to your first wife."

He was amazed she knew what he was thinking. "Listen, you're right about us not being close. But don't worry about it. It's just that I don't feel comfortable with you yet. As you said, we haven't spent much time together. It's probably something we'll get over by talking."

"Then let's talk."

"You first."

"All right. Last Monday, Lottie asked me to lunch. We went to the Mission, and she had two margaritas. About halfway through our enchiladas, she told me you might be needing a new campaign manager."

"Committee chairman."

"Whatever."

"Did she ask you to take her place?"

"All she said was that she'd recommend me if I wanted. She also said something about having some new office space available in a few months if I needed it. She didn't say where and I didn't ask. I told her no thanks, that I wasn't the political type. I also told her that, if she was thinking about leaving the firm, she was making a mistake, but that it was her call and I wished her luck."

"You didn't tell me on Saturday. Why? You felt guilty about not coming to me before?"

"I felt like a kid caught between fighting parents. I didn't want to get in the middle. Besides, I didn't think she'd actually do it."

He watched her for a sign of deception. But it was she who was analyzing him, trying to make this about him again.

"That's what you wanted to know," she said, "if I met with her and why. But there's something else bothering you."

It was time, Nicky decided. He reminded himself to be subtle, not sound like he was standing in front of a witness box. He didn't want to alienate the only person who appeared to be helping him. He said, "Why don't you tell me more about the death of your girlfriend?"

Diz's eyes glistened.

"The reason I ask," he said, "there was one thing you didn't mention. You were a suspect."

CHAPTER 19

As Diz took a piece of paper from Nicky and opened it under the dim moonlight, he resisted the impulse to step behind her and read it. He knew the words by heart.

DEATH RAISES QUESTIONS

Labor Day looked like a nice day to sail on Lake Ontario, with clear skies, a mild 10 mph wind, and three- to five-foot swells.

So Lisa Black, a 23-year-old graduate student at Syracuse University's Newhouse School of Public Communications, rented a 28-foot sailboat in Oswego with Dana Dzikowski, a twenty-year-old senior.

"The two were really excited," said Molly McCauley, owner of Sunset Sails. "Lisa was going to teach her girlfriend the ropes. They came with a big picnic basket." McCauley recalls seeing a bottle in the basket, but does not know if it was alcohol.

McCauley had leased sailboats to Black in the past and called her an "experienced" sailor. McCauley said that the two were wearing the boat's life jackets when they left the dock.

That was the last anyone saw or heard from them until four hours later, when Dzikowski made a distress call over the boat's VHF radio, reporting that Black had fallen overboard.

The Coast Guard immediately launched a 44-foot motor boat from its station at Oswego Harbor. The Coast Guard was joined in the search by an Oswego County Sheriff's helicopter.

Efforts were hampered by a sudden storm, which had increased winds to 35 mph and swells to 15 feet. The Coast Guard eventually found Dzikowski. But it was not until three days later that a recreational sailor spotted a body floating near a breaker wall outside Oswego Harbor.

Oswego Deputy Sheriff Roland Evans waited on shore as Coast Guard divers pulled the body from the water. Evans said the body was clad in a bathing suit but no life jacket. Within a day a positive identification was made.

The Onondaga County Medical Examiner, who has authority to certify deaths in Oswego County, found evidence that the cause of Black's death may have been blunt force trauma to the back of the head rather than aquatic asphyxiation.

Dzikowski claims Black was struck by the boat's boom and thrown overboard. She claims Black called to her from the water to turn the boat around, but that she could not do so. She claims she threw the boat's life jackets overboard in the hope Black would find them, then radioed for help.

Dzikowski could not explain why an experienced sailor like Black would make such a novice mistake. The Medical Examiner found no alcohol in Black's body. Evans said an investigation of the case is ongoing and that the police have not ruled out foul play.

★　★　★　★　★

Diz folded the article and gave it back to him.

"What do you want me to say?" she said.

She was a cool customer, he had to give her that. "There was a criminal investigation."

"They didn't find anything."

"You were never charged?"

"Never even arrested. Check for yourself."

"I tried. I couldn't find anything online, and the courts weren't open because of the holiday."

"It wouldn't have mattered. It takes almost a week for them to get back to you. The statewide search usually takes a day, sometimes only a few minutes, but you might not get everything. If you go right to the county clerk's office, it takes three or four days. But you can check if I was arrested from the police blotters in old issues of the Oswego newspaper. They're on the Internet."

"Maybe I will."

"You'd be wasting your time."

She was disarming, the way she didn't seem offended. He let his guard down, too, easing up a bit. "Why didn't you tell me about the investigation?"

"Because I didn't do it."

"Then why were they looking at you?"

"You read the story. We were 'lesbians.' I couldn't explain her 'novice mistake.' They thought maybe she dumped me or was cheating on me."

"Was she?"

"Jeez, Nick, we were in love."

"And she just fell off the boat?"

Diz's eyes were showing some emotion, as if to say, *I can't believe you're asking me that.* Nicky's heart filled with sympathy.

But he didn't back down—he needed an answer. Her eyes sank.

"The sky got dark. It'd been nice before that, sunny, just like the article said, but I guess things change fast on a big lake. Next thing we knew the wind picked up, the waves got bigger, and we started to tip over. Nothing Lisa couldn't handle. She was calm. I was the one who started to freak. She told me we had to change directions—tack or whatever—so I let go of the mainsheet and jumped up to get out of her way, and—"

She wiped an eye with her bare arm.

"At one point, after I'd been interrogated for something like five hours, without a lawyer, without a break, without even a cup of coffee, one of the detectives said to me, 'See what your sickness has done?' Your 'sickness.' It got to me. Sounded like something my dad might say. I fell apart. Said something stupid like, 'You're right. It's my fault. She shouldn't have died.' That was it—they smelled blood. They talked to my roommates, my teammates, my professors. It was all over the news. It's how my parents found out I was gay. It's never been the same with them."

Nicky told himself not to be a sucker, but he knew what it was like to feel responsible for someone's death. The suffocating weight on your chest that you couldn't remove. The overwhelming fatigue from waiting for things to get better. And the pit in your stomach from knowing that the guilt and depression might return—which, Nicky realized now, they had done recently. He didn't want to get into all this stuff, dredge up painful memories, fall apart all over again. But for the first time, he thought maybe it would help.

"When Corin died, I kept apologizing to Dara. On her birthday, holidays, whenever we were having a good time. I'd be thinking, Corin isn't here. Dara doesn't get to share this experience with her mother, doesn't even know what she's missing. Lottie used to try to reason with me—say I wasn't in the car, that I wasn't supposed to be picking Dara up from practice. But that just made it worse."

They stood there a moment, two lonely survivors, listening to the thud of baseballs on canvas, the maddening Wac-a-Mole tune, the babble of the world beyond. When it had become clear that Nicky had stopped his cross-exam, Diz's face hardened.

"So, what did you do? Plan all of this? Get me to come out here then shove this article in my face?"

He showed her his palms, wanting to say, *Come on, I cut you some slack.*

"No, I want to know," she said. "Was it because you can't understand why I'm helping you? Or was it because Scarlet died by drowning on Labor Day weekend, too? Like I'm some twisted serial killer. Or maybe it was because you thought Lottie and I were lovers."

"Calm down."

"So now you trust me, is that it?"

"I had to ask."

"You think I don't have questions?"

It threw him. "What questions?"

"Are you kidding? Like Lottie and I never talked. Your casual affairs, your flexible moral code. Half the time I wonder why I begged you to hire me."

"You said you'd do it for free." He wanted to lighten things up.

"I changed my mind. And I'm doubling my hourly rate."

"I'll pay it."

"Darn right you will."

"We'll both just have to trust each other."

"You tell me something then. Who were you with the night of the murder—where and when? And I want specifics. I'll need to know when I file a notice of alibi."

"Which is when?"

"Within eight days after the prosecution's demand, which is usually made at arraignment."

"Arraignment? I haven't even been arrested yet."

"How hard is that going to be? All they have to do is find you."

He thought about the State Troopers on the other side of the canvas, how easy it would be for Diz to get their attention. He'd taken a chance calling her. Her phone could be tapped for one. That's why he'd called from a gas station and said, *Meet me on the other side of your greatest athletic achievement.* That was what she'd called the feat of winning a giant Nemo toy the summer before. But even worse, she could be helping the killer. Hell, she could *be* the killer. He didn't even know where she'd been when Scarlet had died. Still, she hadn't turned him in so far. Why not? Maybe she wanted to know who Lilly was, so she could scare her off even more. Put the final nail in his coffin. Would she really do that to him? He didn't know what choice he had but to trust her—he couldn't get through this alone. He drew a deep breath and began.

When he finished, she said, "Wow, you can really pick 'em. She's as ruthless as her husband. Still, I guess anyone who'd cheat on their spouse would screw over their lover. All right, my turn—now I'll give you something."

She slid a backpack off her shoulder and started fumbling around inside it. Why hadn't he noticed it before—had she been hiding it? What was in it? And what did she mean, *Now I'll give you something?* He saw a bulge in the nylon and her hand grab hold of something. His heart skipped a beat. There was a large, heavy object, a glint of black steel, a barrel pointing right at him.

Had he made a fatal mistake? Was this how it was all going to end, behind the Wac-a-Mole game at the New York State Fair?

He threw up his arms, squeezed his eyes shut, and waited for the bang.

Nothing happened.

He opened one eye and saw she was holding her cell phone and Palm Pilot.

"The police can track yours," she said.

He didn't know what to say. "You'll be an accomplice."

"Don't get all choked up on me." She pressed them into his palm. "They're no substitute for a legal defense."

CHAPTER 20

"Don't tell me," Halliday said. "You've come to your senses."

"Put away the cuffs," Nicky said. "I'm just calling to chat."

Halliday stood on the steps to the funeral home, while Nicky stood across the street in an alley. He'd come to find the murderer, someone who knew Lottie and Scarlet well enough to be welcomed into their homes. Still, he wasn't sure what he was looking for—an unlikely couple, a new car, a bounce in someone's step.

Diz had been right—he didn't know what he was doing.

Lottie's family had been first to arrive—a parade of aunts, uncles, and cousins. Nicky had recognized the heavy one called Pizza Tony. Nicky could still see the man's sausage-like fingers laying Scarlet's Italian tile in their master bathroom. When Nicky had asked the damage, the man had said, *For Lottie's partner? A pepperoni pizza.* Nicky had fit easily into Lottie's sprawling ethnic family. It reminded him of his own. It was one of the reasons he and she had become such fast friends.

Nicky thought of when they'd broken up. They'd been lying on the couch in his office. He'd told her that she was his best friend and the sexiest woman he knew, but that he should try one more time with Scarlet. He had, after all, made a vow to her. And, while Scarlet was having second thoughts about kids, Lottie had no second thoughts at all: she'd made up her mind that she was too old to have kids and wasn't going to even try. Lottie had gotten up and grabbed her litigation bag, just like that. At the door, she'd paused and said, *You're a fool, Nick, a silly fool.* The remark had stung. In time, he'd gotten over it, but deep down he'd always suspected she'd been right.

Sal and Monique had been next to arrive, in a shiny Porsche. Nicky had figured it was Monique's since Sal drove a Dodge Viper—an early model, black coupe that Sal called, *The Batmobile.* Nicky identified the Porsche as a Boxster, a silver convertible with sleek curves. Nicky wondered how much aerobics instructors-turned-bartenders made, even ones with economics degrees. She'd worn a low-cut black jacket, a lace camisole, and a short skirt. Sal had worn a shiny grey suit, the kind mobsters wore on TV. They'd climbed the steps to the funeral home hand-in-hand.

Next Diz had pulled up in a white Jeep Wrangler, with mud on the sides and a bike rack on back instead of a spare tire. She'd worn a simple black dress and sunglasses, her hair still wet. She'd crossed the parking lot slowly, looking this way and that, then had planted herself on the steps. It had occurred to Nicky, maybe she'd been waiting for him, sensing he couldn't stay away.

She hadn't stirred until Doc Halliday and Tony Donuts had showed up, stepping out of a brown Chevy Impala in matching grey suits. Nicky wondered if his comment about the Crown Vic had made Halliday switch police cars, or if the car was Tony's. Tony's gut sagged over his belt, his coat sleeves an inch too short, dark circles rimming his eyes. Nicky had wanted to feel pity for the man, but he could still see the fear on Lottie's face after the break-ins. Was Tony her killer? If so, why would he kill Scarlet? Could he really be so cold as to try to frame someone? And if he wanted to get back at Nicky for sleeping with Lottie, why would he wait so long? Tony and Halliday had stopped at the front door to say something to Diz. She hadn't opened her mouth, just lifted her chin and made them step around her, before following them in. Good for her, keeping her game face.

It was she who had inspired Nicky to call Halliday, drawing him back outside for better reception.

"Your number's coming up unavailable," Halliday was saying now. "You haven't fled the state, have you? I'd have to get the Feebies involved."

Nicky had called the operator and told her he was having trouble dialing a number, so she'd dialed it for him. A trick he'd learned from Terence.

"The Feebies? Where are you from, a 1940s gangster movie?"

"Close—Utica."

Nicky wanted to say he'd had some cases there, ask if Halliday knew any of his clients. But that wasn't the reason he'd called. "What was the murder weapon you found at my house?"

"Why're you asking me? You know what it was."

"Scarlet never gave me the receipt."

"Is that why you killed her?"

"You think I killed my wife because she kept messy paperwork?"

"No, I think it's because she was going to leave you and take half your money. But you're admitting you did kill her, right?"

"What did you find?"

"Not only the murder weapon, but the charge on your Visa bill. Dated right before Lottie's birthday. Clever way to get it into her home. Shows premeditation, don't you think?"

Nicky tried to think what he got Lottie for her last birthday. "Those Profiles in Scourge bookends?"

"I didn't get the name at first. Someone had to explain it to me, the reference to JFK's biography. But I figured out where you got them, that airplane shopping catalog. And I know why they caught your eye—bronze busts of Ralph Nader and Erin Brockovich. What feminist crusader could do without them?"

"They were in my house?"

"Don't sound surprised. They weren't all that well hidden in your basement, with that bunch of smelly dolls, you perv."

"You went through my daughter's things?"

"Like those sex toys weren't yours. What about the dresses? Your wife didn't know anything about them."

The dresses were Corin's, which Nicky was saving for Dara. Nicky wanted to ask for a little respect. "Don't you realize the murderer planted them there?"

"Only prints on 'em were yours and Lottie's. The boys at the lab are still trying to figure out which one you used on her. Me, I think it was Brockovich—you can get a better grip on her 'cause of her boob job. Is that how you killed Scarlet, whack her on the back of the head, or did you just hold her underwater?"

Nicky was surprised that the county medical examiner hadn't already figured that out.

Halliday said, "Let me tell you what I think happened."

As Halliday hypothesized, Nicky tried to control himself, make himself focus on the reason he was there. He watched Martin and Tiffany arrive in their new Honda Pilot, a ST. LAWRENCE sticker on the rear window. Tiffany was driving, one hand on the wheel and the other pointing at Martin, her mouth open. Nicky was always a little glad to see other couples fight, to see it wasn't just him and Scarlet. Martin and Tiffany turned off the engine and stayed in the car a moment. Then Tiffany got out and slammed her door, which echoed down the block. Martin hung his head and followed her across the parking lot. Nicky tried to imagine what kind of woman could beat down a rock-climbing, cliff-rappelling, battle-hardened soldier. She wore a black dress, black stockings, and a black hat. Not a bad figure for a monster. She waited on the steps for Martin to open the front door, then strode past him.

Wally McGuffin and Terence Jefferson were next, the odd couple, in Wally's old Lincoln. Maybe Terence was angling for a job, or maybe his aging Hyundai was in the shop again. Nicky thought of car-dealer Billy Fuccillo on those TV commercials, screaming that his deals were *Huge!* For a while Nicky had debated doing an ad playing off the catch phrase, saying his clients' verdicts were *huge*. But Lottie had reminded him of the ethical rule against misleading prospective clients, making promises you couldn't keep. She'd always been there to rein him in. What would he do without her? Wally and Terence had stepped out of Wally's black Town Car, dings in its fenders, rust on its doors. Wally wore the same threadbare suit he wore to court. Terence wore the kind of suit ex–NFL players wore on pre-game shows—three-button, brown, with a huge shirt collar that devoured his tight tie knot.

Next was Laurel Lewandowski and sons, and Marcy DeSalvo and family—all packed inside Marcy's blue Plymouth Voyager minivan, its bumper scraping the pavement. The six of them spilled out the door and across the parking lot, one of the kids shoving another, and Marcy's husband smacking the aggressor on the head. It was the kind of family that brimmed with life, the kind Nicky had always wanted. He felt it was getting too late for him, forty-six years old and twice a widower. Not to mention an imminent guest of the state.

Nicky noticed that Halliday had stopped talking. "Are you done?"

"Check this guy out, with the attitude."

"Do you have any leads? Other than me?"

"I told you how I work. I've picked my theory."

"So you didn't follow up on Tony Donuts' alibi?"

"You don't quit."

"He could be the one."

"His story checks out. I talked to his partner and their girlfriends."

"Did you talk to Lilly? I think she's in danger."

"I bet she is. Wouldn't confirm your alibi."

"That's not what I meant. I think the killer may go after her next. He's trying to set me up."

"Is that how you think this works? You kill off all the witnesses and say their murders are evidence someone else did it? That only works in movies."

"Would you stop a minute? You don't know everything."

"What don't I know?"

"Randy DeVine just started seeing Scarlet."

"How do you think I learned Scarlet was dumping you? Why are you bringing him up anyway? Is he next?"

"So you know?"

"Sure, but I'd be happy to talk to him some more—I forgot to ask if he has any dirt on you. What do they call it? Opposition research?"

"This could all be a scheme to beat me in the election."

"Since when do people die over judicial elections? Besides, I like to stick with what I know. Motive, opportunity, weapon. A few witnesses would be nice, but you're too smart for that."

"Did you talk to Tiffany?"

"She's the one who told me to talk to DeVine. Said you called her like you were looking for Scarlet. That you acted real surprised when you found the body. Even offered her ten grand to confirm your story. Nobody's buying it. Not even the part about jumping in the pool to save your wife. We all know you have a flair for the dramatic from your commercials."

"Talk to my employees and friends. They know I'm not capable of murder."

"Some of them say that. Others say you're a man on the edge, with a lot of anger bottled up. Police psychologist says you might not even be aware of it."

"That's crazy."

"Exactly. Man loses his wife, goes into denial, loses touch

with reality."

"Leave her out of it."

"What's the matter? I touch a nerve, killer?"

Nicky drew a deep breath. He wanted to tell Halliday to not call him that, ask the man why he'd turned so mean. They'd gotten along fine before, like adults. He figured Halliday's change of mood was due to Scarlet, Nicky becoming an embarrassment to the man down at the station.

As Halliday began describing the police psychologist's absurd profile, Nicky watched Trace Lipp arrive in the Hummer that had followed Nicky to Skaneateles. The long antenna on the roof, the black box on the dash—a fuzz buster or police radio. Now Nicky was wondering how much TV reporters earned. And how anyone who was part of the media, supposedly informed, could drive a car that gets a dozen miles per gallon, especially in a time when America's foreign policy problems resulted so much on its dependency on Middle East oil. Nicky could still see Trace in his rearview mirror, swerving between cars with his chin low to the wheel, like he was dodging mortar fire as he raced into Baghdad. Trace got out, slipped a mini notebook into his sports coat, then took out a dictaphone. The guy had no shame.

Barth Crawford followed in a Mercedes, with Porter Boyd in the passenger seat. Barth wore one of his famous black suits, and Porter donned a mindless blue pinstripe. They waited for Judge Nichols and Judge Merritt to get out of a Cadillac before walking in with them. If Barth played his cards right, he might even be able to bill for this. What would the time-entry code be? *Marketing? Judicial Relations?* Maybe Trollope & Secore had a code that just read *Kissing Ass.*

Next was Lottie's client, Maria D'Angelo, the woman whose injuries Lottie had been trying to avenge. She stepped out of a Ford Escort station wagon, wearing long sleeves and slacks, the clothes hanging off her. Her hands seemed shrunken, then Nicky remembered what had happened to her fingers. She had hollow eyes, pronounced cheekbones, and deep lines around her mouth. She floated across the lot and slipped inside the funeral home without a sound.

"So why'd you do it?" Halliday was saying. "Were you and Sal in it together—you knock off his sister, he knocks off your wife?"

"Sal had nothing to do with this."

"Fine, tell him if he comes in, I'll make a deal for him, too. But only until the arrest. The DA has a bug up his ass about that."

"How can you stand in front of Lottie's dead body and pretend to look for her killer when you'd be willing to cut a deal with him?"

"How do you know where I am?"

Nicky's stomach flipped. "Where else would you be? Calling hours are today, aren't they?"

"Like you don't know. Why don't you come by and pay your respects?"

Nicky breathed easier. "Place is probably swarming with cops. Lawyers, judges, maybe a few reporters."

"More than a few."

As Halliday listed the attendees, Nicky watched a Chrysler pull in and felt his heart sink. Stepping out of the car were his brother Alex, his Aunt Athena, and his Uncle Cosmo. Behind them in a Chevy with rental plates were his father and Dara. Alex looked good—trim, starched and clean-shaven, having recently ditched his moustache to fit in with the ex–Microsoft execs. His father looked like he'd put on ten years—his hair white and thinning, his skin sallow, his movements slow. Would he die thinking he had raised a murderer? Then came Dara— the only woman he'd seen yet with mascara-stained eyes. Nicky wanted to cross the street and fold her in his arms, tell her that nothing was going to happen to him. But he didn't believe that.

"Look who's coming," Halliday said. "Like shooting fish—"

Then a screech filled the air. A fire alarm—no, a siren—wailing a few blocks away.

Nicky waited as it grew louder and louder, until his head was going to explode. An ambulance was screaming down the street between them, a flash of red and white, lights whirling. Nicky cupped his other ear with his free hand, only to find he could still hear the racket through the receiver. Across the street, Halliday was doing the same. Then Halliday looked up, wearing a surprised expression.

"I'll be damned. You're here."

As he ran down the steps and into the street, the faces of Nicky's family followed him, turning toward Nicky. Nicky darted back into the shadows and turned off Diz's phone, wanting to throw it in a dumpster, like it was a live grenade. He started to run down the alley, then remembered his bike. He pulled down his helmet, got on, and kicked the starter—again, and again, and again. He cursed. He heard shouting across the street, and in his head Lottie's voice.

She was calling him a fool, a silly fool.

Chapter 21

A Rottweiler leapt at Nicky's throat, sending him back down the steps to the trailer. Dale caught the dog by its collar, his skinny arm straining. "Look what we got here. I thought you'd be in Canada, maybe Mexico."

Nicky was still in shock from the wild beast with snapping jaws. "Why would I go there?"

"I forgot, you didn't do it. That why you shaved off all your hair?"

Nicky looked down at the slobber on his boot, trying to regain his composure. "Do you mind?"

"You're the one getting her all riled up, shouting like that. Try chilling the fuck out. Problem with Rotts is people. Got to give 'em space is all. I used to take her for walks on that golf course back there until they called their lawyer. Now I gotta take her across the street, up past that baseball field. Belongs to the school. I got a right to use it, my mom pays taxes. Used to be all sorts of weeds and shit until they mowed it. She still loves it, though. Sometimes she'll find a carcass and roll around in it. You gotta hose her down before you let her back in the trailer, but it's worth it. You treat her right, she'll treat you right. Put out your paw, let her sniff it."

"I just came to talk."

"You don't like Fluffy?"

Nicky tried to make himself say, *She's beautiful,* but couldn't do it.

Dale yanked Fluffy back inside and locked him in the bathroom. "If you're gonna be rude about it, my mom's at church. Sorting back-to-school clothes for kids. I told her charity starts at home but she only listens to that damn reverend. I think she's got a thing for him, you ask me."

"I didn't come to see her, either."

"Huh. Okay, but I'm not letting you in. You got something to say, go right ahead and do it in the rain."

Nicky turned up the collar of his leather coat and hunched his shoulders, feeling the water pelt his bald head. "I came to tell you that I know who killed Lottie."

Dale blinked. "You mean me?"

"You talked to her Friday night about your mom's case, didn't you?"

"After that thing in court? Nah, I was going to but I decided I overreacted. Realized how similar we are, you and me. Businessmen for one, but you know what else? I bet you do all right with the ladies. I saw your wife on the news. She was at some fund-raiser, had on this little dress. Tight, curvy, long legs. Like she was ready to go. Except you could tell she had a nose job. She must a had a schnozz before. What'd they say was her unmarried name, Liebman? And that partner of yours, she was a looker, too. Rockin' bod, but the kind likes to be boss in bed, am I right?"

"She didn't give you ten grand?"

"You got balls, you know that?"

"You're not denying it."

"The money? What's it matter if I don't? You can't prove it. Unless you're wearing a wire. But that'd mean you went to the cops, which I know you didn't from the news. What I want to know, what's to stop me from punching you in the nose and dialing nine-one-one?"

It was a good question. "I see you got a new TV from that

box by the snow plow."

"Forty-two inches of plasma orgasma. High-definition heaven."

"Where'd you get the money?"

"Paving driveways and painting houses. Work harder than you, jackass. You know how hot it gets on a roof in the summer? Standing on black shingles—sun burning your back, sweat stinging your eyes, shoulders aching from holding the scraper, some fat, wrinkled bitch yelling up at you that you're getting paint chips on her hydrangea bushes. Only reason I'm not up there today is on account of we're using latex. It'll go on fine over wet wood but after a few days it starts to blister. You get a call, 'My house looks like it's about to explode—I'm stopping payment on the check!' Have to haul your crap back there while you're working the next job then get those people pissed at you."

Boy, this guy loved to hear himself talk, stopping only to spit an ounce of brown goop on Nicky's Levis, which Nicky decided only added to their authenticity. That's when he noticed the hunk of chewing tobacco wedged in Dale's cheek. So Dale painted houses for a living. Nicky resisted the impulse to say that's how Hitler got his start.

"Not that I'm gonna paint houses my whole life, especially for no Lyndon Painting Company. I'm just saving to start my own business. Plowing in the winter, lawn care in the summer. Gonna call it Hill 'N Dale Landscaping. Get it? I got a pickup and a plow, but I need the other crap. Mowers, brush cutter, ro-totiller. Hedge clipper, lopping shears, pruners. Chain saw, wood chipper, stump grinder."

Why was Dale listing all the dangerous stuff? What happened to work gloves, rakes, and wheel barrows? Nicky tried not to imagine the havoc Dale could wreak with a chain saw—a hockey mask on his face, body parts flying, blood-curdling screams filling the night. He recalled that wood-chipper scene from *Fargo* and tried to erase it from his mind. He was getting along fine with Dale so far, setting aside the punch-you-in-your-nose part.

"Still," Nicky said, "the timing's funny with the money, don't you think?"

"It was Labor Day weekend. Every store in town had a sale, including Best Buy."

"Know what I think? I think you killed Lottie by accident. She called you with an offer, you called her with a demand—it doesn't matter. You showed up wanting more money, argued with her, maybe tried to scare her. Things got out of hand. That's when you grabbed the bookend. You didn't think to do Scarlet until you saw the news and thought, 'Hey, I can frame that Greek dude.' "

"You've been smoking too much grass from—what is that thing called?—a 'hookah'?"

"That's what they're called in Turkey or India. I think the word in Greece is 'Narghile.' "

"Yeah, I love those things. Real social way to party. Anyway, I was at the Fair Friday night, hanging out with some buddies, getting ready for the Joe Nichols concert."

"These buddies wouldn't happen to be fellas you met in the pen, would they?"

"You wish. I've got better witnesses than that. I was detained by none other than two New York State Troopers."

"When?"

"Between seven and nine, at the Fair Command Post. They kept feeding me coffee, trying to get me to sober up. I yarked all over the midway after climbing onto the Fire Ball. You know, the one that twirls round as it swings back and forth like a pendulum? They strap you in this chair, feels like bed spins. FYI, fried dough and Budweiser tastes better going down. Only reason they didn't arrest me, I 'splained I'd be violating my parole and end up back in the pen. Not bad guys, all things considered."

"You remember their names?"

Dale told him their skin colors and the ethnicity of their last names—*Eye-talian* and *Polack*—the only things that he noticed. Nicky took out a mini notebook.

Dale said, "I bet you think you're pretty smart pretending you're investigating the murderer. Except it comes off like O.J. putting out that reward for the guy who did Nicole."

"I appreciate your astute criminal perspective."

"I'm just telling you, one man to another. Another thing, I like your choice of defense lawyers, getting that Amazon— otherwise the jurors will think you hate women. Shit, are you in for a ride. You know the worst part about being on trial? Fact that everyone else—the lawyers, the judge, even the fat-ass bailiff—they get to go home at the end. You get thrown in a cage with a bunch of spooks and greasers. Still, they probably got fewer kills than you."

"Everyone's so convinced I did it."

"Only because you did. I heard your alibi—you was at the Fair campaigning. I didn't see you at the Fair."

"Evidently you didn't see a garbage can you could puke in, either."

"Maybe not but know what I see now? A guy hiding from the cops. That's why you got that leather coat and sunglasses."

"How do you know this isn't my new look? So I can appeal to the working class."

"Take more than a bike to do that, fancy lawyer like you. What is that, a Harley Wide Glide?"

"A Low Rider."

"With ape hanger handlebars. Like from *Easy Rider.* Or that Clint Eastwood flick, the one with the orangutan."

"*Every Which Way But Loose.*" Nicky felt stupid chatting with an ex-con while the police were out looking for him. But he needed answers, and this was the only way he knew to get them.

"That's the one. Pretty dinged up, but it sounded good when you pulled in. How much she set you back?"

Nicky told him.

"You got taken, my friend. I got a buddy, he builds those things from scrap. Like in that TV show, *American Chopper.* Except cheaper. I'm thinking of getting one when my parole's up. If not from him, then one of them rice-burners. Kawasaki, Suzuki, maybe even a Honda. I like the look of 'em. All pumped up, like a muscle car. Gonna sell my pickup and move south."

Nicky wanted to ask, *What about the landscaping business?* But he didn't want to get into all that. "They don't have pickups down south?"

"Not where I'm going, Key West. Gonna tend bar, been reading a book on it. I'm not a Parrothead or anything. You know what that is? Like a Deadhead, but follows Jimmy Buffet around. That guy drives me crazy if I'm not stoned. And I don't like the idea of all them fags. I knew these guys once, drove an RV down there. Couldn't use the shower 'cause it had a keg in it. So they used the one at the beach. Don't you know those homos kept coming in to check them out? One does that to me and I'll bust his nose. Pop, just like that."

Nicky flinched, thinking of Dale's earlier threat. "I'm sure you'll be a welcome addition to the community."

"You think you're better than me, don't you? Why, because I live in a trailer park? We didn't always, you know. My parents used to have good jobs at the Hotel Syracuse, my old man in the kitchen and my mom cleaning rooms. We lived on Westcott Street. Remember the Orange Grove? Pop used to take me there on Fridays for fifty-cent slices. Let me sip his beer. Then he got sent upstate for boosting cars. That's when my mom sold the house and bought this double-wide. Not a bad place. Million-dollar homes up the street. I've painted a couple of 'em. Men in shorts and polo shirts putting their golf clubs in their trunk in the middle of a weekday, their wives and daughters in the backyard by the pool. Sometimes I'd let the ladder fall just to see them jump up, forgetting their bikini tops was undone. Thing is, those people ain't any better than us. That Jamelske dude right smack in the middle of 'em, with that underground dungeon in his backyard. You know he kidnapped five women over fifteen years? Held them as sex slaves. Know what happened to the house after he was caught? It was bought by some guy, by the brother of the fourth victim. Paid only a hundred grand for it, not a bad house, near that fancy development, Waterford Woods. Said he was going to preserve it as 'exhibit one' in his civil suit against Jamelske. Said Jamelske's worth a million dollars. But then, see, the guy starts *improving* it. Which makes me think, what the fuck's goin' on? He gonna put up some sorta museum? Sell tickets? And people look down their noses at me 'cause I live in a trailer."

Nicky considered this guy, this ex-con, who would probably be back in prison within five years. A punk who saw the world through a perspective of resentment, anger, and violence. Nicky didn't care anymore if he offended Dale. He had to stop wasting time, be more direct. "That's not why I think I'm better than you."

"Is it because I never went to college? You don't think I read? My old man, before he got sent up to Watertown Correctional on his second fall, know what he told me? Boy, he said, never let school stand in the way of your education."

"I'm sure he's got plenty of time to read."

"He calls me on Sundays to tell me what's good. I just finished *The Federal Siege at Ruby Ridge* by Randy Weaver. You know what those goons did to the man's wife? Shot her in the face as she was holding her baby. All because her husband didn't show up for a court date on some bogus weapons charge. For buying, get this—a sawed-off shotgun. Except really it was 'cause they'd tried to make him snitch on the seller but he wouldn't do it. That's when they come after him. You're a lawyer, tell me where it says in the Constitution they got a right to come onto a man's property and shoot his dog."

"I don't know what the Constitution says."

"There, it's not so hard to admit you don't know everything, is it?"

"Where'd you get that tattoo?"

"This little thing? Down on Salina Street. I told my girlfriend I was making a political statement, you know, about the Middle East. Israeli aggression on the West Bank. At first it was that wall, the 'security barrier.' Five hundred miles long. Now I don't got a problem with the idea of a wall. We should have one up ourselves, a big, long one to keep out the wetbacks. But the Israeli wall—shit, the thing wasn't even on their land. What do you call it, trespass. The thing put something like ten percent of the West Bank on the Israeli side. Then they start a war. Kill a thousand Lebanese, a third of 'em women and children. Four thousand wounded. Fifteen thousand homes destroyed. And what do they suffer? A couple hundred casualties? Three billion in property damage, which we'll end up payin' for with our hard-earned taxes. Not that I really give a shit. I was just drunk, trying to impress her. I did, too, except the wrong way. Bitch dumped me. My mom wants me to add four lines on the outside here, turn it into a square with a cross in it. I said, 'Why don't I just put a goddamn tick-tack-toe board on my shoulder?' I don't know, maybe I'll get it scrubbed off before I move to Florida. Don't want to get all those fags' panties in a bunch."

"Where were you on Sunday?"

"Went to Six Flags Darien Lake in Buffalo with my buddies. Someplace they don't harass you."

"Where you can throw up on people in peace."

"You know they got this roller coaster, the Superman something, one of the tallest in the northeast. Seven seconds of zero gravity on the first drop. But you know what, I still like the Mind Eraser better. They got you in this harness, your legs dangling. Kind of like the Fire Ball but faster."

"When did you leave Syracuse on Sunday?"

"Bright and early. Was gone 'til the next morning. I still got my admission ticket, you want to see it. Motel bill, credit card receipts. Even got a speeding ticket outside Rochester. Hey, you don't know a good V&T lawyer, do you?"

"What about Monday morning?"

"Jeez, you're Mr. Smalltalk, ain't you? Went to Green Lakes with the guys to go for a swim, get baked."

"What're their names?"

"So you can lay some bullshit rap on them, too?"

"You want, I can have my lawyer, the Amazon, call the state troopers from the Fair, ask them. She's real persistent, a former prosecutor. Those guys are the same ones you were picked up with before the concert, right?"

Dale finally gave up their names.

It made Nicky feel good, reminded him of what it was like to cross-examine doctors on the stand. For the past few years, the only questions he'd asked them were in depositions, where he'd step carefully, calling them *sir*, keeping his tone friendly—even when they blew up at him. *Why is that relevant?* they'd scream. *I won't answer that!* Nicky would just nod respectfully and move along. Anything to keep a civil relationship with opposing counsel, to fan the glowing embers of settlement. But now Nicky wasn't taking any prisoners.

"Anyone see you at Green Lakes?"

"This time I got a park ranger. Kicked us out because he recognized me from Hillbrook. You know, juvey? He's a retired deputy sheriff. Prick always had it in for me. But I guess I should be grateful he saw me. Hey, know what I just thought? Hold on a second."

Dale went inside, leaving the door ajar, which made Nicky step back further into the rain, fearing Cujo might reappear, nose it open, and start growling. He looked around for cover, at the propane tanks and garbage cans around the corner, the trailers nearby on cinder blocks. He wondered how many kids lived here, how much money it would take to give them clothes that fit, three square meals a day, and maybe a computer to help them with their schoolwork. He decided he was not paying Anna enough to clean his house.

There was a flash of light. When Nicky opened his eyes, Dale was standing in the doorway again, this time with a camera.

"Best Buy had a sale on these things, too," Dale said. "All you do, plug it into the computer, and you can e-mail this puppy to anyone you want. See?"

Dale showed Nicky the camera's compact screen, on which appeared Nicky's guilty face, water rolling off his scalp.

"What I was going to say, I'm probably the only one knows what you look like in that getup. Maybe there's a reward."

Nicky had new respect for Dale. Why punch a man in the nose and call the cops when you could blackmail him? "How much do you want?"

"Hell, how much you got?"

Nicky opened his wallet, and Dale reached out.

"Hold on," Nicky said. "What about the camera?"

"Now you're really tripping. It's worth at least what you got in there."

"The memory card then."

"Whatever."

Nicky put the card in his pocket as Dale fanned out the bills.

"Two fifties," Dale said, "four twenties, a ten and—two, four, six—seven ones. What's that, two hundred? Not bad, and I like a man who keeps his cash organized. But I might still blow you in. Forget nine-one-one, just call that cop on the news. What's his name—Holiday?"

Dale showed Nicky his big yellow teeth.

"Come back tomorrow with ten more," Dale said.

"Hundred?"

"Nice try, dink."

"Grand? The banks will get suspicious, realize who I am."

"Then you're just gonna have to figure out a way to get it, ain't you?"

"It'll take longer."

"Friday then." Dale folded the bills and stuffed them into his pocket. "See? I can be reasonable, just like you. A real pro."

CHAPTER 22

Nicky took a seat and pulled his headphones down around his neck.

"What're you listening to?" Diz said. "George Thorogood? ZZ Top? Maybe some Kiss?"

"The police scanner. Just plug these things into your Palm Pilot and log onto Syracuse dot com."

"Look at you. Did they even have electricity when you were a kid?"

"I thought the haircut was supposed to take off ten years."

"You should keep it—you know, when this blows over."

He liked her optimism. "I think it makes my cheeks look fat."

As he looked into a spoon and pinched the loose flesh on his cheeks, she opened her menu.

"So, is meeting at Dinosaur Bar-B-Que part of your hide-in-plain-sight strategy?"

"I'd like to say it's because I fit in with all the Harleys. But truth is I'm too hungry and tired to care. I slept on a golf course last night."

"You look like it, grass stains on your shirt, wet leaves on your jacket. Smell like chemicals—pesticide or something."

"Where am I going to shower? That punk took all my money."

"I guess I know who's paying for lunch."

The waitress finally appeared, dressed like a biker chick. Black leather bra, skirt, and boots. And matching silver accessories—chain around her waist, studs on her wristband, and skull-and-crossbones on her cap. She cracked her gum and put a hand on her hip.

"Yeah?"

Diz ordered a Mojito chicken breast sandwich, no mayo, with fruit salad and an iced tea. Nicky ordered the Big Ass Pork Plate with barbeque beans and mashed potatoes with gravy.

"And a Mich Ultra," he said, but the woman was already halfway across the room. "The service here is exquisite."

"That's their thing, being rude. Like at a Waffle House. Ever been to one of those? Servers shouting orders to cooks five feet away. 'Adam and Eve on a raft, hash browns scattered smothered and covered, no grits!' Nothing written down but they keep it all straight."

Nicky had heard of them, something about them being sued down south for discriminating against African-American patrons. He'd always wanted to know what those settlements were like. He'd never taken any race cases, although Lottie had gotten into gender cases toward the end. Unequal pay, failure to promote—they were valid issues. Could Nicky somehow parlay Lottie's verdicts into female votes?

"By the way," Diz said, "that diet beer was a good call. It'll make all the difference when you're wolfing down that mountain of pork and beans."

"I'm trying the low-carb thing. Nothing extreme, everything in moderation. The beans and potatoes are only for show. So they don't gain control over me."

"Didn't you see the Atkins autopsy in the paper? He weighed like half a ton."

"Two fifty, and I heard his wife say in an interview that it was because they'd pumped him full of fluids in the hospital. He weighed a buck ninety going in. Not bad for a guy who was six feet tall. He had big bones."

"He had clogged arteries."

"But who knows what they were like before he went on the diet? Maybe he would've died sooner if he hadn't."

"All I'm saying, going low-carb is a good way to jump start your diet but it's not a sound long-term strategy."

"In case you didn't notice, I'm not focusing on long-term strategies these days. Did you bring it?"

She took out a legal envelope. "Your retainer plus a little extra from my savings. Don't act proud. I know you need it. And I know I'll get it back."

"With interest. I'm afraid to go to an ATM. They'll know which part of the city I'm in. Plus they have those cameras. Which reminds me, did Halliday see me?"

"At the funeral? He was too busy almost getting run over as he crossed the street. He was so pissed I don't think he even heard the motorcycle. When word spread that you were outside, the place cleared. He and Tony Donuts grilled me for fifteen minutes in front of everyone. 'Why were you waiting outside earlier? Are we supposed to believe you don't know where Rigopoulos is? How can you represent a murderer?' "

"Good questions."

"I gave it right back to them. I said to Halliday, 'How can you turn the spotlight on Nicky when Tony here used to break into Lottie's house? Torch her coffeemaker? Pour Clorox in her fish tank? Give her dog to the pound?' Tony threatened to sue me for slander. Know what I said? 'The truth is a defense, stalker.' People laughed."

"Halliday said he checked Tony's alibi."

"So did I, unfortunately."

"He also said they found the murder weapon."

"Save your breath, I know it's not yours."

"How can you be so sure?"

"What kind of schmuck would hide it in his own home? And leave his prints on it?"

"Maybe I didn't have time to get rid of it."

"Didn't have time to bury it at Lilly's farm in Skaneateles? Throw it into Onondaga Lake? Pound it to pieces in your basement?"

"Maybe I froze. Halliday says a police psychologist thinks I could be doing all of this without knowing it. Like Dr. Jekyll and Mr. Hyde."

"Her? That woman's a crackpot. Once she misidentified an anonymous letter from the Canal Killer. Said it was from an 'amateur' with no connection with the homicides. The killer later admitted he'd sent it. Another time she didn't let a guy talk to his psychiatrist in a standoff situation. So the man killed his hostages—his girlfriend and her kid—then himself. I won't even go into the number of times she's misused hypnosis to manufacture child-abuse memories."

"Still, they're going to indict me, huh?"

"The DA convened a grand jury. They won't cut a deal after that."

"I suppose you think I should give myself up."

"I'm long past thinking you'll listen to me. Did I even yell at you for calling Halliday at the funeral? If you want to go to jail, I can't stop you."

"The words every client longs to hear. What else did you find?"

"Dale's alibi checks out. The troopers at the Fair remember him from the night of Lottie's murder. He gave them a song and dance about having to take care of his mother. The Park Ranger remembers him, too. Kicked him out for possession, disturbing the peace and littering. Said Dale was lucky he didn't call the Manlius Police. Said he was always too soft on the kid."

"What about Dale's buddies?"

"Dumb and Dumber? They back him up. Thick as thieves those three. Did time together in the pen. Were supposedly in a skin-head gang according to a guard I know."

"He said he was just making a political statement."

"He's a regular Martin Luther King. Still, I checked his rap sheet and his county criminal records. No hate crimes. I talked to the ADA who prosecuted the assault charge. He remembered it, said Dale went ballistic because—get this—a guy picked up his quarter off a pool table down at Shifty's. You know, trying to cut in front of him. Not a race thing, though. Victim was white."

"Jewish?"

"Italian."

"How'd you do all that so fast?"

"I know a guy at a private investigative firm. He has access to the NCIC, the FBI's National Crime Information Center, down in West Virginia. And before you get mad, he doesn't know why I was asking."

"Can we use him to tap the kid's phones?"

"He's not going to break the law. He's a retired FBI agent, for Pete's sake."

"I was just asking. There's someone out there trying to frame me for a double murder, and a police force showing my picture on the news."

"I'm glad all this is finally sinking in. Then I guess I can tell you, I also talked to Lilly."

Nicky didn't know how to react. He'd told Diz not to interfere.

"She's a piece of work," Diz said. "Offered me lemonade when I showed up then turned up her nose when I asked for help."

"What can I say? It was true love."

"Wolf in sheep's clothing, if you ask me."

"She might be in danger. Someone's offing all my exes."

"I told her that on my way out. She accused me of threatening her."

"So did Halliday when I told him."

"He's talking to everyone in the office, plus your family. I'm trying to keep track of them all, getting a debriefing afterward. Problem is I called a few people who hadn't been interviewed yet. When they later refused to talk to Halliday, he read me the riot act. 'Aiding a fugitive is one thing, but now you're interfering with a government investigation?' I told him to go pound sand. I'll talk to anyone I want, thank you very much."

"You go, girl." It was what his daughter would have said. He was trying to loosen up.

"I reviewed Lottie's bank account statements online, using that password you gave me. Worked great. I could see photos of old checks right on the screen. Nothing made out to anyone suspicious in the past year, except there were periodic withdrawals of large amounts of cash. Five, ten, fifteen grand."

"For what? Clients?"

"Why would she give money to clients?"

"As a refund of her fee for verdicts they weren't happy about. Under the table, so I wouldn't find out."

"I'll look into it. You don't happen to know Sal's bank account password, do you?"

"Even if I did, I wouldn't tell you."

"The words every lawyer longs to hear." She poured some Sweet'N Low into her iced tea. "You know what I was thinking? How the bookends got in your house. At first, I figured it might've been the cops, Tony Donuts. Or maybe the murderer just walked in and put them there, with Scarlet being half in the bag most the time. But then I thought, that implies the murderer knew he could do that. So I started thinking, how could he have come back and murdered Scarlet? There was no sign of forced entry, right? Why would she let him in? Same with Lottie. Must've been someone they knew."

Nicky had already come to the same conclusion but he didn't

like it. "Would you stop with Sal, already?"

"Who then?"

"Must be someone we're not thinking of. We just need to dig more."

"This whole amateur-sleuth thing is crazy."

"Going to the cops is too risky."

"You thinking you can find a murderer by—what?—talking to suspects? What do you expect them to say? 'All right, you got me, Sheriff. I'll go peaceably.' "

"Do you have a better idea?"

"We need evidence. Photographs, DNA, eyewitnesses."

"Can we get that private eye involved? Or is that beneath his code of ethics?"

"I'll talk to him."

"I don't want you to get in any deeper."

"I don't care."

"I do. One law-license suspension is enough."

"You think you can stop me?"

"I can stop talking to you. Just give me his name. I'll call you if I need anything."

"Fine." She took out a pen.

After he folded up her napkin, he said, "What else do we have?"

"One more thing, but you're not going to want to hear it."

"Let me guess. Lottie's will."

"How'd you know?"

He held up her Palm Pilot. "I can follow the news on the *Post-Standard*'s Web site."

"Even without pictures, I'm impressed. The will gives half her estate to a battered women's shelter, half to Sal. Rumor is the shelter's going to contest Sal's share, pending the results of the criminal investigation. They know about Sal's debts and his friendship with you. They think there may be some sort of conspiracy between you two, in which case Sal can't benefit from the murders."

Nicky shook his head. A conspiracy to murder? "Am I still listed as the executor?"

"Lottie redid it six months ago, naming Wally."

Wally? What had Martin called him? *McMuffin?* "I didn't know they were that close. Or that she even trusted him."

"He's done them before, and she probably thought she could save the estate some money by not having to hire a real lawyer."

"What sort of fee will he get?"

"The statutory amount. Something like five percent of the first hundred grand, four percent of next two hundred, three percent of the next seven hundred. Unless he serves as the estate's lawyer, too, in which case I think he has to take half his commission as executor. Either way, it adds up, but not enough for a motive. He's had bigger year-end bonuses. Don't ask me why—Lottie picked the amount."

"We're still missing something."

The food came and Nicky ate greedily, filling his stomach for the first time in days. Forget the low-carb diet. He was getting plenty of exercise running from the law.

As he wiped barbeque sauce off his chin, Diz leaned back. "I know you don't want to talk about this . . ."

"Here it comes."

"How close was Sal to Lottie?"

"He was her brother, Diz."

"He just made it out of bankruptcy."

"He'd filed?" Why hadn't Sal told him?

"According to the court in Utica, a voluntary petition for relief under Chapter Eleven in early August. You know, keep his creditors at bay for a hundred twenty days while he reorganized his business."

"What creditors, beer distributors?"

"No, the way I understand it, bar owners have to pay their beer and liquor distributors cash within fourteen days if they're late on one thirty-day invoice. So he was current on them. It was everything else that was killing him. Payroll, insurance, distributors. Utilities, taxes, even the linen company."

"How much did he owe?"

"In total? More than a hundred, I think."

"And he discharged all of it?"

"That's what I've been trying to tell you. Somehow he got a lot of cash."

Nicky hoped Sal had had one of his legendary nights at the casino. Then Nicky slipped his earphones back over his head.

"What is it?" Diz said.

"Something about Dale."

Nicky rose and covered his ears, trying to block out the clank of plates and silverware, the din of the crowd. Out of the corner of his eye, he saw people study him, hearing them think, *He looks familiar.*

He tossed his napkin on his plate and said, "What do you know? There *is* a reward out for me."

CHAPTER 23

"Where are you?" Dara said.

Nicky shielded his cell phone from the rumble of an eighteen-wheeler headed back to the thruway. People passed him on their way in and out of the travel plaza, more concerned with keeping their kids in line than capturing outlaws. He'd considered calling Dara from the road, but didn't have a hands-free mike and didn't want to get pulled over for breaking New York's new law. Beyond the gas pumps, the sky was the same color as the road. Fall was on its way, summer fading into dates on some future indictment.

"I shouldn't say."

"I heard they can't tap your phone if it's digital."

He wanted to ask who told her that, but it didn't matter. "I'm more afraid you'll come and see me."

"And then they'd follow me?"

He didn't want to even think about that. "You have your own problems."

"They seem kind of stupid now."

"Where are you? When I called before, your phone said you were outside the service area."

"In Syracuse, staying with a friend. The police are done with the house, but it freaks me out, looking at the pool. It was never really my home, anyway."

He told himself not to feel guilty for moving after she went to college, for storing her things in his new attic. It'd been Scarlet's idea, anyway.

"I stopped by your hotel to get your things, but the police put yellow tape over the door. The management was upset, said it looked like someone was murdered, scaring off the guests. Some detective tried to ask me questions."

"Don't let him push you around." Nicky felt his blood boil. His temper had grown shorter recently. Was that part of his personal growth, his *opening himself up to others?*

"I deal with parents worse than that every day. 'You're giving too much homework. You didn't let my girl sit with her friend on the field trip. You gave my boy only a B on a project that I did for him.' "

"But this parent has a gun."

"A forty-five with nickel plating. I asked if he was going to shoot me, and he took it out to show me. I told him it was so big, the barrel so long, he must be overcompensating. The other cops laughed."

"They're not all bad." He thought about whether to be upset at his daughter's sense of humor, at its sexual undertones. How had she learned to handle men? By going to bars in New York City, brushing off jerks' crude come-ons? He wished he'd never let her move away.

"I'm glad you called. I've left you a zillion messages. I've been glued to my phone all week."

"I'm sorry." He didn't want to explain that he was using Diz's phone, further drawing her into this mess. What could she be charged with already? Obstruction of justice? Aiding and abetting a fugitive? Accomplice to murder? "Mine ran out of juice. I had to buy a charger, then I had to find someplace to plug it in."

"Can't you just go to a motel? Do you need money?"

"I'm just afraid to show my face."

"Can't you go to Father Benedictos? I'm sure he'd let you

hide out at St. Sophia's. Or maybe call your cousin Markos. Everyone knows he's in the Greek mafia."

"That's all I need, to drag my church into this. Or my family."

"You're going to have to do something. The police are offering ten thousand dollars for information leading to your arrest."

"I'm surprised it's that low. Didn't they offer ten for the guy who torched that temple?"

"That caused millions in damage."

"But no one got hurt. I'm practically a serial killer."

Dara didn't laugh. "Sorry about Scarlet."

"I feel bad she's gone. I did love her once."

"I thought her death would remind you of mom—you know, even more than Lottie's."

"Everything reminds me of your mother."

"You sound different."

Did he? He felt different, less in control. More like his old self.

She said, "I know you didn't do it."

"Thank you, dear."

"They're full of shit on TV."

As he weighed the utility of criticizing her language, she said, "They don't even know you."

He thought they knew him pretty well, after all his commercials and campaigning. "That doesn't matter. What matters is their viewers are the jury pool."

"Can't you get the trial transferred? Like to Rochester?"

He wanted to point out that there was no trial yet, but he knew that was only a matter of time. "My commercials ran in all of upstate New York."

"A victim of your own success."

"That'll be the title of my autobiography. I hear you have plenty of time to read and write in prison. What's the press saying anyway?"

"Your ex-lover was murdered hours after announcing she was abandoning your campaign for Supreme Court Judge and threatening to dissolve your law partnership. And your estranged wife was murdered days after helping police find the murder weapon in your closet and telling you she wanted a divorce."

"It all sounds pretty convincing, now that I hear it. How am I doing in the polls?"

"You don't want to know."

"I thought Randy's affair with Scarlet would get out, hurt him."

"People are more focused on you withdrawing from the ballot."

"I don't know which is going to be worse—being someone's boyfriend in the pokey, or losing to that hack."

"Don't talk that way. What can I do to help?"

"I'm going to have to get out of this one on my own."

"I don't suppose you'd turn yourself in."

"You've been talking to Diz."

"She stopped by. I like her. She cares about you."

"I like her, too." He wondered how Diz knew where Dara was.

"Can I do anything?" Dara said.

"One thing. Don't worry about me."

"Too late."

Another truck rumbled by.

"Can we talk about something else?" he said.

"Well, the invitations are a problem again."

"No one's coming?"

"I wish. They're all coming. Forget the thirty-percent attrition rate the stationery stores tell you about."

"Everyone wants to see the murderer."

"It's sick."

"We'll need a bigger tent and more tables. Write a check to the hotel and sign my name."

"I don't know if that's such a good idea."

"Did they freeze my accounts?"

"No, not that."

"What's wrong then?"

"At this point, I don't even know if there's going to be a wedding. Brady and I got in another fight."

"So?"

"I threw the ring at him."

That's my girl, Nicky wanted to say. "He must've deserved it."

"I overreacted."

"Let me guess. Was it about the invitations, the seating or the honeymoon?"

"He mentioned that he dated one of the girls he invited. So I say, 'Oh, really?' And he says, 'I told you about that.' And I say, 'No, I don't think you did.' And he says, 'Huh.' So I say, 'Huh.' And then I tell him about Nelson."

"The little one?"

"I couldn't help myself."

"But he has Coke-bottle glasses and pimples."

"He was my first boyfriend."

"Brady was jealous of him?"

"It was the fact I kept it from him."

"Why did you?"

"I thought he'd get mad."

"Which he did."

"But he says it was because I didn't trust him. I can't help it. Sometimes he has a temper, like you used to have. They say you marry your dad."

"In that case, call the wedding off."

"I can't believe he made such a big deal about it. It's not like

Nelson poses a threat. I only slept with him once, when I was sixteen, and I didn't even enjoy it."

"More than I needed to know." Sixteen? Wasn't she still playing with those dolls then?

"Sorry."

"So he kept the ring?"

"He must have it on him. I ransacked his apartment."

"The way to let him know you really care."

"He said he's keeping it for a week to teach me a lesson. It's so embarrassing—people keep asking to see it. I don't know what I was thinking."

"You were mad."

"The worst part is it's mom's."

Nicky remembered the day Brady asked him for the ring, cornering Nicky by the fridge as he was getting a beer on Thanksgiving, and telling him he was going to marry Dara. That's how he'd put it. *I'm going to marry her.* Like she didn't have any say in the matter, nor Nicky. Why couldn't Brady have asked for Nicky's permission while he was at it? Or at least his blessing? Had the world changed that much since he was a kid? He remembered asking Corin's father for permission, the big, burly man actually taking time to think about it. He remembered how he later proposed to Corin, getting down on his knee and promising—what had he said? *I'll always love you, take care of you, and be true to you.* He'd thought at the time, *What more was there to it than that?* How little he'd known. But it'd all been worth it. He contemplated whether he should feel angry that some kid was holding his wife's ring hostage, then decided that raising a stink about a piece of jewelry wouldn't bring her back.

He said, "All the more reason to know he'll return it."

"But maybe it won't come with an offer."

"Now you sound like a lawyer. Who says you can't ask him next time?"

"Next time?"

"You've got your whole lives ahead of you. This is just one fight. If you break off the engagement, fine, but you've got to keep perspective. You've found each other. You're in love. You can't erase that in a day. You remember how long you waited to find someone like him? How many losers you dated, as you call them. You'll still be in love in a few months, whether you like it or not. Have confidence in that. Marriage is a marathon, not a sprint."

He liked that. He thought about giving her his *First love yourself* bit, his stock speech when she was a heartbroken teen. Or maybe his *Love is a verb* bit, for when she hit rough times with her boyfriend in college. But Nicky's mouth was dry and his head was starting to pound. Was he actually talking his daughter into marrying this guy?

"I don't know if I'm buying it," she said, "but thanks."

"I'm tired. I've been living on coffee and cigarettes all week."

"You've started smoking again?"

"Marlboro Reds."

"You know how hard it was to quit last time. You drove me crazy."

"They come with the costume."

"You mean the biker's outfit? They showed it on TV. Thanks to that Dale guy."

"I'm a farmer now. Got a pickup truck, a Carhartt jacket, and a John Deere hat. Only thing I'm missing is a gun rack in the back window and a ten-point buck on my plow mount."

"Is that where you've been hiding? Out in the boondocks?"

"It's not so bad out here. The people are nice, a little strange but down to earth. There's this one place called The Coonrod. Heard of it? It's an old hotel they say is the geographic center of the state. The middle of nowhere is more like it. There's not even a sign on the front door. It's real dark inside, hiding pool tables and a bunch of booths with games in them—cards, checkers, backgammon. They have these hot dogs, called Coon Dogs. Steamed in beer, with hot sauce on them. Make your nose run. Can't taste your beer, which is probably for the best—it comes in an old mason jar. When I first sat at the bar, I was making small talk, and I felt this thing crawl up my leg. I brushed it off and kept talking, but I felt it again, this time on my thigh. I jumped off my chair. When I got up, everyone was laughing. The guy behind the bar, the owner, he pulled a broom stick out of a hole. He does it to all the new people. He has so much fun with the place, he won the New York Lottery a few years back but still opens it sometimes. Even has bands. Jerry Garcia used to come and hang out. Can you imagine that?"

"I'm glad you're making friends."

"It gets my mind off things."

"So what are you going to do?"

"I don't know."

"Who do you think did it? Diz said Dale's alibi checked out. And Tony Donuts', too. Randy DeVine didn't have a motive to kill Lottie. And the people in your firm didn't have a motive to kill Scarlet. You know who Diz thinks did it?"

"I know." He was impressed at how much Dara had thought about this. Maybe he should've asked her to be his campaign chairman. Had her take a leave of absence, put her on salary, and get her away from that ring thief. Still, he didn't like her instincts, so quick to point a finger at his best friend.

"I can talk to him if you want," she said. "See what I can find out."

"Stay out of it."

"I'm not a kid, you know."

He didn't press it, sensing she might give in if he handled it right. Maybe if he appealed to her reason. "Someone's killing the women in my life, Dara."

"I can take care of myself, Dad."

He wanted to say, *That's what I thought.*

CHAPTER 24

"Mr. Rigopoulos?" said a familiar voice, making Nicky spin around.

It was one of the boys from the frat house.

"I thought it was you," the boy said. "You look different."

Nicky thought of playing dumb. *Who, me? Sorry, I ain't no Greek fella.* Then tip his NASCAR hat. But the ruse had sounded better on the truck ride out there.

"You, too," said Nicky, fearing that the subject would turn to disguises. He tried to think of the boy's name—Twin Trees, Two Feathers? "Less collegiate, more—what's the word? More like a player. You know, older, sophisticated. I bet the guys at the house don't call you Two Beers in that."

There it was. Now Nicky had to work on the boy's real name.

"You mean the black shirt and pants?" the boy said. "The guys say the silver-tipped belt and boots make me look like a gay cowboy. My girlfriend bought them. Saw someone wear them on that TV show, *Las Vegas*. Wanted me to have an outfit in case we went clubbing. She's from Long Island. That's what she calls it. Like we're going to kill baby seals or something."

"I think it looks hip, Todd," Nicky said, hoping he'd gotten the boy's first name right.

"What're you doing here? Aren't the police, like, after you?"

Nicky looked over Todd's shoulder at the Turning Stone Casino—the crystal chandeliers and richly colored rugs, the soft lighting and hum of voices. The place was huge, the walls more than a football field apart in each direction, and thousands of games in between. Ones he recognized, like roulette, craps, baccarat, and stud poker. And others he didn't, like Let-It-Ride, Big Six, Red Dog, Pai Gow and Sic Bo. At the tables were throngs of people, the sort from the New York State Fair, or Hafner's Farmers' Market, or the Centro bus transfer hub at South Salina and Fayette Streets. *The Great Unwashed* was what Scarlet had called them. But Nicky had always thought of them as working class. Like the way Jimmy Stewart had described them in *It's a Wonderful Life,* when he was giving it to the rich guy in the wheelchair—*This rabble you're talking about, they do most of the working and paying and living and dying in this community.* Still, Nicky was glad that he didn't see any of them working in a blue uniform with a silver badge on it.

Neither did Todd, who said, "Oh," apparently realizing he was talking to a fugitive.

"You're turning white. Sit down."

Todd stalled, then took a seat.

"How did you know it was me?" Nicky said.

"Honest? The sleepy look in your eyes. I recognized it from TV. I always thought it made you look bored."

That was one Nicky hadn't heard before. He leaned over to peer into the chrome edge of a gaming machine, widening his eyes until he looked like a monster. "The things your campaign chairman never tells you."

"Wasn't that Lottie Magnarella?"

Nicky asked himself what Todd was up to. Was the boy trying to broach the subject of the murder investigation, or was he actually busting Nicky's chops? Nicky told himself that if Todd was going to turn him in then so be it. He wasn't going to take crap from the kid. "Have you decided whether I did it yet?"

"Not yet. Did you really go to the Fair after you left the house?"

"You've really been following this thing."

"Everyone has."

"How am I doing?"

"In the election? Last I heard, the Democratic party chairman was telling people not to vote for you."

"Renounce my candidacy? Wes?" Had Lilly told him about the affair?

"He said that, if he can't get you to withdraw, he's going to circulate a petition to add another liberal."

"Spoil the election."

"I don't get it. Can't the County Board of Elections just remove your name from the ballot?"

Nicky drew a breath and shifted into teacher mode, trying to forget the empty expressions he saw whenever he finished a lecture at the law school. "Only if I plead to a felony. That's because if I'm convicted my office would automatically become vacant by statute."

"What about getting a judge to intervene? Grant some sort of protective order?"

"You mean injunction? Whose side are you on?"

"I'm just a curious college student."

"Did the curious college student get my signs up around campus?"

"I did because I gave you my word, but someone tore most of them down."

The Young Republicans, Nicky thought. A few rows over, a gaming machine flashed and rung. Nicky believed Todd about the effort and was grateful.

"I went to visit a friend," Nicky said, "after I left the house."

"Who?"

Nicky gave Todd the look his father used to give him when he asked for the night off to go on a date.

"I'm just asking. I'm wondering if you're going to use her as an alibi."

"I guess friend wasn't the right word for her."

Todd didn't say anything. Nicky decided the boy was too young to have experienced first hand things like infidelity, betrayal, and treachery. He would have to become an expert in them if he was going to get into politics.

After a moment, Nicky said, "Are you here with your girlfriend? Sorry, I forgot her name."

"I didn't tell you what it was. Ariana. She doesn't like to come, says it's depressing. Reminds her of home. I'm with some guys from the house. That's Over Time over there, working the blonde dealer. Good luck with that. That's Sporty Spice with the gel in his hair. And that's Potsie playing the five-cent slots. He said the guys shouldn't call me Two Beers while we're here in case the injuns think we're making fun of them. That's the word he used, 'injuns.' "

"My daughter's going to marry one of you and it scares me."

"We're not so bad, one on one."

"When is someone ever one on one with a frat boy?"

"What do you call this?"

"But your buddies are out there, waiting to come over, drop trou, and do a group chug."

"Where did you hear that?"

"I was at the Zeus ritual, remember?"

"Did you even have fraternities at your college?"

"I went to Le Moyne undergrad then SU Law. I remember you guys at parties. Muscling your way up to the keg, starting fights."

"What did they do to you? Steal your girlfriend or something?"

Nicky let out his breath. "I'm just having a bad life."

"What are you doing here anyway?"

"Trying to catch the guy who's setting me up."

"He's here?"

"Over there, at the blackjack table, the high-stakes one behind the ropes."

"No way. With the goatee?"

"The one next to him."

Todd squinted. "Isn't that Sal Magnarella?"

"Don't tell me his picture's been in the news, too."

"When I was a freshman, he used to get up on the bar on Friday nights and sing the SU fight song. I heard he had a bunch of sports bars back in the day. Players, Score, The Dome, except people called it the Do-Me. And there were a couple of dance clubs—I can't remember the names."

Back in the day? How old was Nicky getting? "Orange Crush and Fannyslappers."

"Those are the ones. A little more risqué than Lucky's."

"I didn't realize he's such a celebrity."

"Are you kidding? He's a legend. Isn't he your friend?"

"I thought so."

"For what it's worth, Double-Down is kicking his ass."

"Is that who's across from him? I didn't recognize him without a beer in his hand. How much are those black chips worth?"

"A hundred bucks. The purple ones are worth five hundred."

The dealer added a purple and three blacks to Double-Down's pile, and cut Sal's pile in half.

"What are you expecting him to do?" Todd said.

"I'll know when I see it."

"You've never done this before, have you? You keep staring at him and he's going to come over and ask you out. Sit down there with your back to him and I'll sit here and tell you what's going on. We'll pretend we're playing slots."

"Pretty crafty."

"I scope out chicks for my frat brothers all the time. Then I go in as their wing man—you know, talk to the other girl, usually the fat one. I'm not trying to be mean—she's usually the more interesting of the two, smarter. But, once I walk her back to her dorm room, that's it. I stick out my hand and say I have to get up early and go to ROTC. They look at me funny, but they don't say anything. Two taboos—saying something against guys with disabilities and guys in the Service. Support our troops, and all that."

Or maybe the girls think he was wounded in action. Nicky scrutinized the boy's scruffy haircut and sloping shoulders and wondered if he himself would have bought such a lie. "What do you get out of it, the scam?"

"Free drinks. I haven't bought a beer in two years."

"They should call you Free Beers."

"Some of them do."

Nicky took out a plastic account card and inserted it into a machine called Pot O' Gold. The touchscreen monitor showed a flock of games. He decided it was like reading a Chinese menu, a half dozen ingredients mixed into a zillion combinations. The names alone were enough to give him a headache. Black Gold 21, Triple Sevens, Jacks or Better, Wild Joker, Joker Poker, Superball Keno, Deuces Wild, Supergold Bingo, Lightning Keno, Touch 6 Lotto, Toucheasy Keno, Superpick Lotto, Shamrock 7s, Supergold Bingo, 8 Ball Poker, and Spinball Bonus.

"These things should come with a manual." Nicky picked Triple Sevens and pressed *PLAY.* The reels spun into a blur of color, making him dizzy.

"The one Potsie is playing is easier. Seventh Heaven."

Nicky liked that Todd could see over his shoulder and tell him what Sal was doing. Besides, Nicky was up fifty cents. Maybe the secret to gambling wasn't abstinence but just being cheap. "I'd buy you a drink but the place is dry."

"Them Injuns. Can run a billion-dollar resort but can't handle their liquor."

Nicky didn't want to talk law but didn't want Todd to leave. So he let the subject turn to the Oneida Nation's casino-funded land claim—a federal lawsuit against Oneida and Madison Counties for the return of more than a quarter-million acres or for fair compensation for the land. Todd talked with some intelligence about a 1985 Supreme Court decision holding that the Oneidas could sue New York State for unlawfully taking their homeland in 1795. He presented arguments for and against the additional claims of the Wisconsin Oneidas—now fifteen thousand strong—who had been ousted from New York State two hundred years ago.

When Todd ran out of opinions, Nicky said, "How are we doing?"

"He's smiling. He won the last hand and is up a few grand. A pretty girl just joined him."

"Blonde with a big rack?" Nicky had heard one of the frat boys use the term the other night to describe a potential object of his affection.

"Brunette."

Nicky snuck a look. The girl was young and thin, with a white tube top and a sequin miniskirt. Not Monique.

"Hey," Todd said. "Do you want my help or not?"

"Sorry. Do they have hookers here?"

"Out in the parking lot. Fifty bucks for a 'happy ending,' according to Over Time. Don't tell me you're interested."

Nicky pushed *PLAY* again and watched the reels spin, wondering who the girl in the tube top was, whether Sal and Monique had broken up, and if so, why? Maybe Sal was cheating on her. If so, what else was he lying about? Maybe Monique had found reason to think Sal had killed his sister. Nicky tried to brush away the guilt nibbling at his conscience, telling himself no one was above suspicion, that his freedom was at stake. Todd's attention began to wander from Sal's direction.

"Where you from?" Nicky said, wanting to bring Todd back but keep him off the subject of land claims.

Todd was from Poughkeepsie, his father an engineer at IBM and his mom a high school art teacher. He had an older sister who played pro soccer. Todd had come to SU wanting to go on to med school, become a pediatrician or maybe a neuroscientist. But he'd almost failed out his first year, tackling biology, chemistry, and calculus all at once. His second year he'd switched to classes that didn't require as much *heavy lifting,* as he put it, and he was graduating a semester early with a major in poly sci and minor in history. What else did Nicky want to know? His favorite historian was Howard Zinn. He recently gave up his hobby of trying to figure out who killed JFK. And he had a job lined up with Congresswoman Kara Corbett as an LC, which was Hill-speak for legislative correspondent. Nicky almost asked if kids graduated early these days in a rush to make money or just because they hated learning.

"Impressive," Nicky said. "Don't people usually start out as staff assistants?"

"I paid my dues. Worked on her last campaign, stuffing envelopes and making cold calls. Then I interned two summers, doing typing, getting coffee, even attended a few hearings."

"You did all that and graduated early?"

"The internships were for credit. Had to write a paper at the end of each one. You know, 'What I Did on My Summer Vacation.' Besides that, I loaded up on an extra class here and there during the year. It's not that hard if you skip a few parties."

"She's got a great future. Won by a landslide."

"Thirty-nine points."

"Do you know what issues you're going to handle?"

Todd told him.

"You want to make politics a career?" Nicky said.

"You mean do I want to run for office?"

"Not necessarily." Nicky thought he'd touched a nerve. Under all that acne the boy was already bitter about life. It'd taken Nicky two dead wives and a daughter on the brink of a bad marriage for him to get there.

Todd raised his hand and lowered his head. "Sorry, everyone asks me that. The thing is I do, but not because I want to be famous or anything. It's just that we're facing serious problems, as a country. Not just in Iraq and Afghanistan, but domestically. The environment, health care, education. And it's not like the problems are independent. Oil companies hold the patents on alternative power sources, preventing entrepreneurs from using the technology, which ruins our environment, keeps us dependent on foreign oil, drives our foreign policy in the Middle East. Drug companies bilk us on prescription medicines, which jack up our health care costs and divert tax dollars from our school systems. And don't even get me started on gay marriage. It's a total red herring. Look at the issue from strictly an economic perspective. Married couples are statistically more likely to have greater incomes and own homes, and less likely to have substance-abuse problems. Plus gays are better educated and more likely to be employed. Why wouldn't we want them to get married?"

Nicky was taken aback by the boy's energy, the strength of his convictions. He was too tired to argue. He said, "I guess some people would say there's more to it than that."

"You mean the fact that the word 'marriage' carries a societal stamp of approval? I don't deny it—that's why gays are making such a big deal about it. But if that's why Bible thumpers are against it, why not let gays at least have civil unions?"

Nicky shrugged, thinking the issue, like most issues, was really about money—people not wanting to pay benefits to gay lovers—but not knowing if saying that would set the kid off on another tirade.

"The point is," Todd said, "with the exception of some computer geeks who volunteered for the Howard Dean campaign for a few months, no one my age is getting involved. All my friends want to do is make money. Work as financial analysts, marketing managers, software engineers. Not me. I'm good at this, and I can help people."

"I know what you mean." Nicky felt embarrassed, hearing for the first time what he himself must sound like to others.

"The only thing I worry about," Todd said, "I get nervous talking in front of large groups of people. I took this communications class last semester. We studied all sorts of stuff—note cards, proper diction, debate skills. At the end of the class, we had to do five speeches. Commemorative, informative, demonstrative, persuasive and—what was the last one?—impromptu. Only ten minutes long, but I, like, threw up before each one. I'm serious, my face was all white. Afterward, they played back the video and everyone critiqued us. One girl told me I needed rouge."

"I was the same way when I started trying cases. I couldn't stop my hands from shaking. I held a pen like Bob Dole. Thing is you get over it with practice. Just focus on what you're trying to say and not on yourself. Remember, it's not about you. It's about the message."

Then the two started really talking, covering everything under the sun. New York State taxes, NAFTA, the president, Hillary, the Democratic party, the Republican party, the War on Terror, the Middle East. Nicky shook his head when the kid started ranting about the Patriot Act. The abridgement of civil liberties wasn't exactly a hot issue in central New York. Nor was terrorism in general at the top of the area's problems right now. Sure, there was that Iraqi doctor in Manlius convicted of violating US sanctions by using a charity to send money to Iraq. Now he was rotting away at FCI Fairton in Pennsylvania. And there were the Nine Mile 1 and Nine Mile 2 nuclear power plants in Oswego, not unrealistic targets of sabotage. And someone always had a relative or friend stationed at Fort Drum who was deployed or about to be deployed. But, other than that, to a lot of people in the area terrorism was just something in the back of their minds during the day and on TV at night.

For a minute Nicky felt on top of things again. He was still free, tracking down suspects, crossing them off his list one by one. He was there at the casino, surveilling Sal with someone else's help, at least until Todd came to his senses. And no one had recognized him yet, waving down a drone in a suit, until Nicky was taken by the arm to the security office where state troopers would come get him. Maybe coming to Turning Stone hadn't been such a crazy idea. Maybe he would actually find a clue here that would lead him to the killer.

Then something happened, the Pot O' Gold machine in front of him lighting up, bells ringing, sirens blaring.

He'd won.

Fingers were aimed at him, and he imagined what he looked like to Sal, even in his disguise with his back turned. He leapt off his chair toward a row of slots, landing on his belly, and bumping into something. A blue-haired lady hit him on the head with her purse, not taking her eyes from her screen.

Todd came around and withdrew Nicky's card from the machine.

When the ringing in his ears stopped, Nicky crawled to his feet and returned to his chair.

"A little advice," Todd said. "If you want to avoid suspicion in a casino, don't run from a ringing slot machine."

Todd offered Nicky his card back.

"Keep it," Nicky said, blowing out his breath. "How's he doing now?"

"His chips are gone, and so is the girl."

That's how it works, Nicky wanted to say. Did Lilly even miss him?

He heard Sal's voice, then turned around. The table in front of Sal was bare and green, and the dealer was rigid, his white-sleeved arms protecting a tray of chips.

"That was fast," Nicky said.

"Double-Down says he can lose a semester's tuition in fifteen minutes."

Nicky was just about done with Todd. "Do his parents know?"

Sal said something to the dealer.

"That's why he became president of the house," Todd said. "Free room and board. His dad doesn't have any idea. Just sends him checks."

"He'll make a fine corporate exec someday."

Now the dealer was saying something back to Sal.

"He applied to that show, *The Apprentice,* a few years back, 'cause he started a real successful house-painting business when he was growing up, Lyndon Painting Company. Supposedly sold it to someone for a lot of money. Says he got cut on the final audition after coming back drunk from a three-hour lunch with Omarosa. Remember her? She has her own Web site. No one at school believes him."

Lyndon Painting Company? Wasn't that the company Dale worked for? Was Nicky on the wrong track here? Maybe he should be following around Double-Down.

Sal began shouting, gesturing wildly, and Double-Down and the man in the goatee scooped up their chips and stepped back from the table. Heads were starting to turn. Two men in blue suits with ID badges on their pockets appeared by Sal's side. As they reached to help him to his feet, he brushed them off.

Nicky rose and said, "That's my cue." He turned to Todd. "If you're going to sell me out, speak now or forever hold your peace."

CHAPTER 25

"How'd you get in?" Sal said from the darkness.

"You still keep your key under that fake rock," Nicky said, feeling the wall for a light switch. "You can tell the thing is plastic, even at night. I finally peeled off the price tag."

"Jesus, you shave all your hair off? You look like Ghandi gone country."

Nicky hoped that was an improvement over Saddam. He waited for his eyes to adapt, watching a soft glow appear in the bay window, light from a neighbor's front yard lamp. Sal's silhouette took shape on the couch, where he sat holding what looked like a bottle of rum. Nicky found the switch but nothing happened.

"I sold the lamps," Sal said.

"And the end table?"

"Furniture, stereo, microwave. Stocks, CDs, IRAs. Then I got into the heavy stuff. I refinanced, took out a home equity loan, even sold some of the bar to my ex to cover back alimony."

"Which one?"

"Number two, the dental hygienist, Joyce. She's the one got her jaw broke on Jerry Springer during that episode about sleazy doctors. Used the settlement to buy a condo in Lauderdale at the start of the boom. Now she's into West Palm, flipping 'em every six months. Said she'd take a quarter of Lucky's to diversify her portfolio. Like it was a mutual fund. Sheldon told me to jump on it."

"Your bookie?"

"His day job is a CPA. The only thing I kept was the TV and couch, so I could watch the games. It's a pull-out so I kill two birds. I let my son take it when he came up for the funeral, slept on one of those air mattresses. He says to me, 'Mom's going to move us in with a dentist who calls me Conrat. Can I live with you next summer?' Broke my fucking heart."

"All this is part of the bankruptcy?" Nicky scanned the room for somewhere to sit down but Sal was right—the place was empty. The only spot was on one end of the couch, but Sal's fat ass was planted right in the middle.

"The what? No, the bankruptcy's part of this. How'd you find out about that?"

"It's public record."

"For someone who's looking. Bankruptcy. Fucking pain in the ass. Had to go through—get this—'credit counseling' before I filed. What a racket. You probably want to know how I got it discharged."

"Not if you don't want to tell me."

Sal poured some more Goslings. The bottle was half empty, and there was no ice in Sal's glass. Nicky wanted to ask Sal why he didn't drink it right out of the bottle. Maybe it would be like admitting he had a drinking problem, too.

"There's a glass in the sink," Sal said.

Nicky didn't know if Sal was changing the subject or preparing Nicky for a long story. He wanted a drink but not with Sal. "When did you start drinking again?"

Sal looked at his watch. "Six months ago."

"You have any more blackouts?"

"You mean ones when I kill women and don't remember?"

"I'm just asking. I saw you tonight, at the casino."

"Was that you diving for cover when your slot machine went off? I thought some hick had gotten into the moonshine. You see I was up ten grand? Started off slow then got hot. I was so close I could smell it. Then—" Sal flipped his wrist like he was dismissing a friend's offer to split a check.

So close to what? Nicky wanted to ask. "It looked like you blamed the dealer."

"That putz? All I ask for is some lousy respect. All the cash I drop."

He took a drink.

Nicky said, "You understand you have a problem."

"No shit, Sherlock. I gamble alone, stay until I'm broke, and can't sleep at night. I keep worrying Sheldon's going to send over a goon. Or I think about how to get my hands on some cash—sell stuff around the house, take out a loan for the bar, maybe finagle some sort of insurance claim. You know what money is to me? Something that lets me play longer. It's whacked."

"What are you going to do about it?"

"That I don't know."

"Does Monique know about this?"

"She says she needs some space, until I get control of myself. Says she learned from her mom that a woman can't save an addict. Smart girl. It took Lottie ten years to learn that."

"But she did in the end."

"It's why she wouldn't loan me the ten grand."

"But she loaned you money before that."

"Five here, ten there. And I paid it all back. Most of it anyway. She said I worked the rest off helping her around the house. Funny thing is, we were a lot alike, her and me. She liked to roll the dice, too. In court."

"Can you see a professional?"

"They don't do anything for me. They have no idea what it's like."

"Isn't there some place you can go?"

241

"You mean like Gamblers Anonymous? I tried that, remember? Quit during step eight: 'Make a list of all persons you've harmed and be willing to make amends to them.' It was my first ex that did it; called me a con artist. I say, 'I send you a check every month. Can't you do me this one little thing? Accept an apology?' She says, 'I spent five years listening to your bullshit. Try it on someone else.' I said fuck it, who needs this, and declared myself healed. Then I put a bet on the Super Bowl, just a small one, like normal people. Except I'm not normal people. I was into Sheldon for five grand by the time March Madness rolled around. Sometimes I see another guy from my group at the track. Joe Z. That's how we knew each other. Hello, my name is Sal M. We used to sit around and wait for each other to break down, tell each other we're not bad people. Now we can't look each other in the eye."

"How much do you owe?"

"More than I got. Sheldon's going to call a guy from Utica to break something. Says it's nothing personal. Actually asked whether I'm right-handed or left. So I figure I got that going for me, a bookie with a heart. Tell you the truth, I'm not going to put up a fight. I still got my health insurance."

"Didn't Lottie leave you something?"

"The will hasn't been—what do you call it?—probated. I talked to that crook, Wally. He said it'll be a week before he draws up the papers and files them with the Surrogate's Court. Then it'll be a month while he closes up her business—meaning your firm, I guess—and does her tax returns. Then it'll be a couple months for the government to audit the returns. I went through all this when my parents died."

"Can you get a partial distribution before then?"

"The Harbor House, that women's shelter, they say they'd contest it. Doesn't matter. I'd just piss it away."

"What about that blank check I gave you?"

"That's how I got out of bankruptcy. I went to the roulette table, put it on black, won, and let it ride. Got to a hundred and walked away. Hardest thing I ever did, leaving a hot table, but Monique made me."

A hundred grand in cash? Nicky wondered if Sal had paid taxes on it. "I'll write another one."

"I don't think it'd look too good to the DA to find a bunch of payments from you to me after Lottie's death. Besides, you'd have to dip into your war chest, which is going to take a hit when you get your lawyer's bill after this whole thing is finished."

"I don't care."

"I appreciate that, I really do. But what they tell you in the program is relying on others ain't the answer. I have to take responsibility for my actions. 'Make a searching and fearless moral and financial inventory of myself,' it's called. Step four. What I learned about myself, I'm just going to go back and get in deep again. It's what I do."

"What is it, chemical?" Nicky felt funny asking, never having gotten into it before. He had been embarrassed for Sal, sensitive of diminishing the man's self-respect. Now they were past self-respect, Nicky standing there in denim overalls and shitkickers, like it was Halloween.

"Like an adrenaline rush? Nah, this shrink once said it's psychological. From my feelings of inadequacy. Something about my old man withholding his approval. Blah blah blah. All I know, I'm always thinking of what I'm gonna do when I make a big score. Buy all new shit. House, car, clothes. Then go somewhere warm for a while and get a tan, maybe lose some weight. Then come back and invite everyone out to my new summer house, onto my new boat. Blow the rest on charity. It's crazy, I know. The funny thing is I don't care. The only place I feel like myself these days is at a blackjack table. No one coming to me with a problem, with some bill to pay, with some cheesy line about being sorry for my loss. Just me and the cards. It's killing me, but I can't help it."

Sal covered his eyes and his shoulders shook. Nicky moved to the couch, awkwardly leaning over and patting Sal's back. When Sal had wiped his eye and stopped swearing, Nicky got the telephone book.

After he hung up, he said, "I got a recording. There's a meeting tomorrow at noon at the United Methodist Church on Butternut Street."

"I know where it is," Sal said.

"Will you go?"

"I'd be lying if I made any promises. Maybe if you, you know, go with me."

Nicky clapped his hands together. "Where's that air mattress?"

Sal stood up. "You sure you want to stay here? What about the cops?"

"I parked up the street and came in through the back."

"But they could come by."

"Didn't they already talk to you?"

"I told them to get a warrant."

"Then they don't have probable cause yet."

Sal started to protest, then his shoulders slumped. "You don't have to do this. You got your own problems. Christ."

The two men stood in the dark for a moment, listening to a car approach, its tires making a swishing sound on the wet pavement. When the noise had passed, Nicky said, "I don't want to be an asshole, but I have to ask."

"The answer's no." Sal fell back onto the couch in a heap. "I don't know who whacked Lottie, or Scarlet while we're at it. I wish I did. Maybe he could do me, too."

CHAPTER 26

The next day, a few minutes before noon, a gold Tahoe forced Nicky's pickup onto the shoulder of Butternut Street. The door to the Tahoe opened and discharged a large, powerfully built black woman. She came over and stuck a pistol in Sal's face. After Sal had gotten in the back of the Tahoe, Nicky got in the front beside Sheldon, who was clipping his fingernails.

"How'd you do on Sunday?"

Nicky didn't know who Sheldon was talking to.

"I don't know what I was thinking, letting you piss more money away."

Sal said, "I came out five grand ahead."

"Where's it at?"

"Back at the house."

The black woman smacked Sal on the side of the head. "Quit your lying. We mean business."

Sal's cheek reddened. "Who're you?"

Sheldon turned around in his seat. "Sal, meet Daleesha."

"*Daleesha?* Are you da-serious?"

"You wanna da-die?" said Daleesha.

"What happened to Dominic?"

"Lamaze," said Sheldon. "One of those all-day things. Renata's due in six weeks. He's freaking out. Wants to take—get this!—paternity leave. I had to bring in Rambo here."

"Dominic's a knucklehead," said Daleesha.

Sal looked at her. "I guess she's big enough. Gotta be six

feet. And I like the tattoo. How much she weigh?"

"More than you, cream puff."

"You lift weights?"

"I get plenty a exercise slapping round deadbeats."

"But you're a girl."

"Mr. Sheinbaum's an equal opportunity stoonad."

"You're not even Italian."

"Maybe I'm Sicilian. Or black Irish. What do you care? You owe us money."

"I owe him money."

"How do you think I get paid?"

Nicky cringed, wanting to direct Sal not to answer that.

"Well, you're too ugly to be a ho."

And before Nicky knew it Daleesha smacked Sal again, loud and hard. She had long fingernails, covered in kiwi-green polish, complete with tiny black seeds. Something from a salon. Still, her hands were too fast for Sal. He groaned, covering his ear. When he took his hand away, there was blood on it.

"Fucking popped it. All I hear is ringing."

"It's a skill," Daleesha said into his good ear. "Picked it up in the 'hood. My baby brother had to learn sign language."

"I'm sorry," Sheldon said. "She gets a little excited. It'll grow back in a few weeks. Keep it dry and get some antibiotics. The last guy got vertigo so you might not want to drive for a while."

"So help me Jesus," Sal said to Daleesha, "you do that again . . ."

"You'll do what?" She stuck her pistol back in his face. "Bleed all over Mr. Sheinbaum's sport virility vehicle?"

"You don't know how to use that thing."

"A SIG-Sauer P245? You better hope I do. Or else I might miss and shoot you someplace funny, the foot or knee, maybe the crotch. How would you like that, big guy?"

"Fucking Christ, I'd like to see you try."

"You swear too much."

"You're offended by profanity?"

"Just the taking-the-Lord's-name-in-vain part."

"But you'll break people's kneecaps?"

"The Good Book says, 'Render unto Caesar that which is Caesar's, and render unto God that which is God's.' This here's Caesar." She waved the pistol. "So start rendering."

"Do you two have to fight?" Sheldon said, popping a Rolaids. "My reflux is killing me. GERD. Doctor says it's the stress. I quit caffeine, got a masseuse, and started taking Zantac, and I still feel like I swallowed a plate of peppers. Listen, Sal, I'll take what's left of the bar and we'll call it even. I know I'm leaving money on the table, but it's part of my new personal philosophy. Don't sweat the small stuff. We can go to my lawyer right now and do the paperwork."

Nicky tried to imagine how Sheldon would get along with Sal's ex-wife. Probably great. He could manage her portfolio.

"Or what?" Sal said.

There was a muffled pop, like a fastball hitting a catcher's mitt. By the time Daleesha returned the forty-five to Sal's face, smoke curling up from the silencer, he'd retreated to the corner of his seat.

"Jesus," he said, clawing at his foot.

She had shot off the top of his sneaker.

"What're you doing?" Sheldon said. "This is a lease. You see the size of that hole in the floor? What am I going to tell the dealer? I went over a rock? What if you'd hit the gas line?"

"I couldn't help myself. The man talks, I see red."

"You just missed my toe," Sal said. "What happened to breaking my hand?"

"You want I should smash your knuckles first? I can do that. I got a crow bar in the trunk."

Sal turned to Sheldon. "I thought you said this was nothing personal."

"It's not, Sal, relax. I'll still do your taxes. By the way, you open that 529 Plan for Conrad like I told you?"

"Why do you want my bar? Why not my house?"

"And fight the bank for it? I know they're sending you notices. Daleesha's been checking your mailbox."

"Full of filth," Daleesha said. "*Penthouse* and *Hustler,* and some names I can't say, being a lady."

"Plus," Sheldon said, "house sales are public. This way, we can keep it on the QT."

Sheldon ran his eyes over Nicky, as if noticing him for the first time. "Hey, I know you. You're that guy from the news. The Lady Killer."

"Who?" Nicky said.

"You made the front page this morning. The headline was *Trifecta,* with a photo of you at the track. They found the third girl last night. Lilly somebody."

"Longacre? She's dead?" The air left Nicky's chest and his head grew light, the car starting to spin.

"They're right," said Sheldon to Sal. "He is good at acting surprised."

"He didn't do it."

"That so? Tough luck. He doesn't happen to have an alibi?"

A surreal feeling came over Nicky, picturing Lilly in some morgue, while he listened to the others talk about him like he wasn't there. He imagined her lying on a steel table, under a green sheet, her skin paler than usual. She'd seemed so fragile when they were lovers, her voice soft and small, her arms long and thin, like he would break them if he didn't hold her just right. Then she'd toughened up that last day at the farm, her face hardening, her voice taking on an edge. Was he somehow responsible for this by breaking up with her? Was he killing all the women in his life through his selfishness? No, he had to remember: someone was doing this to him. "How did she die?"

"Two in the head. Sheriff found her Volvo station wagon by a stop sign on some road in Skaneateles. Funny name, near some horse farm. They ran the plates, found some blood on the bumper and popped the back. There she was, under a horse blanket, in all her gory. Ballistics results haven't come back yet, but they think you used a nine millimeter. They found two shells in the grass. If I was going to pop someone, I'd use a revolver. Semiautomatics spit the shells out the side. Guys always panic, forget to pick 'em up."

Nicky had to force his brain to work. "They think it was planned?"

"Sheriff wouldn't say, but they showed some detective on the news—I guess he's investigating the two other murders. He said it could be anything from road rage to a hit. There was a dent in her rear bumper that her husband didn't recognize. Someone could have rear-ended her, gotten her out of the car, then whacked her. You ever hear of that, Daleesha?"

"Not me. I don't run with them violent types."

"When was she killed?" Nicky said.

"Some time last night," Sheldon said. "Around midnight, I think."

Nicky thought about how Todd could cover him from ten to eleven, and Sal from one on, but no one in between.

"And they think I did it?"

"How did that article start off? 'Nikomedes Rigopoulos is one of the city's top personal injury attorneys, a dark-horse candidate for Supreme Court Judge, and fast becoming a triple-homicide suspect.' It said you argued with her couple days ago."

"She was his girlfriend," Daleesha said. "That's what the news said. They interviewed some barn worker."

"Barn hand," Sal said. "They shovel shit in the stalls, replace it with hay. My little girl, she was crazy about show jumping until she discovered boys. Now all she does is hang out at Carousel. Smoke cigarettes, actually got in a fight last week. They should move up the curfew on that place. You got any kids, Nick?"

Nicky looked out the windshield at the grey sky. Lottie was gone. Scarlet was gone. And now Lilly was gone. He had to do something, identify her body, talk to Diz, at least get a hold of a newspaper.

"Don't sweat it," Sheldon said. "I won't drop a dime on you, as they say. But I better get my money or I can't tell what will happen to Sal. I'm serious. I don't know what Daleesha's going to do next. She doesn't listen to me. Isn't that right, Daleesha?"

"Huh?" said Daleesha.

Nicky had to stop this, get control of the situation. "It's okay. I'll pay."

Sal sat up in his seat. "The fuck you will."

"You'd do that?" Sheldon said to Nicky. He turned to Sal. "You should be proud to have a friend like that. I've been doing this for twenty years and no one has taken it on the chin for a deadbeat, no offense Sal. But they're usually happy to see the guy squirm, teach him a lesson."

Nicky said, "Sal doesn't need to learn any lessons from you." He couldn't help himself, Sheldon acting like he owned Sal, like he was above the law.

"I'm not going to argue with you. What I want to know, you got that sort of money?" He eyed Nicky. "Yeah, you got that sort of money. You're dressed like a hick, but I've seen your commercials, slick with those special effects. On all day because your clientele doesn't work. My favorite one, you're standing in front of that crunched up car beside that kid in a wheelchair. You look right in the camera and say, what is it? Something like, 'The drunk driver took his legs, then the insurance company tried to take his hope.' Talking right to the future jurors, so you got 'em before you ever step into court. And what happens when they give you a verdict? You take one-third. And you've been doing that—what?—fifteen, twenty years? It adds up. I can see it in your eyes. That sleepy look, like you see on people who don't care. Millionaires and hardened criminals. So let's go, drive to a bank."

Nicky and Sal exchanged a glance.

"Wait a minute," Sheldon said. "You can't. Your picture's all over the news. Makes you look like, I don't know—"

"That Ghandi guy," Daleesha said. "Don Hensley."

"You mean Ben Kingsley. No, his nose isn't big enough. I was going to say Saddam. You know, with the bags under the eyes. The man must've gone a month without sleeping when they found him. Can you imagine what he smelled like?"

"Like he was sitting next to me," Sal said, looking at Daleesha.

"Smell this," said Daleesha.

She pointed the SIG at Sal's knee, and Sheldon reached over and touched her wrist. "Come on, you two, you're worse than my kids."

Nicky wanted to suggest they get someone else to withdraw the money, his daughter or his brother, but he didn't want to involve them. "I'll withdraw it as soon as I'm arrested. You're betting I'll get caught, right?"

"I'd give you ten to one. And you know what? I actually think you'd pay, assuming you make bail. But I'm asking myself, How's he going to pay if he's been charged? Can't the government freeze your assets in case you're convicted and ordered to pay—what's it called?—restitution. You know, compensate your victims' families? Not Lottie's family—that would be Sal here, because their parents are dead, and Lottie was divorced with no kids. See? I know my clients. No, what I'm wondering about is your wife's family. And this Lilly person."

"They're not my victims, so no."

"The cops don't know that."

"They will."

"How? They're not even looking for the guy. They think you did it."

"I'm going to find him."

Sheldon chortled. "Is that what you two are doing out here, trying to find the guy who whacked Sal's sister and your wife?"

Nicky glared at Sheldon, feeling an odd sensation swell inside. Was it hatred? No, it was something else. Violence. Nicky couldn't remember the last time he had the urge to lash out at someone. He wanted to actually hit the man, grab his oily hair and bang his bulbous head on the steering wheel. To his credit, Sheldon just grinned back at Nicky, like he was used to being reviled.

"Tell you what," Sheldon said. "Why don't I just take those?"

"My keys?"

"Not all of them, just this one, with the Jaguar logo. What year is it?"

Nicky watched the man pry the key from the chain. Then Nicky answered, throwing in the model, mileage, and color.

"Nice," Sheldon said. "Where's it at?"

"My garage. Robineau Road. It was my wife's. No dings, but she didn't keep up the engine. Needs new belts and an oil change. Plus the inspection's overdue. And be careful—there's half a bottle of peach schnapps that falls out of the glove compartment when you open it, in case you get pulled over."

"You see?" Sheldon said to Daleesha. "The man's looking out for us. All because I talked to him with respect. No shouting, no pepper spray, no switchblades. See how reasonable people can be you treat them right?"

Nicky thought of Dale, how reasonable he was.

"You know what would be reasonable?" Nicky said. "If we could consider that key a down payment and have until Monday to get the rest."

CHAPTER 27

Sal's office contained a large oak desk with locked drawers. Nicky found the key under the straw skirt of an electric hula dancer. The doll was perched atop an immense digital sound system, which was wedged between a softball trophy, a box of T-shirts, and a stack of old menus.

As Nicky had expected, the desk drawers were a mess. Manila folders holding piles of loose papers in no particular order and topped with yellow stickers bearing handwritten notations. *Invoices to Be Filed, Bills Due, Accountant, 30-Day Notices*. No wonder the bar was having money problems. In the bottom drawer, under a pile of blank checks and time cards, he found an envelope holding a half dozen spare keys and a dingy business card from Executive Escorts. On the back of the card was penciled a series of numbers and words. *Magnar0258, jets69, Godfather.*

Nicky turned on Sal's computer and typed the last word into the password prompt. As he was logging on, he noticed, next to the printer, a second monitor. He switched it on.

Up popped a screen split into four boxes. The boxes showed a bird's-eye view of three registers and the back door. Nicky remembered Sal saying he bought a security system that had cost a mint. Monique stepped into view, her cleavage inches from four stacks of cash. Nicky suspected this was Sal's favorite program. He punched the *ZOOM OUT* button until the screen showed all three bartenders. They were busy chitchatting with a respectable happy hour crowd. He panned back all the way, until he caught a glimpse of the stairway to the second floor, which was vacant.

He checked Sal's E-mails first. Dirty jokes from his buddies, lame promises to his son, and Internet purchase confirmations. Nothing about Lottie. He pulled down the log of Web sites visited. Porn, sports, and gambling. Again, no big surprises. Finally, he opened an accounting program and scanned through a spreadsheet.

The bar had a mind-boggling number of monthly expenses. Payroll: thirty grand. Beer: ten grand. Food: nine grand. Liquor: seven grand. Rent: four grand. Gas and electric: two grand. Soda and juice: a grand. Insurance: a grand. Cell phones, TV and security system: five hundred each. Nicky figured Sal had to do sixty-five grand in business each month, after taxes, just to break even. And that wasn't including the cost of cleaning, trash removal, and extermination services, and the rent on the refrigerators, ice machine, and ATM machine. Nicky lost interest in the identifiable expenses when he noticed the series of checks made out to cash. The last one was for ten thousand dollars, dated the day of Lottie's murder, when she'd supposedly written a check for the same amount.

Had Sal taken checks from Nicky *and* Lottie that day?

His pocket beeped, giving him a start. It was Diz's cell phone, playing the tune to Gloria Gaynor's *I Will Survive*. Not a bad theme song, Nicky decided. The caller had a 206 area code. It was his brother Alex.

"Nicky, finally," Alex said. "Whose phone number is this?"

"You really want to know?" Nicky said.

"Where are you?"

"Safe."

" 'Safe'? What're you, in the Witness Protection Program? What's going on?"

Nicky gave him the *Reader's Digest* version of events from the past week. To Nicky's surprise, they seemed to calm Alex down.

"I wanted to stick around after the funeral," Alex said, "but that lady lawyer made me leave."

"Diz?"

"Said it would only draw you out of hiding, get you nabbed."

Nicky wondered why Diz would say that. He thought she wanted him to go to jail, anything to make her job easier.

"It was Dad who fought her on it," Alex said.

"How is he?"

"He's going in for his third prostate thing next week. When he's done with that, they're gonna give him a new hip."

"How are his spirits?"

"What do you think? Dara and I keep telling him everything's going to be okay, but he knows. He gets the Syracuse paper sent to him by mail. He says he read you're going to be disbarred."

Nicky hadn't heard that one, but it was the least of his worries right now. "Everything *is* going to be okay."

"Sure, I know. You should call him, though."

"I'm waiting for some good news to give him. You going down to visit him this fall?"

"You really want to talk about that?"

"Takes my mind off things."

"You sure you should be taking your mind off things?"

"Diz says I'm fooling myself. Says, 'Denial ain't just a river in Egypt.' "

"She right?"

Nicky sighed. "People don't want to hear about your problems. They want to talk about themselves."

"Then you're talking to the wrong people."

"I guess you're right. I mean, look where I am. Maybe if I'd turned myself in and made a statement, I'd be out on bail, free to walk the streets like a normal person."

"And the cops would be looking for the real guy who did this."

"Don't get your hopes up."

"That's what Diz said, they have it in for you."

"So let's talk Florida."

Alex said that late November was probably best for him. He had to attend a tournament in Ft. Walton, near Pensacola, from the twenty-sixth to the twenty-eighth. He could fly into West Palm, hang out a few days with their dad, then catch a puddle jumper to Tallahassee and rent a car from there. That way the League would pay for the cross-country airfare. He had Nicky's knack for working the angles. He told Nicky to bring his clubs.

"I've been taking lessons," Alex said. "Learned how to draw the ball. Just firm up your grip, close your stance, and swing inside out. Plus I got this new Titleist driver. Well, last year's model, off eBay. Hundred bucks. But I'm hitting the ball fifty yards farther off the tee. The titanium face, it sparks when you make contact. Seriously, I'm going to kill you." After a pause, he said, "Sorry."

"Drive for show, putt for dough," Nicky said. "I'm surprised you have time to practice."

"You mean with B-school? Piece a cake. I decided to go at night at SU." Out there, *SU* meant Seattle University, a mid-sized Jesuit school that had attracted Alex because it had reminded him of Le Moyne College in Syracuse, where he'd gotten his undergrad degree in economics, three years behind Nicky. "First-year course load isn't so bad."

As Alex talked about Business Calculus, Nicky logged onto the Internet, went to the *Post-Standard* Web site, and started looking for the article Alex had mentioned about disbarment. Nothing but a few abbreviated stories about the murder investigation. He went to the Lexis Web site and punched in his credit card number. He knew Halliday was probably in the process of subpoenaing Nicky's bank account records, or even records of his account at Lexis in order to track down the Internet Service Provider address of the computer Nicky was using. But he didn't care anymore. He opened the news file and started running searches.

"All in all, things are great out here," Alex said. "Best move I ever made. Hey, why don't you come to the Left Coast? Land of mountains and evergreens."

"And tort reform. The way they cap damages, I'd have trouble making a living."

"That's California, not Washington. You could try it out first, get away for a while, clear your head."

"Cross state lines, bring in the FBI, maybe make the national news."

"No one would know. You could take a bus. When you get here, I got an extra bedroom in my apartment. Way up high with a view of the Space Needle and Mt. Rainier."

"Just like from that show *Frazier.*"

"Except that view was at an impossible angle. I'm telling you, the city's awesome. We've got Microsoft, Starbucks, Boeing, hospitals, biotech labs, you name it. More companies than you could sue in a lifetime."

"Sounds nice."

"Well?"

Nicky heard the hallway floorboards moan then the doorknob squeak. He whispered, "I'll have to check my calendar."

CHAPTER 28

"You said he was here," said a woman. "Was this just one of your ploys? 'Cause if it was, it worked."

The door to the office clicked shut. Nicky heard the rustle of clothing, then Sal's voice.

"Not now, hon. He's around. See, my computer's on. He must a found my password." Sal raised his voice. "I wonder if he thought to look for the safe, behind the TV. Has lots of incriminating evidence in it."

Nicky heard two raps on the desktop above him.

"Come out, come out wherever you are."

Sal was using that voice from *Cape Fear*—De Niro, or Robert Mitchum if you preferred the original. He knew that, if he didn't give in, Sal would keep going. Maybe say, *I know where you live, Counselor.*

He crawled out and climbed to his feet, brushing off his hands and knees. "What are you doing here?"

"Making sure you got in the back door. Besides, I brought reinforcements."

Monique curtsied. "Thanks for taking him to that meeting. He just told me. I couldn't believe it." She took Sal's arm and kissed his cheek.

He said, "She's taking me back on a trial basis."

"I'm happy for you," Nicky said, drawing the curtains.

"Hey, you're logged on the Internet. I didn't know you could pull up newspaper articles."

"You gamble online?"

"Casino dot net. It's offshore. Curacao, in the Dutch Antilles. I'm bringing Monique next year."

"How do you know they're not cheating you?" Nicky wanted to ask if there was a gaming commission overseeing it. Was he the only one who saw the dangers lurking in the world?

"They use an independent auditor. Reviews the results every month. Pricewaterhouse, I think."

"And they deduct the money right from your credit card?"

"The Web site I used before took it right from my bank account."

"Your creditors probably loved that."

"Why do I get the feeling you're changing the subject from that article on the computer?"

"It's nothing." Nicky reached for the mouse.

"Hold on." Sal brushed away Nicky's hand, leaned on the desk, and inspected the screen. Nicky straightened up to see over Sal's shoulder.

LICENSE TO KILL?

In addition to facing life imprisonment for murder, attorney Nikomedes Rigopoulos is facing more mundane problems: the loss of his license to practice law.

Several clients of the law firm of Rigopoulos & Magnarella, LLP have filed complaints with the Fifth Judicial Department's Grievance Committee regarding Mr. Rigopoulos's representation of them. "Basically," said Dale Pardy, "the jerk promised us the moon, settled our case for peanuts, and won't return our calls." Mr. Rigopoulos has been unable to be reached for comment, and is sought for questioning in three murder investigations.

If Mr. Rigopoulos fails to respond to Mr. Pardy's complaint, or if the Grievance Committee determines that his conduct was improper, he could be cautioned, admonished or reprimanded. In addition, if his misconduct is deemed serious enough, his case could be referred to the Appellate Division of the New York State Supreme Court for action, which could include suspension or loss of his law license. Mr. Rigopoulos's law firm has already lost all of its other attorneys—Carlotta Magnarella having recently been murdered and Walter McGuffin and Martin Newberg having resigned.

Even the firm's legal opponents have voiced complaints. "A firm sues your client and drags its good name through the mud," says attorney Bartholomew Crawford of Trollope & Secore, LLP, "the least it can do is return your calls when its lead attorney dies and you ask who you're dealing with."

Mr. Crawford's client, Onondaga Furniture of Willow Glen, is one of numerous defendants in a multimillion-dollar personal injury suit brought by Rigopoulos & Magnarella. Having recently lost a critical motion in the case, the company has scheduled a press conference for Monday evening at a Skaneateles Town Board Meeting, where it is expected to address the status of the case against it and the community's concerns about its future.

"One thing the company doesn't have to worry about anymore," said Mr. Crawford, "is dealing with Tricky Nick."

There was that nickname again, this time in black and white. It made Nicky want to scream.

Sal said, "What do you care about this shit? You're facing

hard time. You lost your wife, your partner, and your girlfriend."

"It's my firm. I built it. Besides, if I'm not a lawyer I can't run for Supreme Court."

"Get your priorities right."

"Look who's talking."

"Why are you so worked up?"

"Who else did you tell I was here?"

"Only her. She won't talk."

"It's true," Monique said. "I tell hardly no one about Sal's kinky sex life."

"I just wanted to know could we help. Find the guy who's setting you up. I got to thinking after I dropped you off. I appreciate what you did, putting your ass on the line with Sheldon. I didn't want you to think all I care about is the money. Far as I'm concerned, we don't catch the guy by Monday, I'm not letting you walk into some bank to get nabbed, broken knuckles or not. You got any leads?"

Sal and Monique waited, wide-eyed and innocent.

"I don't know," Nicky said.

"Come on. You gotta have something. You've been looking all week."

"I keep running into dead ends."

"What about that lawyer of yours? She's what you call the common denominator in all this. Worked with Lottie, was in that book club with Scarlet, and was going at it with Lilly last week. A cop I know, friend of my dad's, said they have a witness saw Lilly throw her off the place."

Nicky wondered if Diz's visit to Lilly was worse than Diz had described.

"I can follow her around," Monique said. "She lives downstairs from me. My apartment overlooks the parking lot. I noticed a ding in her front bumper. She drives that white Wrangler, right? Could be nothing, but you never know."

Nicky wanted to ask how much Sal had told Monique. He couldn't believe these two were here, much less that they were grilling him about his theories of the case. He'd planned to play his cards close to his vest and hunt down leads, one at a time. Now nothing was going right. He couldn't take it anymore.

"Want to know what I think? There are more suspects than you can shake a stick at. Diz could've had a lesbian thing going with Lottie, gotten jilted, then killed her out of anger. She could've done Scarlet because she knew about it, then Lilly to ruin my alibi. And she could be representing me only to get evidence to turn over to the police. Then there's Tony Donuts. He could've killed Lottie out of jealousy, then killed Scarlet to frame me, then found out from Halliday that Lilly was my alibi. He probably had the easiest access to a gun. And there's always Dale Pardy. He was pissed at Lottie, could've talked his way into my house and learned about Lilly from Scarlet. Other suspects are Randy DeVine, Wes Longacre, and evidently half my former clients. But you know who tops my list right now? You and your girlfriend here."

Nicky heard his voice change, shed all civility until it was cold and quivering.

"You could have done your own sister to erase a debt or get your inheritance, then done my wife because you thought she was my alibi, and then done Lilly because you *knew* she was my alibi. What I don't get is why you want to get close to Diz. Is it to plant some evidence on her or maybe kill her, too?"

Sal looked at him with half-closed eyes, the sort of expression Nicky imagined he himself had, people telling him he always looked bored. Then Sal surprised Nicky, showing a more mature side of his personality, saying, "You're tired. Why don't you get some sleep? We can talk in the morning."

"I don't want to talk in the morning."

"You have everything you need. The couch isn't a pull-out

but it's comfortable. There's a pillow and blanket in the closet. You've probably figured out there's a bathroom behind that door. There's coffee in the drawer under the pot there. You hungry?"

In fact, Nicky *was* hungry, but he didn't want to change the subject.

"I'll bring up a menu," Monique said, "just in case."

Nicky regretted having raised his voice. He wondered if anyone had heard him. He cracked the door and checked the hall.

"The upstairs ain't your problem," Sal said. "It's outside you got to worry about."

"What are you talking about?"

"That's the other reason we came up, if you'd let us explain. That reporter from the track, the one with the fruity name, he's across the street at the coffee shop. At one of those outdoor tables. He's trying to be sly, with his nose in a newspaper, but it's so obvious. He's been there since lunch, sucking down lattes. I'm surprised he's not going to the can every five minutes."

"I'll go out the back."

"Monique saw a guy strolling up and down the alley."

"I was bringing out the trash," she said. "I didn't get a good look at his face, but I thought I saw a holster under his jacket."

Nicky parted the curtains. Below, a man drew on a cigarette. "Doc."

"The guy that came to my place?" Sal said.

Monique checked the window. "Now I recognize him. He came to my place, too. Kept talking to my chest. When I stopped him from coming inside, he twisted my arm behind my back and told me he liked it when girls play hard to get. So I banged my head against his chin, kneed him in the balls, and shut the door in his face."

"You never told me that part," Sal said.

"I don't tell you a lot of parts."

"How am I going to get out of here?" Nicky said.

"I told you, that's the reason I brought her up," Sal said. "Go ahead, honey. You showed him your pom-poms. Now show him your brains."

CHAPTER 29

Game day, a half hour before kickoff, two uniformed cops appeared in the doorway to Lucky's. The bar had never seen so much action. It was packed shoulder-to-shoulder with men in blue and orange who were armed with obnoxious sports gear—pennants hanging from sticks, foam hands making the number-one sign, hard hats holding beers and dangling plastic tubes. The SU fight song blared on the stereo, a half dozen pre-game shows playing on TVs hung from the ceiling. Above the bar hung a banner that read *FREE BEER!* But the main attraction was on the bar, standing in only a blue miniskirt and orange body paint. The letters SU were never more admired in the sports-loving town.

Monique shook her pom-poms and cried, "Hold that tight end, strip that ball, sack and tackle, maul maul maul!"

The cheer was lost in the clamor, but the men got the message. They raised their fists and let out whoops.

"Eat more wings and drink more beer!" Monique cried. "Tip your waitress, pinch her rear!"

She put extra emphasis on this last word, jutting out her hip. The invitation to grope the staff was too much for the men. They lost control of themselves, pushing their way to the bar. That was enough for the cops, who started yanking shirt collars and clamping necks, parting the orange sea. Their journey was slowed by tables and chairs, which were scattered about like mines.

In the middle of the crowd, Nicky raised himself on his toes and checked the mirror behind the bar. At first, he didn't recognize himself—the blue face paint, the orange wig, the black sunglasses. Then he found his nose, large and arched. He lowered his head and swam upstream to the end of the crowd, which had left some space along the far wall.

At the front door, he couldn't resist turning around. He wished he hadn't. Across the room, standing in the back doorway, was Detective Halliday, eyes aimed in Nicky's direction. Nicky wrestled with the impulse to run. Telling himself he had time, he strolled across Walton Street, down South Franklin, around the old Armory Building, and up the steps to the railway station.

On the train, he locked himself in a bathroom and took deep breaths. When the train stopped moving, he got off and trekked up the hill, joining thousands of fans from campus parking lots.

Inside the Dome, he went to his seat on the ten-yard line, first level, and watched the teams warm up. A pretty young woman sang the national anthem. During kickoff, he stayed seated, happy the people around were standing. As Miami returned the ball—crossing the twenty-yard line, the thirty, the forty—Nicky gasped. Across the field, in the opposing stands, a uniformed cop was coming down an aisle. Nicky jumped when his pocket beeped. He answered Sal's cell phone.

"Ol' Saint Nick," said a voice.

"Halliday?"

The crowd sat back down.

"That was some run, huh?" Halliday said. "You have a good view from Sal's seats?"

Nicky told himself to be cool. "You don't know where Sal's seats are?"

"I'm waiting for the Box Office to call me back. They said they were busy. You believe that shit? People have no respect for cops anymore."

"Don't hold your breath. There are fifty thousand seats in here."

"But only a few thousand season ticket holders. Besides, that's what computers are for, right? Find a name with a punch of a button."

"Do you really think I'd use Sal's tickets? I could've gone to a scalper."

"That's why I have a dozen cops combing the stands for you."

"Only a dozen?"

"With more on the way."

"Good luck. I see two levels to this place, three in the end zones. Each level must have two or three dozen aisles."

"They don't need to be in every aisle to see you. They know you shaved your moustache and put on an orange wig and blue face paint."

Nicky wanted to know how they knew that. Had Halliday seen him at Lucky's? But, if he'd asked that, he'd definitely be implicating Sal, with his coincidental free-beer deal and peep show. Nicky said, "Luckily, so are a hundred other guys."

"Ninety-nine. I just found one and took his wig. Told him he could pick it up at the end of the game at Gate IOU."

"Why are you telling me all this? Aren't you afraid I'll leave?"

"You don't think I have guys posted at the exits?"

Nicky sighed. "What do you want?"

"If you mean, what's my latest deal, don't bother. It's off. No, the reason I'm calling, I want your professional advice. About a case I'm working on."

"I know the one. I think you've got the wrong suspect."

"Wait, hear me out. I've got an office full of employees who'll testify the guy was pissed at Lottie for threatening to bail on his political campaign because he was screwing her clients. I've got a friend of Lilly's who'll testify he asked her to lie about his alibi on the night of Lottie's murder, and that Lilly dumped him because he wanted her to leave her husband. And I've got Randy DeVine and Tiffany Newberg who'll testify he was pissed at Scarlet for cheating on him with his political opponent and threatening to file for divorce and take half his money. That's motive for all three murders, in case you're keeping track."

Nicky had to admit, it sounded pretty good, the way Halliday presented it.

"What about opportunity and weapon?" Nicky said, trying to stall Halliday while he considered what to do. If the man was talking, he couldn't be looking very hard.

"The opportunity's there for all three, unless you're concocting an alibi for Lilly's murder. We have the weapon you used in Lottie's murder. You didn't use a weapon in Scarlet's murder, unless you count alcohol and the pool. And I'm working on tracing the nine millimeter to you. Frankly, I like the creativity you showed on that one, making it look like a stranger did it. But your mistake was using a semiautomatic. I don't know, maybe it's all you could get your hands on with such short notice. But if you'd used a revolver, say a thirty-eight, the shell casings—"

Nicky had heard this one before. He scanned the crowd. A cop was coming down the next aisle over. Nicky bent down and pulled off his wig, stuffing it into the back of his jeans under his jersey. Halliday was still talking, telling Nicky about a case he once had.

"The guy was so stoned," he was saying, "that he walked out into broad daylight with blood streaked across his shirt. You know, from wiping his hands? Thank God most people who commit crimes are stoned, scared or just plain—"

Nicky stopped listening again, waiting for the cop to pass him. When the man was gone, Nicky interrupted Halliday.

"Do you honestly think I'm that dumb?" He was aware of the people around him. He wanted to ask Halliday how anyone could think he could commit one murder to cover up another one? Twice?

"I don't think you're dumb, just deluded. I know from talking to Dale Pardy that you think you're innocent. And before you say it, I know he's a lying, no-good sack of shit, but the DA can bring all that out on direct and take the punch out of Diz's cross. I've seen that happen. The judge will tell the jury to take Dale's testimony for what it's worth. Anyway, he's not the only one. Martin Newberg also says you think you're innocent. He honestly thinks you believe it, too. His wife Tiffany is another matter. She thinks you're faking. Between you and me, I think she's psycho."

Another cop was at the bottom of the aisle, scanning the seats below Nicky. Didn't these guys keep track of ground that had already been covered? The cop's eyes ran over Nicky's row until they came to Nicky—making his heart stop—then moved on.

"So, let me get this right," Nicky said, "I'm some sort of sociopath?"

The guy in front of Nicky turned around, and Nicky lowered the phone, rolled his eyes, and mouthed the word *women*.

"You're a complex man, Nicky Rigopoulos. You've even drawn Diz, Sal, and Monique into your tangled web of lies. I've got people watching them twenty-four-seven, by the way. I have half a mind to pick them up for harboring a fugitive. Face it, you have nowhere to run."

Halliday was right, if that was true. Nicky started thinking of hiding places. The locker room, a janitor's closet, an elevator shaft. But how was he supposed to get into any of those places? Then it came to him. Why hadn't he thought of it before?

The firm's private box suite.

It was one of only thirty-eight in the Dome and cost a mint, the price recently rising from thirty grand to forty-eight. But it was worth every penny, not to entertain clients—personal injury plaintiffs weren't the sort you had to woo with imported beer and jumbo shrimp—but to schmooze the judges and their law clerks. Invite their wives and kids, watch them admire the signed photos on the walls, get them talking on the drive home about how nice Nicky was.

The suite was large enough to live in for a few days, with all those cushioned seats, a plush couch, a widescreen TV, a refrigerator stocked with beer and soda. Nicky wondered if it was too late to order cold cuts from the Dome's catering service. He decided it would be too risky. He tried to think whether the suite had a storage closet. He could take in cushions from the couch and curl up until the game was over. Dome Security wouldn't check it before they closed up. He would be home free.

He scanned the crowd for cops, then took off his sunglasses and peered over the faces above him. His stomach sank. The suite's lights were on. And it was occupied. Nicky made out four figures, two male and two female. How had they gotten in?

Then he recognized them.

Martin Newberg and Barth Crawford were sitting beside Tiffany Newberg and Maria D'Angelo, eating hors d'oeuvres and drinking green-bottled beer. What was happening?

Sure, lawyers could socialize with opposing counsel. Syracuse was a small town. You couldn't help but run into your opponent here and there—at the grocery store, shopping mall, maybe a cocktail party. You'd be cordial and exchange a few words. But would you invite him to the big game? Even if Martin had kept in touch with Barth from when he'd interviewed at Trollope & Secore a few years before, why would he drag Tiffany and Maria along? There was no reason for non-lawyers to be cordial to opposing counsel. Maybe Barth was the glue that held the four together. Had Nicky been on the wrong trail? Had Barth murdered Lottie to strong-arm Martin into settling, then murdered Scarlet and Lilly to frame Nicky? Could the case mean that much to Barth?

Tiffany said something to Maria and roared riotously. Maria recoiled, regarding Tiffany like she was crazy. Then Tiffany's mouth dropped open and she extended a hand. Nicky followed her finger across the Dome to the JumboTron in the far corner of the third level.

Shit.

There on the fifteen-by-twenty-five-foot color screen, for the world to see, was his blue open-mouthed face, his big nose, and his naked eyes. Luckily, the fans around him jumped up and started waving, mugging for the camera. But it was too late.

"Bingo," Halliday said over the phone.

Nicky had forgotten the thing was on. He whirled around and saw a couple of uniformed cops jogging across the end zone, headed his way. He turned off the phone and climbed between the fans behind him, bolting up the aisle.

In the mezzanine, people waited in line for overpriced Dome Dogs, or stood around closed-circuit TVs watching an SU linebacker intercept a pass. Nicky weaved through them, keeping his knees up so as not to trip, feeling his chest tighten. He would definitely have to hit the gym when this was all over. He just hoped it wouldn't be in a prison exercise yard.

When he'd circled around to the northwest corner of the Dome, he slowed down and searched for black caps and silver badges. Finding none, he ducked into a bathroom and scanned under the stall doors until he found a pair of gleaming Italian leather loafers. He locked himself in the adjoining stall.

"How do you like the game?" Sal said.

"Eh, you know, a little boring."

"Tell me about it. Monique wouldn't even let me bet her a back rub. She's got this idea that she shouldn't put out until I'm completely cured of my addiction."

"Abstinence makes the heart grow fonder." Nicky took off his jersey and kicked it under the stall wall, along with the wig.

"Or go wander." Sal handed Nicky a wet wash cloth, a Sky-Chiefs baseball cap, and an orange SU basketball T-shirt.

"No offense, but I don't know if you could do better than her."

"So she tells me. By the way, I couldn't find a mirror, but you can check your reflection in the toilet paper dispenser. Make sure you got all the paint off."

"The sweat on my face did most of the job."

"Relax. Enjoy the game."

Nicky heard Sal's door open, then watched through a crack as Sal strolled out of the far exit of the bathroom. Nicky counted to sixty, then opened his door, and strolled out of the other exit.

A man in a black uniform was staring at a TV hanging from the ceiling. SU was trying a forty-yard field goal. As the ball tumbled end over end toward the left goal post, Nicky slipped behind the man, through the revolving door and into the sunlight. Just like that. He couldn't believe it.

The outside of the Dome was unpopulated and tranquil. No black uniforms, no Detective Halliday. Nicky breathed the sweet air of freedom, and put his sunglasses back on. That's when he saw it, trouble dead ahead.

Tony Donuts.

CHAPTER 30

"Come on," Tony said, grabbing Nicky's arm.

Wait! Nicky wanted to say. *This isn't fair! I made it!* But Tony pulled Nicky close so Nicky could smell the man's cheap cologne and feel something poke into his side.

"No, I'm not just glad to see you," Tony said. "That's a Browning automatic. Don't get any ideas. Only a nine millimeter, but holds thirteen rounds, able to fire as fast as I can squeeze the trigger. In case I'm aiming at a moving target."

A nine millimeter? Wasn't that the gun that killed Lilly? Nicky's brain started working.

"Who said anything about moving targets? Hey, where are we going?"

"Down there." Tony was looking across Irving Avenue, at the farther of two parking garages. "I'm going to take you in."

"To the police station? Okay, but do you really need that thing? Don't you have some handcuffs?"

Nicky felt his heart pound. He took the concrete steps from the Dome one at a time, hoping for someone to appear, anyone—a driver passing by in a car, a student lugging his backpack up to the library, a patient walking out of the VA hospital up the street.

"No one home," Tony said when they passed the vacant ticket booth in the first garage. "Everyone's watching the game. Finally, a team with half a shot. We should've dumped that stiff long before we did."

Nicky didn't know who Tony was talking about.

" 'We tried hard,' he used to say on those post-game shows. Like the other guys had been at the beach all summer. But people would get offended if you knocked him. 'What?' they'd say. 'Fire Coach P? But he's done so much for us!' 'Really?' I'd say. 'Like what? Gotten us to the Music City Bowl? The Insight-.com Bowl?' And that's if we were lucky enough to get invited. Shit, we used to lose to bottom-feeders like Rutgers, Temple, and East Carolina. What do you expect? In there." He jabbed the gun into Nicky's back and pushed him in a side door to the second garage.

Tony huffed and wiped his forehead. He was in worse shape than Nicky. Inside the garage, Nicky headed for the stairwell, getting an idea.

"Uh huh," Tony said, pushing him toward the elevators, "that way. I've had enough of that shit. Climbed that fucking Dome a dozen times looking for your Greek ass, while those uniformed kids stood around the exits."

Nicky watched the doors close and wondered if this was how it was going to end, bleeding to death in a dirty elevator with its emergency phone ripped out.

"They look like pro athletes," said Tony, his fleshy neck spilling over his dingy shirt collar. "Fresh out of the academy, with their brush cuts and tribal arm tattoos. Except they're dumb. Waiting for you inside the exits. Like you're going to try to make it out if you see a guy with a gun waiting for you. So I thought, fuck this, pick an exit and wait outside, around a corner, where he can't see you. Maybe have a smoke, take a load off. And what do you know? It's my lucky day."

"Why'd you pick Gate L?" Nicky said, feeling funny making conversation with an armed stalker. At first, he'd thought maybe he could distract Tony, but then what? Run? Call for help? He'd decided to try to loosen the guy up, appeal to his soft side. He had to have one—Lottie did once love him. What was it captives were supposed to do? Humanize themselves? Get their captors to sympathize with them? But, jeez, this was the best Nicky could do—*Why'd you pick Gate L?*

"Same reason as you. Close to the cars, or the 'hood if you make it across the track. The other side of the Dome puts you out onto campus. Get lost in the students, fine, but it's Saturday. Lots of the buildings are locked."

The doors opened at the fourth floor and the twinge was back in Nicky's ribs.

"That way," Tony said, prodding Nicky. The garage was packed with cars, but no one was around. Nicky could hear the wail of an ambulance bringing someone to the VA, or maybe beyond that to Crouse Hospital. Tony pushed Nicky toward the far left corner of the garage, the most secluded part. The other side overlooked Van Buren Street, where Nicky would have been able to shout down to pedestrians walking on the sidewalk. But the left side overlooked a strip of grass that separated the two garages, about half a football field in length, hidden in shadow. Nicky looked out into the other garage, which also was packed but vacant. Had Tony parked here on purpose?

They approached a Ford Explorer, red and dented with maps strewn across the backseat, and Nicky tried to remember the car Tony had driven to Lottie's funeral.

"This one yours?" Nicky said, then felt the air leave his chest.

Next thing he knew he was against the Explorer and the top of his head was throbbing, his eyes flooding. Tony was holding the Browning like its steel grip was a hammer.

"That's a relief," Tony said. "I thought maybe that Explorer might have an alarm, but the way you knocked it, I must've picked a winner." He put his foot on the bumper of the Suburban on the other side of Nicky and rocked it. "This one, neither. That's what I like to see, my police instincts still sharp."

"What're you going to do?" Nicky was trying to stall the man. There had to be a way out of this.

"That's not the question. What you really want to know is what you're going to do. Jump over that rusty steel rail and that short concrete wall, but then what? Must be a good forty or sixty feet to the bottom. So you're asking yourself, how hard is the bottom? Broken-ankle hard or broken-neck hard?"

"The other cops will be out looking for me. I can scream."

"Big deal. They hear you, I'll say this is where I found you. No, I'll turn you over, eventually. First I want a little quality time together, just you and me. And if I should happen to get caught, or you should happen to die, then I'll have to file a report, maybe go before internal affairs, but what the hell? I've been there before."

"Why are you doing this?"

Tony hit him across the mouth, hard, and it was a moment before Nicky realized that he was on all fours, licking a split lip. Nicky looked up just in time to see Tony's fist, then it was dark again.

When Nicky came to, he was curled up in a ball, hearing Tony's shoe on his back, his stomach, his arms. Nicky hardly felt a thing. He didn't know which was worse—the idea of what Tony was doing to his poor body or having to listen to Tony's grunts and demeaning insults. *Greasy, olive-sucking goatbanger. Uncut, mono-browed beef curtain.*

What sort of Neanderthal used the term *beef curtain?* And what did it mean, anyway? Was it supposed to be some reference to people's love of lamb? His *people.* Nicky's thoughts, buoyed on a sea of numbness, drifted to Wally, the man's love of the Irish, and Martin's disdain of them. Was that what this was about—racism? Nicky peeked between his raised forearms, and instantly wished he hadn't. Three things floated between his wrists—the Explorer's front left tire which was spotted with blood, Tony's face which was twisted and damp, and Tony's shoes which were black and polished. Nicky remembered Todd's silver-tipped boots at the casino. He told himself to be grateful Tony wasn't a gay cowboy. The light grew dim again, and the blows stopped.

Was he dead?

Then Tony's lips were next to his ear, the man's breath warm and sour. "You wanna know why I'm doing this? I'll tell you why. You killed my wife."

You killed my wife. The words echoed in Nicky's ears.

That's when it hit him. His senses were almost gone and his brain was half dead, but he was still with it enough to come to a fascinating realization. *Tony didn't do it.* He couldn't have. If he'd killed Lottie, why would he want to avenge her murder? Tony could lie about the reason he hated Nicky, but not in the heat of passion, when people spoke the truth. It was like that exception to the hearsay rule for excited utterances. Nicky was proud of his legal reasoning, but the revelation did him little good. The look in Tony's eyes had morphed into madness. He took out the Browning and glanced over his shoulder. Nicky knew he had no choice.

If Tony wasn't already a killer, he was about to become one.

Nicky stretched his leg and hooked his foot around Tony's ankle, then slammed his other foot against Tony's knee. There was a loud pop. Tony swore and lurched backward. As he teetered on the steel rail, Nicky scrambled to his knees and grabbed Tony's feet, lifting. Tony dropped the Browning and clawed at the smooth concrete wall.

He swore the whole way down.

Nicky knelt there a moment, hearing his own panting. He couldn't shake the feeling that Tony would return at any moment—scale the walls, pop out from a parked car, plunge from the ceiling. The man was barely human, knuckles dragging on the ground. Nicky looked for the pistol, finding it at his feet. He stared at its dull black luster, deciding whether to go there. The last thing he wanted was to give people another reason to think he was a killer. He waited for the nausea to pass, then climbed to his feet and looked down at Tony. The man was lying on his side at the rear of the garage, like he'd fallen on his ass and rolled down the hill until his huge gut had stopped him. Nicky saw no blood or bone, but he waited for Tony to groan and reach for his leg, just to be sure he was still alive.

"What do you know?" he shouted at Tony. "Broken-ankle hard."

Nicky spat blood, tucked in his shirt, and replaced his baseball cap. He didn't like the face gaping back at him in the Explorer's side-view mirror, but he was glad to be alive. He took the stairs to the first floor, feeling the muscles in his thighs and back ache. He limped out the rear exit, onto Stadium Place, and looked both ways.

No Tony Donuts.

He crossed the train tracks, passed under a highway, and meandered through streets littered with trash and lined with brick apartments. The low-income neighborhoods he'd once promised himself he would clean up. In the safety of Sal's car, he took out Sal's cell phone, and punched some numbers.

"Okay," he said. "Now what?"

CHAPTER 31

"On behalf of Onondaga Furniture," said Barth Crawford from the podium, "thank you for having us."

The gallery let out a sigh. It was seven-thirty on a Monday night in the Skaneateles Town Hall, and they had been there a half hour. At one end of the room sat seven men and women around three sides of an oak table covered with papers. The town supervisor sat in the middle, flanked on one side by three town councilors, and on the other side by the town clerk, town attorney, and a fourth town councilor. On the other end of the room, on plastic chairs organized into uneven rows, sat three dozen citizens. They mostly wore jeans and T-shirts with faded logos. Doug's Fish Fry, the Annual Turkey Run, the Antique Boat Show. But the two front rows were filled with people in suits—Porter Boyd and Maria D'Angelo, Martin and Tiffany Newberg, Wally McGuffin and Terence Jefferson, Laurel Lewandowski and Marcy DeSalvo, Sal and Monique, and Diz and Dara. In the hallway that transected one end of the room stood a half dozen tardy citizens. Among them were Trace Lipp and his cameraman.

The meeting had started with the pledge of allegiance, then an explanation by the supervisor that this was a specially scheduled meeting, not one of the board's regular Thursday night meetings. As a result, there would be no reports about the highway department, water department, recreation department, transfer station, animal control, and budget. Those subjects would be covered at the next meeting, where the board would address several issues. These included the alleged runoff of water from a public road into a private property owner's basement, the corrosive effect on a three-hundred-yard section of iron pipe by a stretch of what an engineer called *hot soil,* the planned advertisement of the new aerobics room at the fitness center, the increased incidence of unauthorized dumping at the recycling station, a recent invasion of several homes by bats, and the rising mileage and monthly repair costs of the town's fleet of rescue trucks.

The crowd had been pulled back from the brink of unconsciousness by an abrupt and rousing debate between the board's sole Democratic member and his Republican colleagues over the feasibility of improving the town employees' health-insurance, sick-leave, and pension benefits. Order had been restored by the supervisor, who had warned the board's Democratic member about using board meetings to campaign for re-election.

This had been as good a segue as any for the introduction of the board's first special guest, Wes Longacre—the County's Democratic party chairman and election commissioner. Wes had purportedly been invited to talk about the upcoming primary and general elections. He had sat in a special seat behind the supervisor and clerk, not quite at the table, but at least separated from the rabble across the room. He had spoken softly, barely above a whisper, about the town's transition from mechanical to electronic voting machines, and the mind-numbing details of Election Day. Eight hundred fifty anticipated voters in each of the primaries, forty-two hundred anticipated voters in the general election, eight polling places, twenty-four election inspectors . . . The crowd had found itself back on the road to unconsciousness, but no one had showed it. Not to a man who had just lost his wife.

The next item on the agenda, according to the supervisor, had been a public hearing on another important community issue. Apparently prompted by the term *community issue* and inspired by the TV camera, a mother of three had risen and begged the town to put speed bumps on her street. A spry octogenarian had followed, snapping about having been repeatedly ticketed despite his handicap parking permit. Before the supervisor could call the hearing to order, a man in a safari hat had announced that the entire town was under invasion. *Alien aquatic plants!* he'd said. *They're clogging our estuaries, choking our motorboat engines, lowering our property values!* Finally, the floor had been yielded to Barth Crawford, who had stepped behind a special podium wedged between flags of the United States of America and New York State, in the middle of the far side of the room.

"First," said Barth, "my client would like to extend its deepest sympathies to you and your family, Mr. Election Commissioner."

The TV camera lighted up Wes's face. He clenched his jaw and gave a nod, eyes shining.

Barth said, "The economic problems Onondaga Furniture and its employees have faced the past two years are overshadowed only by the loss you must feel right now. That realization is what inspired Onondaga to reach out recently to one of its former employees, Maria D'Angelo, to try to heal the scars that separate us. It is also what inspired Onondaga to resume discussions with the Town Board about a proposed deal involving a reduction in Onondaga's property taxes. Those efforts have resulted in a decision by Onondaga, which is the subject of my announcement here tonight. Encouraged by an economic future that is free of the uncertainties of litigation, Onondaga Furniture has decided . . ."

Barth paused to find the TV camera, which was stationed in

the hallway near the rear exit, with a dramatic view of the board members, podium, flags, and concerned citizens.

"To rebuild its factory and recall its employees," Nicky said from the hallway.

All heads turned toward him.

He stepped out from behind a photocopy machine, which had been removed from the boardroom to make way for more chairs, and he walked down the hall, feeling camera lights on his face. As he crossed the room toward the podium, he heard mumbling then Dara say, "Daddy."

Pandemonium broke out.

Wes Longacre shot to his feet and thrust out a finger. "Sonofabitch! You murdered my wife! You seduced her then killed her!"

Wes made it halfway around the oak table before being clotheslined by a board member in a denim shirt and caught by a board member in a coat and tie. It was an inspiring display of bipartisan cooperation—Democrat and Republican working together to keep the peace.

Nicky hadn't expected Wes to be here. An *important community presentation* about electronic voting machines? The man's attendance was clearly a ruse to garner support for Onondaga's announcement—the widower of one murder victim united with the client of another murder victim. A spectacle Trace Lipp couldn't miss. Still, Nicky knew, Wes was a reminder to all of the victims of Nicky's infidelity.

He told himself to be calm, but Wes's words rang in his ears. *Seduced* her. Nicky had never seen it that way before, Lilly practically ripping off his clothes the first time they were alone. But he knew that was the word for it, like the way a scoundrel preyed on lonely women. Except his target had been married women. They'd been safe—always afraid to leave their husbands, and able to be dumped out of fairness to the kids. He knew Wes was right enough.

In the middle of the room, Martin, Wally, and Terence held back the gallery, which appeared about to burst forth and trample them. Unconsciously, Nicky ran his tongue over his lip, still swollen from the Saturday before. He wasn't afraid for his own safety. He knew that whatever he got he had coming, ruining all those marriages. It was his daughter's safety he worried about. He stepped into her outstretched arms and pulled her tight. His precious Dara. She sniffled in his ear. He wanted to tell her so many things. He loved her. He wasn't such a bad person. He'd never cheated on her mom, always known how lucky he was. But this wasn't the time. He pulled her arms away and pushed on.

Barth wasn't yielding the podium, so Nicky stopped and faced Wes.

"You're right, I am a sonofabitch." He waited for the room to settle down before continuing. "I had an affair with your wife and I'm sorry. It was a mistake. It was wrong. And I'm ashamed. But you're wrong that I killed her. The person who killed her did it because they knew she could prove my innocence. They did it to frame me."

The crowd started up again, some of them heckling him this time. *Liar! Shyster! Psycho!* There were boos and hisses. Nicky forced a smile. He'd known this wasn't going to be easy.

"The person who killed Lilly also killed my law partner and wife. They killed Lilly to cover their tracks. But they went too far. They made a mistake. I know who they are."

People started shouting again. *Sure! Who? Tell us!* Some men in back pushed forward, stumbling over the plastic chairs in the next row. People spilled out into the hall. They grew red in the face. They told each other to shut up. But Martin, Wally, and Terence held the line, joined by Porter Boyd. Eventually, the mob's faces registered the realization that, while they weren't going to reach the lawyer-turned-murderer-turned-fugitive, he wasn't going to escape, either.

"You have a captive audience," Barth said to Nicky, unfolding his hands. "Please, give us your last words before you're hauled off in handcuffs."

Nicky took Barth's place at the podium and gazed out at the faces before him—some enraged, some scowling, some expectant. The room was crowded and hot, and smelled musty, like a lake house or ski lodge. Nicky had hoped people would sit, give him some time, but that wasn't happening. He glanced at Diz and Sal for reassurance, but felt only anxiety. He knew that, if they were there, Halliday wouldn't be far behind.

"Onondaga didn't settle the case because of Lilly's murder. If anything, the opposite is true."

Barth smiled and cocked his head, clearly humoring Nicky. "Lilly was murdered to settle the case?"

"Lilly was murdered to cover up Lottie's murder, which was committed to settle the case."

"Let me get this right. Are you accusing me, before all these people, of killing opposing counsel for financial gain?"

"No, I'm saying the murderer killed Lottie in order to take over the case, and then settle it. You're just the bloodsucking leech that took advantage of it."

Barth seemed unable to decide whether calling a lawyer *a bloodsucking leech* was defamation. After all, the truth was a defense, like Diz said. Apparently placated, he stepped back. No further questions for the name-calling murder suspect. But then people started mumbling again. What had the Greek guy said? The murderer took over the case?

It was a moment before Martin realized people were looking at him. "Me?" he said. "You think I did it?"

"At first," Nicky said. "Your alibi about being home with your wife at the time of the murder wasn't completely true."

"I got back at eight. Ask Diz—she dropped me off at work at quarter of and saw me drive away. I went straight home."

"But your wife wasn't there."

"Tiff?"

Nicky wanted to remind the former Army captain that the camera was rolling, and whatever he said would have to square with what he said under oath. But Nicky didn't want to look like a bully. He just let the idea hang in the air. He wasn't confident the makeshift jury knew the significance of Tiffany's absence from home at the time of Lottie's murder, but it didn't matter. Halliday would know.

Tiffany glared at Martin. "Go on, tell him."

Martin knitted his eyebrows.

"Thinking how to cover for her?" Nicky said.

"No. She left early to pick up cookies for book club."

"She wasn't home when you got there?"

"We wanted to keep things simple."

"She leave before a quarter of eight?"

"She didn't pick up when I called on my way home."

"And book club started at eight-thirty?"

"Your wife was in it."

"So Tiffany left forty-five minutes before book club started?"

"What's the big deal?"

"She ever bring snacks to book club before? Did anyone ever bring snacks?"

Some people exchanged looks, not sure where Nicky was going.

Nicky turned to Maria D'Angelo, one of the few people in the room who had sat back down. She stiffened in her chair under the sudden attention.

She wore a long-sleeved turtleneck, large sunglasses, and a curly black wig—anything to hide her scars. He'd met her only twice before—when she'd signed the retainer agreement in the firm's conference room, and a year later when he'd run into her in the elevator. She'd just gotten out of her deposition and had that vacant look in her eyes. He'd offered to buy her a cup of coffee. She'd smiled and said, *No, thank you, really.* So he'd walked her to her car, holding an umbrella over her in the rain. He'd sensed a certain integrity about her then, and he was betting—yes, that's what it was, mere gambling—that she would show it now.

"No," Maria said. "Lottie always made dessert. Tried to keep everyone on the low-carb thing. Crustless cheesecake, sugar-free fudge, you name it."

"Everyone was doing the diet, even Tiffany?"

It was a threadbare sweater to pin his hopes on, he knew, but it was all he had. Tiffany looked down at Maria with exaggerated curiosity. Maria wasn't flustered. She'd been through too much.

"She's the one who got us all started on it. She was a fanatic. Whenever we caved and ordered pizza, she just ate the toppings."

Tiffany's expression had disintegrated to one of disdain. Nicky knew he was scoring points.

"You showed up at Lottie's house at the same time as Tiffany that night, right?"

Maria nodded.

"Did Tiffany have any cookies with her at the time?"

Now Tiffany was glaring at Maria. Again, Maria ignored her. "Not that I remember."

Martin didn't miss a beat. "Come on, you have to be kidding. We're talking about some lousy cookies. Maybe she ate them on her way from the store in a moment of weakness. Or left them in her car."

Maybe she never had them at all, Nicky wanted to say. But he knew everyone was thinking it. "Do you even know what kind they were?"

Martin threw up his hands and scoffed.

"Half-moons," Tiffany finally said. "From Wegmans. They were delicious."

People agreed—Wegmans did have an excellent bakery.

Nicky was happy Tiffany had spoken. Now they were getting to it. He said to her, "How many did you get?"

"Are we honestly talking about this?" Martin said.

But Tiffany waved him off. She looked Nicky in the eye. "A half dozen."

"And you ate them all?"

"What can I say? I eat when I'm down. My friend did die."

"Did you pay with a credit card?"

"Cash."

"Use your shopper's card?"

"To save a few pennies?"

"You keep the receipt?"

"Sure, I had it laminated."

There was some snickering. People were loosening up. Some had even sat down.

"Did anyone see you at Wegmans?" Everyone knew you couldn't walk into the place without tripping over your next-door neighbor or fifth-grade social studies teacher.

"I don't know. Why don't you subpoena the surveillance videos? It hasn't even been two weeks. They probably haven't been taped over yet."

Nicky didn't say anything. It was the sort of comment that showed she'd been thinking about this, and he wanted to let that idea sink in.

Martin seized on the silence. "She picked up cookies, she didn't pick up cookies, give me a break."

It was time for Nicky to show his cards.

"If she wasn't at the store before book club, where was she?

And why would she lie about it? Maybe she went to Lottie's early, to give her a piece of her mind about your hours and salary. Like she did to me earlier that day. Even my secretary heard her."

"Bitch on wheels," said Laurel Lewandowski, happy to pile on. "I thought she was going to start swinging."

"Maybe she did," Nicky said. "At Lottie's place. Lottie puts up a fight and things get out of control. Tiffany takes off, waiting up the street for someone else to show up. A pretty good alibi."

That was it—Nicky's theory in a nutshell. He was trying to keep it simple, like Martin said. He expected more heckling, but there was none.

"How can you stand there and attack her like that?" Martin said.

It was the question Nicky had been waiting for. "Have a seat, and I'll tell you. If you don't think I've proved my case, I'll wait quietly for the police."

A few people shrugged and sat down. But Martin folded his arms and remained standing.

Nicky had known it would come to this. Win or lose, no compromise, like the way he used to practice law. The mornings before trial, as he walked around his kitchen in the mumble tank, Corin would put her hands on his shoulders, kiss him on the mouth and say, *Don't forget to take out the garbage.* It had always made him laugh, given him a sense of perspective, even self-respect. Like, *What have I got to lose? I'll give it a shot.* It was a feeling he hadn't had in a long time. He hoped he was about to get it back. He cleared his throat, stepped away from the podium, and faced the gallery.

"I'll be brief. Motive, opportunity, weapon. Who has them more, Tiffany or me? You decide."

Nicky was conscious of the TV camera in the corner. He

knew that someday soon all this might be played to a real jury.

"First, motive. Tiffany's was money. She was deep in debt. You're thinking, 'Who isn't?' But she owed more than a quarter million. What from? You name it. New house in Fayetteville, new SUV, new clothes, country club dues, infertility treatments, even a show-jumping horse here in Skaneateles, boarded at Lilly's farm. Bottom line is Tiffany was in default on her student loans and her credit cards were canceled. How do I know? Exhibit One, a copy of her credit report."

Diz was already passing around copies, just like they had planned.

"That's private information," Martin said.

"I blocked out her Social Security number, birth date, and credit card numbers. And to ensure accuracy, I used each of the three major credit reporting agencies—Equifax, Experian, and Trans Union. Go ahead, take a look. I've highlighted the 'balance due' sections."

Nicky wasn't surprised to see people taking the reports. Who could resist a peek at someone else's finances?

"Now you're asking, 'So what?' How would killing Lottie solve Tiffany's money problems? The answer is that with Lottie out of the way, Martin would inherit the Onondaga Furniture case and its one-third contingency fee. Onondaga's last settlement offer was six million. Tiffany pushed Martin to accept it. Again, how do I know? Exhibit Two, a photo of Tiffany getting cozy with Barth Crawford at Saturday's game. The photographer will testify to the fairness and accuracy of the picture."

"Here," Diz said, lifting her arm. She passed around color copies of the photos.

"Next, opportunity. Tiffany was friends with Scarlet, welcome in my home anytime. The day after Lottie's murder, Tiffany came over and planted the murder weapon, a bookend, in my attic. She returned the next day to ask Scarlet what my alibi was, then get her drunk and push her in the pool. She knew it would look like I did it. The next morning, she told Martin that the police had found the murder weapon in my home, knowing he would tell me and I would go home to find out what it was. Then she called the police to catch me there with Scarlet's body. A few days later, she eliminated my alibi for Lottie's murder. She waited outside Lilly's farm, forced her off the road, then shot her. Again, how do I know? Exhibit Three, photos of the dent in the front bumper of Tiffany's new car, and the dent in the rear bumper of Lilly's car. A perfect match."

Again, Diz passed around color copies.

"Finally, weapon. The bookend we already covered. I doubt it has any prints—Tiffany probably wiped it clean. The same with any liquor bottles or glasses from my patio. But it's in murdering Lilly that Tiffany made a mistake. She used a Beretta nine millimeter, standard-issue in the Army, where Martin served for over ten years. He still has one. Again, how do I know? Exhibit Four, a blown-up photocopy of his pistol permit, on file with the Onondaga County Sheriff's Department."

Nicky waited for Diz to pass around copies.

"That's his little photo in the corner, and the serial number of the gun."

Martin gave Tiffany a wounded look.

"You're wondering if she borrowed it recently," Nicky said to Martin.

"He's delusional," Tiffany said to Martin.

"Am I? Martin isn't coming to your defense. And neither is anybody else."

"They don't believe you."

"Let's take a vote."

Over Tiffany's shoulder, the gallery stared back at him. The mother of three who had pleaded for the speed bumps stood up. People waited as she looked down and smoothed the wrinkles in her skirt.

"I think she did it," she said.

A young man next to her reached for her arm, but she pulled it away. "She wears too much makeup, like she's trying to hide something."

The octogenarian fanned the air with his cane. "Makeup? You can't go by that. You have to stick to the facts, the evidence. Like the photos. How do you explain them?"

"They were just watching a game," Porter Boyd said. "And you should see the bumpers of my wife's car. Covered in scrapes from every parking garage in the city. No, what I want to see is the ballistics results. You know, from the slugs that the cops recovered. I saw on the Science Channel they're, like, ninety-nine percent accurate."

"I don't have to wait for ballistics results," said the man in a safari hat. "I think she did it. Who buys cookies when they're on a low-carb diet? And where's the receipt? But I think we're missing the bigger picture here. What about the weeds? They're coming!"

There was an argument about whether most people keep their grocery receipts and for how long, and whether circumstantial evidence was enough to convict someone of murder. Several people shouted *Guilty!* while some others shouted *Innocent!*

"When you all decide," Tiffany said, picking up her purse, "give me a call. Until then, I'll be at home. I've been to sorority rush functions that were less painful than this. Marty, stay if you want, but you'll have to get your own ride."

And with that Tiffany was across the room and halfway down the hall in her pearls and high heels. Nicky was amazed. People had wanted to lynch him, and they were going to just let her go. But Tiffany didn't have any such luck. Before she reached the rear exit, she pitched forward, throwing her purse into the air. Next thing Nicky knew, she was on the floor. No one moved to help her, not even Martin.

The hand that finally reached out belonged to Detective Halliday.

"The cameraman should've taped down that cord," he said. "It's a trip-and-fall hazard."

"Have you just been standing there?" she said.

"Long enough."

"Are you going to let go of my arm?"

"I don't think so. Not until we straighten this out."

A sheriff's deputy said, "Want me to arrest her?"

"And him, him, and him," Halliday said, pointing at Nicky, Sal, and Martin. "I'll sort them out later."

Nicky let a deputy take his arm, and told Dara not to worry.

"I'm not going to lie to you," Halliday said. "I still don't like you. But I don't like the chief jumping on my ass, either. Your theory holds water, you'll be back chasing ambulances in no time."

CHAPTER 32

"She would be proud of you," Dara said.

Nicky was kneeling on the November ground, feeling the frost melt against his suit pants, soaking through to his skin. He put down a bouquet of blue and yellow irises, Corin's favorite, and stood up.

"Why?" he said. "Because of the way I carried on with women after she died?"

"The way you carried on at all after she died," Dara said. "The way you made your dream come true."

Coming out of anyone else's mouth, these words would have sounded corny to Nicky. But Dara always had a way of turning the sentimental into the serious. She swept a strand of jet-black hair from her coffee-brown eyes, just like her mother used to do. Then she stomped her feet and cupped her mouth, her wedding ring ablaze in the final rays of the setting sun, which cast the bare treetops behind her in a ghostly light. Flakes of the season's first snow sparkled on her navy wool peacoat. Next to her, Diz turned her back on a gust of wind, showing Nicky the white cross of her red ski-patrol jacket. He led them carefully down a slippery hill.

"My dream was a joke," he said.

"You won, didn't you?" Dara said.

"Thanks to the boys of Delta Tau Chi. One of them tried to vote twice, he was so drunk."

"You reached people, admit it."

"People only voted for me because I told them not to. What do they call it? Spoofing. Like on those reality TV shows where people call in to vote for the most obnoxious contestant."

"The election wasn't a spoof, Dad."

"You were on your honeymoon. It was absurd from the day they let me out, Trace Lipp ambushing me in the parking lot like that for an interview."

"When you *apologized* and turned everything around."

"A disgusting display of self-flagellation," Diz said.

"I just expressed my regret at having ruined so many lives," Nicky said. "My infidelity, my greed, my selfishness."

"Get over yourself," Diz said. "Tiffany was a wack-job. One of those Texas moms who kill their daughter's cheerleading rivals. A character from *Desperate Housewives*. She was going to do Lottie at some point and pin it on someone."

"Somehow that doesn't lift the suffocating weight of guilt from my chest." Nicky pulled the door to the Jaguar shut and started the engine.

"It was the plea to the electorate that really made the difference," Diz said from the backseat. "I can't believe they bought it."

"Because I told them the truth, that they shouldn't vote for me because I was unfit for public office?"

"No, because you didn't go through the minor formality of taking your name off the ballot."

"I was a little busy. Bar disciplinary hearings, backed-up cases, Dara's big day. Then those phone calls and letters."

"Like that one to the editor, begging you to stay in the race? I still think you wrote it."

"Please, I'm not that eloquent."

"But it worked," Dara said, "got people talking."

"That's why I did the commercial," Nicky said. "To *explain* why people shouldn't vote for me. I'd cheated on my wife. I'd evaded arrest. Hell, I'd raised people's insurance premiums for a living. I told them plain and clear, 'If you elect me, I'll degrade the office, ignore the law and contribute to the decline of our society.' What can I say? People loved it. What did Trace Lipp say? 'Finally, a campaign promise we can count on.' "

"And thus began the 'Don't Vote for Nick' campaign," Diz said. "Pathetic."

"If it was so pathetic," Nicky said, "then why did you take over as campaign committee chairman?"

"Chairperson."

"Is that where all those signs came from?" Dara said. "The ones with the circles and lines through them?"

"They're collector's items," Diz said. "People are buying them on eBay. There are even some posters people had made, blowups of Nicky's mug shot. Did he tell you he's considering using the shot for his photo in next year's bar association directory?"

"I can't explain it," Nicky said. "Only that people picked me, and I'm not going to let them down."

"Stop," Diz said, "before I get sick."

"What does your pal Eliot think about all of this?" Dara said.

This invocation of the governor's name injected a tone of seriousness back into the conversation.

"Do you mean will he appoint me to the Appellate Division if I do a halfway decent job as a Supreme Court Justice? Who knows? I doubt it. But I don't care anymore. I just want to do a good job and play with my grandkids."

Dara let out a groan as Nicky pulled out into rush-hour traffic. She said, "Before we get into that again, can someone please explain what's up with Tiffany. Why hasn't she confessed yet?"

"She's a tough cookie," Diz said. "If you'll pardon the pun."

"But you guys came up with all that evidence. How could she think she was going to get away with it?"

"She tried to pin it on Martin. Poor guy had to throw her

under the bus to keep from getting indicted."

"But how did Halliday know which one to believe?"

"He got a warrant and started doing tests. Ballistics, fingerprints, DNA, even subpoenaed the phone records of the nine-one-one call. Proved Tiffany called for an ambulance even before she heard me drop the phone and dive in the pool."

"And she still refuses to plead. It's like she's pathological."

"What Diz is modestly leaving out," Nicky said, "is the way she twisted Halliday's arm to keep after Tiffany. Not to mention the way she ran around town before the board meeting getting all that evidence."

"See?" Dara said. "She does like you."

"He's all right," Diz said. "He gets under your skin. Like eczema."

"The worst part is how stupid Tiffany was," Nicky said. "Thinking Martin could get the D'Angelo fee without having both me and Sal assign it to him first. Sal would've never agreed—we probably would've had to pay taxes on it as a gift."

"So it'll be yours now," said Dara, "the fee?"

"And Sal's," Nicky said. "I'm going to give my share to Vera House, that women's shelter Lottie loved."

"Which should yield a nice tax write-off," said Diz.

But Nicky was focusing on the road, which was covered with a mat of glistening leaves.

"When did you get this back?" Diz said, patting the back of Nicky's leather seat.

"Yesterday. Sheldon put a thousand miles on it back and forth to Atlantic City."

"You didn't say anything?"

"It's only a car."

Nicky skipped over the obscene withdrawal he had made from his Merrill Lynch money market account to cover Sal's gambling debt. The only thing that mattered was that Sal was going to keep his kneecaps and his bar, and that he'd made every meeting of Gamblers Anonymous since that first time. He'd even stopped drinking. With Monique's help, maybe he would be himself again.

"Aren't you generous?" Diz said. "I should give you my bill."

"I told you I'd pay it. Even offered to give you the firm."

"And I told you, I already have a dysfunctional family."

"You should see what he offered to give me," Dara said.

"I heard. Spanakopita?"

"It's just a run-down building right now, but he said he'd pay for the renovation. Grandpa even offered to come home in the summers and teach Brady and me the ropes."

"You going to do it?"

"We're thinking about it. Brady fancies himself an entrepreneur. And Dad offered to throw in our old house. Already bought it, in fact."

"He must really want you back."

"He doesn't have to bribe me. I like it here."

"Not me," Diz said. "I'm done with this place."

"You're moving?" Nicky said, turning the rearview mirror to find Diz's face.

"New York. You know, meet a nice girl, settle down. Watch out."

Ahead, a light had turned red against the black sky. Nicky sucked in his breath and slammed the brakes. But he had already started to slide toward a pair of red taillights. He jerked the wheel to the left, causing the car to fishtail. Then he identified his inevitable destination, a neon-green Ford Focus. He braced for impact, locking his elbows and shutting his eyes. When he opened them, the front right bumper of the Jaguar was resting against the rear bumper of the Focus. The two were joined by merely the softest of kisses.

The only sound in the night was the back-and-forth of

Nicky's windshield wipers.

"Houston," Diz said, "the Eagle has landed."

Nicky let out his breath. "Are you okay?" he said to the two remaining women in his life.

"You kidding?" Dara said. "I work bumpers harder than that parallel parking."

The driver of the Ford opened his window and craned his neck out of it. A cigarette hung from his lips, and his chin showed the start of a beard. He raised his eyebrows then opened his door, placing an unlaced work boot unsteadily on the ground.

"Here we go," Diz said.

Nicky lowered his window, flipped on his hazards, and switched off the engine.

"I know you," the man said. "From TV."

Nicky cringed even before the man's hand shot to his neck.

"Ooh," the man said, trying with dramatic effort to turn his head. "That hurts. Maybe someone should call an ambulance— you know, just in case. I mustn't of noticed it in all the frenzy." He opened and closed his hand. "Hey, my fingers are numb. The seatbelt must a threw out my shoulder." The man stared at the three incredulous faces in Nicky's car, until headlights passed over him, lighting up the flakes of snow in the air. He looked up. "Anyone see that? Millions a specks a light, like stars. I feel dizzy. Help me. Help me, Jesus."

Nicky watched the man drop his cigarette, stomp it out, then lie down by the side of the road, turning onto his hip so as not to get the seat of his jeans wet, and finally resting his head back onto a pillow of snowy leaves. A car pulled over on the other side of the road, the driver wearing a frown and lifting a cell phone to his ear.

Nicky returned his attention to his tort victim and future judgment creditor, whose eyes were rolling back in his head and whose feet were twitching now. Not a bad performance, all in all, Nicky decided. A little over-the-top, but one that just might work . . . on the right jury.

"Maybe I'll stick around for a while longer," Diz said. "Looks like you're going to need a good lawyer. And I could always use a good laugh."

ABOUT THE AUTHOR

Mike Langan writes novels that draw on his experience as a former litigator at law firms in Washington, DC, and Syracuse, NewYork, and as a law clerk to a federal judge. He received his JD from George Mason University School of Law, where he was notes editor of the *Law Review*. Before becoming a lawyer, Mike received his MFA in creative writing from George Mason University, where he was a graduate fellow, and his BA in philosophy from Colgate University, from which he graduated *cum laude*. He has published several short stories and legal articles, and has taught college courses in both English and law. He lives with his wife and two daughters in the Syracuse area.